COMMAND & CONQUER
TIBERIUM WARS

COMMAND & CONQUER
TIBERIUM WARS

KEITH R. A. DeCANDIDO

BALLANTINE BOOKS • NEW YORK

A Del Rey Books Mass Market Original

Copyright © 2007 by Electronic Arts Inc. Electronic Arts, EA, the EA logo, Command & Conquer, and Command & Conquer Tiberium Wars are trademarks or registered trademarks of Electronic Arts Inc. in the U.S. and/or other countries. All Rights Reserved. All other trademarks are the property of their respective owners.

Published in the United States by Del Rey Books, an imprint of The Random House Publishing Group, a division of Random House, Inc., New York.

DEL REY is a registered trademark and the Del Rey colophon is a trademark of Random House, Inc.

ISBN 978-0-345-49814-4

Printed in the United States of America

www.delreybooks.com

OPM   9 8 7 6 5 4 3 2 1

To all the folks at the Palombo Bakery.
They know why. . . .

"War both needs and generates certain virtues; not the highest, but what may be called the preliminary virtues, as valour, veracity, the spirit of obedience, the habit of discipline. Any of these, and of others like them, when possessed by a nation, and no matter how generated, will give them a military advantage, and make them more likely to stay in the race of nations."
—WALTER BAGEHOT, *Physics and Politics*

"You've never lived until you've almost died, for those who fought for it, life has a flavor the protected will never know."
—ANONYMOUS

HISTORIAN'S NOTE

This novel takes place simultaneously with the game *Command & Conquer Tiberium Wars*.

ONE

The tank screamed over the ridge, crushing the grass and bamboo under its treads, guns blazing as it spit bullets and shells into the large temple and its occupants. Several of the bullets ripped into the distinctive emblem of the Brotherhood of Nod that hung over the door: an uneven hexagon, with a red background, and a scorpion tail curled in a backward C in the center. It was almost as if the tank had specifically been aiming to rip that logo into tiny pieces.

The concussive report of the tank's weapons echoed into the night, even as dozens of GDI troops ran in front of the tank in order to secure the remains of the building.

But then a green-tinged explosion ripped through the air, sending dozens of those GDI troops flying backward. Their screams, however, continued long after the blast, for that green tinge indicated that Tiberium had been used in the explosives. Soldiers—combat veterans all—still screamed like children as the infectious crystalline substance that had been spreading inexorably across the globe for fifty years burned through skin and muscle and bone.

However, the GDI attack did not diminish, and even as their comrades fell, the second wave of troops attacked and then a third. Grenade launchers sent more conventional explosives flying into the bullet-ridden temple, and soon Nod soldiers ran out, coughing and bleeding.

Taking refuge behind the pencil cedar and podo trees, several black-clad soldiers armed with bizarre-looking weaponry fired on the tank and the troops, but the GDI soldiers had numbers and better aim on their side. One by one, they picked off the remaining Brotherhood of Nod fanatics.

The first wave of troops to successfully enter the Nod temple was confronted with an unexpected sight: a laboratory, filled with test tubes, computer stations, boiling chemicals, a centrifuge, and more. The lead soldier, a battle commander, ordered her people to start confiscating the equipment.

It was the last order she would ever give.

Another explosion ripped through the air, consuming the building in a massive plume of fire.

A voice said, *"Although the destruction of the Brotherhood of Nod's Kenyan HQ resulted in the loss of three dozen GDI troops, and the injury of hundreds more, it was still one of the decisive victories of the Second Tiberium War when the 45th Infantry Division overcame Nod forces. Battle Commander Ilona Grunwaldt was given a posthumous Medal of Honor by GDI after the war's official end.*

"Examination of the wreckage revealed genetic material belonging to Kane, the psychotic leader of the Brotherhood, thus confirming reports from GDI's Intelligence and Operations Division that he had been in the stronghold. Nod's very quick subsequent fall and Kane's own lack of public appearances or netcasts since the engagement in Y-2 lends credence to the belief that Kane saw

*the text on the screen and took his own life rather than
face defeat and a war-crimes trial that would end with
his execution at GDI hands."*

The voice-over, and the accompanying holo of the 45th's
successful mission, faded from the center of the lounge,
and Jasmine Martinez had to admit to being disappointed
in herself, while at the same time impressed with GDI's
propaganda machine. She'd been a reporter for W3N,
one of the largest news agencies, for several years, and
had seen the footage of the 45th taking down Kane's
stronghold in Kenya dozens of times. Yet she found herself completely immersed in it. The sights, the sounds,
they had been so *real*. She wondered what it would be
like if they ever figured out a way to convey smell in
holos.

They had been playing these various propaganda docu-
mentaries for the last hour or so in the lounge of the
GDSS *Philadelphia*, GDI's largest orbital space station,
and the site of the Energy Summit. They were only there
in the lounge because GDI's Director General, Lia Kinsburg, was supposedly going to be stopping by for a brief
chat with the press. In real terms, this meant that Kinsburg would walk in, say something vague, and then
leave, but still and all, every member of the press felt
obliged to be in the lounge to wait for her.

When Kinsburg finally entered, accompanied by a
short, stooped-over, elderly bald man who looked vaguely
familiar to Jasmine, she tapped the side of her glasses to
activate the cam. Even though little of substance would
be said in front of live cams, not recording could cost Jasmine her job.

Most reporters kept the cam going all the time, figuring they could just carve out the good stuff in the editing
room. Jasmine usually cited a feeble desire to conserve

battery power, but the truth of the matter was she *hated* the editing process, and tried to keep it as simple as possible. The notion of sitting in a dark cubicle plowing through hours of dull chaff to find a micron of wheat filled her with a nameless dread.

Well, okay, not nameless. It's called "laziness." The voice in her head that said that sounded a whole lot like her father's.

Those other reporters also thought they might miss something important if they ever turned the cam off. In all her years of reporting for W3N, Jasmine had yet to see anything spontaneous happen in front of her.

She activated the cam, and put the drone on standby in case she needed a second angle or herself in a shot. Given that there were over a dozen reporters in the room and they were restricted to one corner of the lounge, the drones were invaluable for getting some variety to the footage.

Of course, GDI didn't care about their angles or visuals. They just wanted to maintain security, which was why the drones almost never got to go anywhere interesting, and were vaporized if they tried. Said vaporizing would be accomplished either by automated security or one of Kinsburg's four bodyguards, who were as well armed as anyone short of GDI infantry.

Jasmine had had one of her drones vaporized once. That was when she found out how expensive they were, as W3N took the cost of replacing it out of her paycheck.

Several of the reporters spoke at once and asked variations of the same query: "Director Kinsburg, can you give us a preview of tomorrow's speech?"

Kinsburg, a woman with deep lines in her face that bespoke both advanced age and advanced stress, had sharp blue eyes and a shock of dark-flecked-with-gray hair atop her head. She smiled, showing perfect, flat teeth, while walking over to the table that included finger food and drinks that the reporters weren't allowed to touch. "I wouldn't want to give away too much, Alfred—don't want you sleeping through it because you knew it all already." Kinsburg's voice showed only a hint of her Danish accent.

Everybody tittered politely, even though the joke wasn't all that funny. Kinsburg was the most powerful person in the GDI, which given the state of the world these days, meant she was the most powerful person on the planet, so when she let loose with a witticism, even half of one, you laughed.

"But yes," Kinsburg said as she poured herself a cup of coffee, "I can at least drop a few hints. I'll be talking tomorrow about what we've gotten out of this summit."

Somehow, Jasmine managed not to roll her eyes. They already knew that the speech tomorrow would be the summary of what the Council of Directors and other assorted GDI advisors had been discussing for the past several days behind closed doors here on the *Philadelphia*. Indeed, the speech had been the last item on the summit's agenda for months. The reporters had been given platitudes and clichés from most of the Directors between sessions, and a few carefully selected details had been leaked ahead of time, but none was of any consequence.

Kinsburg went on: "I can tell you that GDI will have a new watchword when this is all over. For the last five decades, we've been forced to emphasize defense against the onslaught of Tiberium and against Nod and the other forces that would destroy our way of life. Tomorrow, that will change, and for the better."

Then Kinsburg indicated the older man next to her, whose face Jasmine had been failing to place for the last several minutes. "I have one other happy announcement. This is Dr. Ignatio Mobius, a name I'm sure you all recognize."

Of course. Most of the pictures of Mobius were from his younger days when, if nothing else, he had hair.

"I'm pleased to tell you all that after my talk, Dr. Mobius will receive the GDI Medal of Honor for his valiant work in trying to solve the ongoing Tiberium crisis. As I'm sure you all know—"

But you're going to tell us anyhow, Jasmine thought uncharitably.

"—Dr. Mobius was one of the first scientists on the scene when Tiberium was discovered fifty-two years ago, and he has remained at the forefront of Tiberium research ever since, both with NATO and later with GDI. The world owes Dr. Mobius a huge debt, and it's one we can only begin to repay with the medal he will be presented with tomorrow."

With that, Kinsburg took her coffee mug and departed, her bodyguards at her side, Mobius behind her. For her part, Jasmine stared longingly at the coffeepot. Her ration chip covered coffee in theory, but there'd been a shortage this year, and B-2, the Blue Zone where Jasmine lived, was one of the regions that didn't get any. She wondered who she had to bribe to get a cup here.

She also wondered why Mobius didn't say anything. True, he wasn't a young man, and she had a suspicion that the main reason why he was being feted tomorrow night was because they weren't sure how much longer he would be alive to receive his medal.

Because she was from W3N, everyone assumed that Jasmine had some inside knowledge that nobody else had. Indeed, before she worked there Jasmine herself had assumed this to be the case, which led to massive disappointment when she took the W3N job after four years doing local news and sports in Boston and found that, though she was employed by the largest news-gathering organization in the world, she got the same lockdown from GDI as everyone else.

However, the assumption remained in the ether, so two local reporters immediately walked over to her with questioning looks on their faces. One was Amelia de Guardiola, a short woman from Lisbon in B-5, and the other Giancarlo Trøndheim, a tall, gangly man from Helsinki in B-1.

Amelia asked, "You know what the big word'll be, Jasmine?"

"No, but I bet we're all gonna get a *lot* of screen time trying to figure out what it is."

Carlo laughed. "I bet it'll be 'Tiberium.' "

"Kinda anticlimactic, don'tcha think?" Amelia asked.

"S'why I figure it'll be it. C'mon, you don't think it'll be something original. This is *GDI* we're talking about."

"I'm just worried it'll be 'war,' " Amelia said.

"You think?" Jasmine tried not to sound excited, then admonished herself for the feeling.

Sadly, the admonishment came too late, as both Carlo and Amelia fixed her with incredulous looks. "You *want* war?"

"No, of course not, it's just—" She sighed. "I became a reporter right *after* TWII ended. Covering summit meetings is as exciting as my job gets these days."

Amelia shuddered. "I prefer boring."

With that, she and Carlo found other people to talk to. Jasmine sighed. She couldn't really blame her colleagues for thinking ill of her. The Second Tiberium War was a brutal conflict that exacted an appalling death toll. Indeed, the only good thing that came out of it was that Nod was crippled and Kane killed.

It had been twelve years since the cease-fire. GDI had spent more than a decade since then trying to stave off Tiberium. These days the world wasn't organized into countries and continents, but into Blue Zones, Yellow Zones, and Red Zones, depending on the level of Tiberium infestation. Blue had none, Red had too much, Yellow was somewhere between those extremes. Unsurprisingly, most of the world was Yellow. Jasmine, Carlo, and Amelia were all fortunate enough to be living in Blues.

Nobody lived in Red Zones, of course. The levels of Tiberium were far too high for humans—or anything, really—to survive.

Her earpiece crackled. *"Jasmine, you there?"*

It was her boss, Penny Sookdeo. Tapping the earpiece, she said, "Yeah, chief?"

"Anh told me that Kinsburg just talked to you guys. Why am I not seeing anything from you?"

"I was in the middle of putting it together, chief, I just—"

"Your drone isn't active. Try again."

"Putting it together in my *head*. You know me, One-Take Martinez."

"I don't have it ready to go online in five, I'm sending Wu up there."

Penny signed off before Jasmine could reply, which was probably just as well. *Annabella Wu isn't half the reporter I am. She's got* no *stage presence.* Jasmine would sooner see that tibehead Cassandra Blair. At least she had the Aussie accent working for her.

In all honesty, Jasmine hadn't been planning on filing any kind of report on Kinsburg's not-a-statement, simply because the Director hadn't said anything of substance. She would rather have done an examination of Kinsburg's *actual* speech rather than her teasing about a magic word that was going to herald a radical shift in GDI policy.

Besides, the "radical shift" had already happened. Recruitment in the GDI military was down, but so were the number of skirmishes they'd been engaged in. Whatever word Kinsburg was going to hit with in her speech tomorrow was probably going to be something that acknowledged that this change had been going on for a decade.

Maybe it'll be "peace."

Of course, there was also Mobius's award. That was worth mentioning.

Jasmine tapped the inside of her wrist, which shifted the drone from standby to active. The small ball-bearing–sized item on her belt buzzed to life. Retrieving the Hand from the other side of her belt, Jasmine used the trackpad to move it away from her belt and into position so that it was facing her. The Hand verified that the gyros and flight systems were functioning normally, the battery was almost fully charged (putting it on standby had drained about four percent), and the lens was clean.

Then she glanced behind her. She didn't really want to give W3N's viewers a shot of an empty lounge that she herself was only allowed to be in twenty percent of. The wall they were all up against had a bunch of really ugly paintings on it that Jasmine wouldn't force her biggest enemy to look at unwillingly. One was a space-scape that had way too many colors for something that was supposed to be just black, and the other was a neo-Impressionist rendering of the skyline of New York City from around 2020. It was Jasmine's considered opinion that the neo-Impressionists should all have had their hands cut off at the wrist to avoid contaminating the art world any further.

That left her with either a bird's-eye view—which was a little too radical for a brief report on a meaningless bite—or a shot that included the other reporters in the area.

After a moment's thought, she decided to torture her viewers with the alleged artwork. Penny always yelled at her when she included non-W3N reporters in a shot, because it reminded viewers that they could be watching someone else. Since Penny was already hacked off at her, it was best not to go with that.

She checked the image the drone was getting on the heads-up display on the inner-left lens of her glasses, was satisfied that her lustrous dark hair looked good, and that the four pigtails (two on either side of her head) were evenly spaced and neatly tied and visible from in front of her, and then started recording.

"This is Jasmine Martinez, reporting from the GDI Energy Summit on GDSS *Philadelphia*. Today is the final day of talks among the GDI Directors as well as several military, economic, and scientific consultants. Tomorrow, Director Kinsburg will give her summation address to let us know what the fruits of this summit are, but today she shared with this reporter—" Again, Penny didn't like the acknowledgment of other reporters, so she made it sound like Kinsburg was only talking to her, not a dozen people. "—that her speech will reveal GDI's new watchword. Speculation is running rampant as to what that watchword will be, but the Director made it abundantly clear what it *won't* be."

Jasmine then paused the drone and used the Hand to call up Kinsburg's speech, inserting the final bit of it: *"For the last five decades, we've been forced to emphasize defense against the onslaught of Tiberium and against*

Nod and the other forces that would destroy our way of life. Tomorrow, that will change, and for the better."

"Whether this means GDI will be taking a proactive rather than reactive stance against the continued onslaught of Tiberium, or something even more radical, remains to be seen. Director Kinsburg also announced that Dr. Ignatio Mobius, one of the world's leading experts on Tiberium, will be receiving a GDI Medal of Honor for his tireless efforts over the past five decades."

Again, she paused the drone, this time splicing in: *"The world owes Dr. Mobius a huge debt, and it's one we can only begin to repay with the medal he will be presented with tomorrow."*

"'This is Jasmine Martinez reporting for W3N."

She watched the entire thing one time to make sure there weren't any flubs, not to mention verifying that a fly hadn't buzzed in front of the drone or something. The one and only time Jasmine forgot to look over the footage before linking it to Penny was the time her drone glitched and was recording about ten degrees off from the feed going to her HUD. Since then, she made sure to check the footage at least once before linking it.

Satisfied that it was fine—and proud of her proactive/reactive line—she linked it to Penny.

Her editor's voice sounded in her ear less than a minute later. *"Not bad. I like the proactive/reactive bit. Nice to see they're giving Mobius the one-foot-in-the-grave award. So what do you think the word is?"*

Knowing Penny appreciated bluntness, Jasmine gave the answer that she was too polite to give Amelia and Carlo: "How the hell should I know? I'm just a reporter."

"Yeah." Penny's voice sounded weird when she said that.

"What's that supposed to mean, Chief?"

"Uh, sorry, Jasmine, something going on down in B-2. Some military movement. I gotta check it out. Keep up the good work."

Jasmine breathed a sigh of relief. When Penny ended conversations with those words, it meant she was in a good enough mood that she wasn't likely to crawl in her ear for the rest of the day. *Of course, it could just be that she's distracted. Wonder why there's mobilization in B-2.*

General Zachary Harkin was just finishing up his link with Intelligence and Operations when Director Kinsburg came into his office.

Or rather, Harkin's temporary office. Normally, as the ranking military officer on the *Philadelphia,* Harkin would get the biggest office on the station. However, with the Directors all on board, that office had to, by protocol, go to Kinsburg. To her credit, the Director herself had apologized for the necessity, and had even offered to forgo commandeering Harkin's place of work, but Harkin himself wouldn't hear of it. It wasn't *that* much of a sacrifice. The power needs of a space station were such that none of the offices were particularly large, and there wasn't much of a qualitative difference between a workplace that was one hundred and twenty square feet versus one that was a "mere" one hundred even.

Besides, as long as Harkin had access to EVA, the GDI military computer and artificial intelligence, he could work in a hole in the ground.

The only thing he missed was the oak desk, which had been in his family for the past four generations. Being a military general paid fairly well, but if Harkin ever found himself hard up for cash, he suspected that he could sell the desk for several thousand credits. With Tiberium consuming so much of the Earth these days, plants had become a necessary resource to keep the world's oxygen supply from depleting, and so wooden luxury items were no longer made new. Existing ones had become increasingly rare and therefore quite valuable. There were times when Harkin wondered how his ancestors could have wasted so much plant life—but then, who could have predicted Tiberium? Besides, he was one to talk, with his prized oak desk, which he'd sworn on more than one occasion would never leave his side until he died. When Harkin had declined the offer of keeping his office during the summit, Kinsburg had offered to at least detail some of the soldiers to move the desk, but Harkin had refused that as well. His self-indulgence went far enough to *have* the desk, and that only because of familial pride. Taking soldiers off more important duties to haul his desk around was a waste of resources. Forcing soldiers to do your personal bidding was the first step in breaking down discipline, and Harkin knew that they couldn't afford that, especially now when things were comparatively quiet.

Kinsburg asked as she entered, "Good news?"

"And bad, unfortunately. The good is that In-Ops has officially downgraded the Nod threat level to 'low.' "

Nodding in appreciation as she sat down in the guest chair, Kinsburg said, "Good timing. I'll have Ella drop that into the speech."

Harkin remained standing, mostly because he hated sitting at the generic metal desk that was in this office. "Honestly, we could've done it weeks ago, but some of the other generals were objecting."

That got a rare genuine smile out of Kinsburg—not

the fake one she gave the reporters. "I assume by 'other generals' you mean Jack Granger?"

Not wanting to speak ill of a fellow general to a civilian, even if that civilian was the woman he reported to, Harkin only said, "He was one of those objecting, yes." In fact, it had mostly been Granger who was convinced that Nod was still a threat, even if Kane really was dead—and Granger was also one of many who didn't believe that the Brotherhood's charismatic leader had truly been killed. This was despite the fact that Granger and Harkin were both among the few who knew that Kane's death had taken place not in Kenya, as had been reported to the public, but in Cairo at the hands of a GDIUP battle commander named Michael McNeil. Still, even though McNeil had stabbed Kane in the heart, a body was never recovered, and that more than anything had led to Granger's skepticism.

Harkin was starting to come around to that point of view as well. "The bad news is that Granger just sent some troops to North Carolina."

Frowning, Kinsburg asked, "Why?"

"A routine stop of a produce truck got pixelated in a hurry. Turned out to be a Nod truck—and the driver blew himself and the truck up."

Kinsburg leaned forward in the chair. "Were any of our people—?"

Shaking his head, Harkin said, "One of the shields was wounded, but she'll be okay."

"My God." Kinsburg leaned back and rubbed her forehead. "We haven't had a kamikaze in, what, a year?"

"Two. And In-Ops's sat-scan turned up some energy readings that are off the grid. So Granger figured he'd play it safe and send a team in. It's coded Op Alpha Green."

"Keep me posted," Kinsburg said. "If Nod's operating so close to a Blue, that threat level change may be premature." North Carolina was in Y-6, the Yellow Zone that took up a large percentage of North America, right near the southern border of B-2.

"And it may be a false alarm. We're not even sure it really *was* a Nod truck, especially since the evidence is so much shrapnel. It could've been some off-net who wanted to kill himself in front of an audience. Let's see what Granger's people turn up before we change the message."

"All right, Zach, if you say so." Kinsburg let out a breath. "Besides, I'd rather tell people Nod's threat is low tomorrow. Even if it's only true for a couple of days, it'll increase confidence in what we're doing, especially when we announce the resonator program."

"Of course, Lia." Harkin nodded in understanding, knowing how important it was to reassure the civilians that things were under control, whether they actually were or not. That was why GDI, a secret alliance formed under a special United Nations order, had kept Tiberium a secret when it was discovered in Italy—which was now the center of R-1, by far the largest of the eight Red Zones. In fact, they had only revealed the truth about Tiberium's existence to the general public when Kane forced them to tip their hand. Harkin was of the considered opinion that what the general public didn't know wouldn't hurt them.

Then Harkin's door buzzed. Kinsburg had just walked right in, but as the Director General, she had access to any room on the *Philadelphia* that wasn't privacy-sealed, something Harkin usually never bothered with. Everyone who had clearance to be in this part of the station wasn't somebody he'd want to keep any business from, and nothing personal happened in his office, regardless of which physical office he was in.

Everyone else, though, buzzed first. The buzzing was accompanied by a holo rising from the desk showing an image of who was on the other side: a short, stocky woman with steel-gray hair cut short, fierce blue eyes, and enough lines in her face to make a convincing scowl. There were also two laugh lines that were well worn. This was Dr. Elisa Scarangello, one of the scientists advising the GDI Directors during the summit, and also Harkin's wife of twenty years.

Touching the upper right-hand corner of the holo caused the door to slide open and let her in.

Elisa crossed the threshold, then stopped when she saw who was in the guest chair. "I'm sorry, Zee, I didn't know you had company. I can come back later."

That prompted another smile from Kinsburg, but this was the flat-toothed one she used for the general public. "Not at all, Doctor, I was just leaving. Your husband was briefing me on a situation that I'm sure he'll tell you all about."

In a tight voice, Elisa said, "I happen to have level-five clearance, Director, and my husband has never—"

"Of course he hasn't." Giving Harkin a nod, Kinsburg said, "Keep me apprised, Zach. We'll talk again tonight."

With that, she left.

Elisa watched the door slide shut behind the Director, then turned to her husband with a scowl that had intimidated many a lab assistant. "Must that tibehead always bait me like that?"

"Apparently." Harkin spoke in a neutral tone. The last place he wanted to be was between his wife and his boss.

"You know what I just found out? The reason why Boyle's been buffering on the funding for the resonator project is because he's acting on direct instructions from Director Lia ficken Kinsburg her own self. Can you believe this shite?"

"No," Harkin said automatically. Now he did sit in his chair. It was best to get comfortable when his wife went off on one of her foul-mouthed rants.

"I've seen that speech she's giving tomorrow. After yelling at me for two days about the 'lavish expenditures' of the program, that moron's made it the cornerstone of her talk, and *she's* taking all the credit for it! It wasn't even her ficken idea, and she fought it from point one!"

"But she *is* doing it," Harkin said.

"Of course she is. When every single ficken person in the room is beating her over the head with it, including half the goddamn Directors, of *course* she's gonna say yes! She's worried it's gonna be Florida all over again."

"Understandable," Harkin said even as he noticed the purple light flashing on his desk indicating an incoming call. He tapped the hold button, knowing better than to interrupt Elisa when she was like this. With space at a premium, their cabin was tiny, so the option of sleeping in the living room was right out, which meant that answering the call would result in him putting a cot in here.

However, to her credit, Elisa saw it and understood what it meant. "Sorry, you need to work."

"That's all right."

"Zee, my love, you're a general. You have better things to do than listen to me while you're on duty." Now she let loose with the smile that could brighten an entire Red Zone. "I'll chew your ear off tonight."

Chuckling, Harkin said, "Fine."

She turned toward the door, then turned back. "Oh, before I forget, why I came in here—"

"It wasn't to scorch Lia?"

The scowl came back. "No. You know Manfred, my old assistant?"

Elisa went through lab assistants the way most people went through underwear. Harkin had stopped trying to keep track of them decades ago. "Of course I don't."

"Well, he proposed to that tech he's been dating, and there'll be a celebration in the staff lounge tonight. I promised to be there, and it'd mean a lot if you put in an appearance."

"What time?"

"Nineteen, after the shift's over."

"I'm supposed to be getting a briefing from In-Ops at nineteen, but I'll come down after that."

"Thank you." The smile returned. "It'd mean a lot to Manfred and Natale both to get your blessing."

Harkin raised his eyebrows. "I'm not blessing anything. I don't even know those two."

"Then consider it a good-luck charm for their marriage."

The light on his desk changed from purple to amber. "Fine, I'll do it. Now I need to take this."

"Fine." She moved to the door. "I love you, General."

He blew her a kiss. "I love you too, Doctor."

As soon as the door shut behind her, he touched the light, causing another holo to appear over his desk. "This is Harkin."

The holo showed the pleasant Asian features of Sandra Telfair from In-Ops. "*General, just wanted to ping you to let you know that initial reports from North Carolina have come in. It's definitely some kind of Nod staging area, but we're not sure of the force yet.*"

Harkin scratched his chin thoughtfully. It could still be nothing. It didn't do to get worked up over this kind of thing, especially since their intel came from one kamikaze truck. "Thanks, Sandra. Keep me posted. How's General Granger holding up?"

Telfair looked serious. *"Chewing through his desk, like usual."*

"Jack's never been happy unless he has something to worry about." Harkin let out a very long breath. "Let's just hope he's worrying about nothing."

Jasmine shifted her weight in the metal chair, trying to find a way to get her arse to conform to it in such a way that she wouldn't be in pain for the next three days but also would be able to sit still for the duration of Kinsburg's big speech.

She suspected that those two twains would never meet. It was something her father always said, and the only twain she knew was the last name of the guy who wrote the *Adventures of Huckleberry Finn.* Either way, though, she made a note in her Hand to pick up some ointment for the inevitable aches in her hips and thighs and arse that this speech were likely to cause.

She used the Hand to maneuver the drone into a good position. As a W3N reporter, she was seated front and center, so her cam had a perfect view of where Kinsburg would be standing. That left her with several options for the drone. Finally, she decided to guide it over to where it would focus on the nine seats behind the podium. The other eight members of the Council of Directors and Dr. Mobius would all be sitting back there while Kinsburg made her speech. Jasmine was curious to see what their reactions would be. Not that all eight Directors hadn't already read over and approved the speech—probably each had their own bits they wanted in or out—but sometimes you could get some interesting involuntary reactions out of people. As career politicians, the Directors would be less prone to it than, say, the athletes she used to interview back in Boston, but even the best politician slipped every once in a while. A politician slipping was always cause for speculation, which got people clicking to W3N. Higher clickrates made Penny happy, and Jasmine knew that it was always best to keep Penny happy. The alternative was too terrible to contemplate.

The press room on the *Philadelphia* was small, of course, as were most of the rooms on the space station, but it was also the room in the station with the biggest window. One of Jasmine's first reports for W3N was about the construction of the station, and she had interviewed one of the engineers about how difficult and expensive (and risky) it was to put windows in, since transparent substances were less sturdy than opaque ones, and the environment outside the station was the unforgiving vacuum of space. Even the glasteel used for the windows wasn't as tough as the alloys used for the rest of the station. When Jasmine asked why they bothered doing it at all, the engineer just smiled and said, "Just *wait* until you see the view."

Jasmine had had to cut most of the engineer's interview, laden as it was with incomprehensible jargon, but she made sure to keep that part.

And he'd been right. Seeing the entire planet laid out below them, with the majestic emptiness of space above and behind it, was simply breathtaking. (Literally for some: Carlo Trøndheim had suffered an asthma attack when he first saw it.)

Indeed, the only thing that spoiled the view was that, even from this high up, you could see the toll that Tiberium had taken. When Jasmine had first come up here after the station's completion, the press room's window showed Europe, western Asia, and northern Africa, and the center of Europe was a sickening greenish-yellow blot on what once had looked like a pristine blue from outer space. Today, though, they were over North America. Peering at the eastern seaboard, she chuckled and thought, *I can see my house from here . . .*

Amelia sat down next to her. "Any word on the word?" she asked.

Jasmine shook her head. "I talked to a couple of aides last night after dinner, but they were locked."

"Me, too. My boss actually started a viewer poll. So far, seventy-five percent say it'll be 'peace,' and twenty percent say 'unity.' The other five percent are about a hundred different words."

Unable to resist a grin, Jasmine asked, "Not 'Tiberium'?"

With a chuckle, Amelia said, "We got one for that, and I wouldn't put it past Carlo to click that one in himself."

GDI Press Liaison Takashi Chao walked through the door behind the podium and approached it. "Ladies and gentlemen, if you'll take your seats, we're about ready to start."

The reporters who'd still been standing all took their seats. Jasmine smiled to herself. Most of them probably wanted to avoid the discomfort for as long as they possibly could, but Jasmine knew it was best to get used to it before you sat so you didn't squirm and make your cam move. (Although some, Jasmine knew, were relying entirely on drones, and some were only making audio recordings, so that wasn't as much of a factor.) Jasmine tapped the side of her glasses and activated her drone as well.

Once everyone was settled, Chao said, "Ladies and gentlemen, may I present the Council of Directors of the Global Defense Initiative and Dr. Ignatio Mobius of the GDI Science Division."

Everyone applauded politely. Most of the people in this room had spoken to at least one or two Directors dozens of times in the last week alone, and it wasn't that big a deal to be in the same room as them. The applause did get a bit louder when Mobius—who was the last to enter—came in.

Jasmine wondered if Chao ever started a sentence with words other than "Ladies and gentlemen." Somehow, she doubted it.

Seven of the Directors, male and female both, wore fairly standard euroamerican formalwear: collarless button-down shirts, slacks, moccasins, all made of cotton or linen. The exceptions included Director Mokae, who was in charge of B-10, B-13, and B-14 in Africa, who wore a vibrantly colored dashiki and hat that made him stand out from the others; and Director Delgado, who wore a dark blue dress and high heels, a surprisingly old-fashioned outfit. Delgado, who was responsible for the smallest territory of any on the Council, being in charge only of B-8 in South America, was also something of a traditionalist, so Jasmine wasn't entirely surprised by this. Mobius was also wearing an old-fashioned suit of a type that was fairly common back in the late twentieth century when Mobius was a young man.

Mobius and eight Directors sat in the seats behind the podium, while Chao made way for Lia Kinsburg.

Jasmine had positioned the drone so that it caught each of the Directors as they came in, and she thought she had seen something. She used the Hand to play what the drone had gotten on her HUD, and sure enough,

Kinsburg looked like she had the weight of several worlds on her shoulders when she walked through the door. That look faded within a second, and she had on the same toothy smile she'd favored them all with in the lounge yesterday. *I wonder what that's all about.*

"Good afternoon people of the press, and through you, people of the world. This has been a great week for us here, and it is our fond hope that that greatness will extend to all of you on the planet that spins below us as we look to the future."

Clichéd, but not bad, Jasmine thought.

"Fifty-two years ago, a substance was found in the Tiber River in Italy. That fateful day in 1995 changed the world forever, and not for the better. The substance, which the scientists of the time named Tiberium, has become the dominant force on planet Earth, as it has inexorably crept across the globe, transforming—one might say corrupting—everything in its path."

As if we don't know all this already. Jasmine sighed, wondering when Kinsburg was going to get to the infamous word.

"Tiberium has been more than a crystalline menace that has rendered parts of the planet uninhabitable, that has changed weather patterns and altered the way we live our lives. Tiberium has also been a force for change, bringing the nations of the world together. Unfortunately, it did not bring them all together under the same banner. Two terrible wars have already been fought, even as our scientists have tried to find a way to stem the tide of Tiberium. Our military has also been forced to fight for our freedom against the deluded terrorists who see Tiberium not as the natural phenomenon it is, but as some sort of ridiculous holy force to be worshipped."

Jasmine could see several other reporters shifting in

their seats, including at least one who was using the same type of spec-cam she had. *Hope you've got a drone for secondary footage, especially since that was a particularly quotable line.* At least, it was for some. Jasmine didn't see any need to repeat something that everyone already knew, which was all this speech was so far.

"Today, though, that changes. After the Second Tiberium War, we were victorious. The Brotherhood of Nod is decimated, its leader dead. Today, we no longer wait for Tiberium to destroy us. Today, we no longer wait for terrorists to attack us. Today, we take action. Since its inception, GDI has always been about defense. Defending ourselves against the encroachment of Tiberium, defending ourselves against the Brotherhood of Nod, defending ourselves against the changes that both these things have wrought on our world. Today, that changes."

Finally. Jasmine noticed that the other Directors seemed to tense, or at least sit up straighter. So did her fellow reporters. This was what they'd been waiting for.

"As of now, GDI has a new watchword: preservation. No longer will we stand idly by and wait for this strange force to work its influence on us. We've been studying Tiberium for fifty years now, and we're closer than ever before to understanding it and controlling it, and without the distractions of military action against the Brotherhood of Nod, we can overcome Tiberium's power and take back our world."

Giving Amelia a sidelong glance, Jasmine wondered if any of the five percent of her viewers who voted for one word picked "preservation." It certainly wasn't one Jasmine herself would have thought of. She wondered if they really meant it, or if it was wishful thinking.

"Recently, we discovered that Tiberium has a vulnerability. Even now, our top scientists are working on a program that will exploit this weakness. We will use sonic resonators to beat back Tiberium. Our initial intent is to halt the flow of Tiberium in the Yellow Zones and keep it out of the Blue Zones, but our long-term goal is more ambitious than that. We were once told that, left unchecked, Tiberium would cover the planet by 2112. Now we have a new prediction: GDI will make all the Red Zones habitable again by 2112."

Now that *quote will be all over the planet by tonight,* Jasmine thought with a smile. She was willing to bet that Kinsburg had deliberately instructed the scientists to fudge their estimates so the target date would match that old prediction for Tiberium takeover. Certainly it seemed ridiculous on the face of it that Reds could become in any way habitable in a mere sixty-five years.

"The human race didn't ascend to the top of the evolutionary ladder without making some amazing strides. We've split the atom, we've sent humans into space, we've mapped out the human body down to the smallest component, we've found ways to extend our lives and our knowledge beyond all possible imagining. And we will conquer this as well. Tiberium is simply the latest in a series of challenges that we have met, and will continue to meet."

Just as Jasmine started linking to Penny—normally she'd wait until she edited the footage down, but she wanted her boss to see this—the station suddenly shook.

Jasmine barely had time to think that the *Philadelphia*'s spin should have kept it steady when the world exploded around her.

When Kinsburg had begun her speech, General Harkin was standing at the back of the press room. He'd, of course, read the speech and even seen Kinsburg rehearse it, so he had no real interest in hearing it now. Mostly, he was here for the view of Earth from the largest window on the station. He hadn't wanted to be assigned up here at first—though he hadn't objected, as he never objected when given an order—but his first view changed that.

This is what we're fighting for. He thought those words as he looked down on the Tiberium-ravaged planet of his birth; he had said them to his wife the first time she had visited the *Philadelphia*. Elisa had said it herself when she was assigned here months after that, and he'd always been grateful to have her by his side.

Now, with the resonator program under way, things were starting to look up. After decades of frustration, they had finally found something that could beat back Tiberium: sonics had succeeded in stemming the Tiberium tide, and GDI's resources had been turned to developing sonic weapons. True, Nod was still a threat. He'd gotten a report from Granger that there was quite the Nod stronghold in North Carolina, including a manufacturing plant and more soldiers than In-Ops thought they had in the Western Hemisphere, much less in one location.

By morning, their threat level would be revised upward to "medium," but he wanted to keep it low at least until enough news sources talked about the speech. Afterward, no one would care as much. Keeping things palatable for civilians was part of a general's job, after all.

Suddenly, his earpiece crackled with the voice of Sandra Telfair. *"General, the Goddard Space Center's been demolished."*

"Who's responsible?" Harkin subvocalized, which was enough for the pickup to transmit to Sandra, but wouldn't disturb the speech.

"We think it's Nod, but that's not the point. Goddard's—"

"Responsible for our A-SAT defense as long as we're over North America. Fotze. We need to . . ."

"*Need to what, General?*" Telfair said anxiously after Harkin trailed off.

But Harkin was too stunned to speak, because looking out the window, he could see the missile that was heading straight for the station.

I love you, Elisa, was Harkin's last thought before the *Philadelphia* rocked to the side. The earsplitting sound of metal being rent asunder echoed through the air, even as that air rushed out. Harkin felt himself yanked across the room by the explosive decompression. Years of training told his body to go limp without his even thinking about it, but it didn't matter. In a moment, he'd be in the vacuum of space, assuming he made it that far.

A sudden increase in heat told him he wouldn't. The last thing Zachary Harkin felt was fire from the missile warhead detonation consuming his flesh and bones.

"Excuse the interruption, but we're getting breaking news on the Philadelphia. *Apparently, just moments ago, there was an accident. Obviously, something has gone terribly wrong. We're going to do our best to confirm what we're all seeing but at this time, we have no idea what possibly could have caused a tragedy of this magnitude. We're going—"*

Kane turned away from the holo of W3N's William Frank, which was being intercut with footage of the fiery remains of the GDSS *Philadelphia* tilting out of its orbit and starting its inevitable plummet earthward. He looked at the acolyte who was seated at the computer terminal. "Are we ready yet, Brother Eamonn?"

"Yes, sir. The overlink will commence at your instruction."

"Good." He looked back at the holo, where Frank was babbling on.

"—*still don't know what caused this horrible accident*—"

"Oh, you're about to," Kane whispered.

"—*but we're getting reports now that all one thousand and forty-seven passengers aboard the* Philadelphia *are presumed dead, including all nine Directors and at least a dozen other members of GDI leadership*—"

"Excellent." Kane was waiting for confirmation that the Directors, the scientists, and the military personnel on board the station were all dead. "Now, Brother Eamonn!"

Eamonn tapped a key on his pad, and nodded to Kane, who took a deep breath as the drone hovering in front of him activated. The holo of the W3N cast was replaced with Kane's own bald head, goatee, and penetrating eyes. His deep voice rung out over the speakers.

"The destruction of the *Philadelphia* was *not* an accident. It was a merciful bullet to the head of a malignant ideology. It was the death of fear and the birth of hope. Rejoice, Children of Nod! The blood of your oppressors will flow and fifty years of tyranny will finally end. Transformation is coming. A new day will dawn. The future—is *ours*."

With a nod, Eamonn shut down the transmission. Kane knew it would never be traced. Eamonn was too talented for that. If he weren't, he never would have been allowed into Kane's inner circle.

And so it begins, Kane thought, eagerly looking forward to the bloodshed that would follow—and what it would, in turn, lead to . . .

TWO

Private Ricardo Vega sat in the small, airless room in Fort Dix where he'd been ordered to report after he was done with Basic Training. About half of his Basic class—half the ones who made it to the end, anyhow—were in the room with him, along with plenty he didn't recognize, making about thirty in all. Vega could hear air-conditioning ducts working in the ceiling, but they weren't doing a whole helluva lot of good. He had already removed his black-and-gray fatigue shirt, draped on the empty chair next to him, and sweat was still trickling down the back of his neck and staining the black undershirt he wore.

Most of the other recruits, male and female alike, had done likewise. Vega noticed one guy he didn't know who was practically drenched in sweat. Next to him was a woman who wasn't sweating at all. It took him a second to recognize her as Autumn Marveille from Basic. She'd had short brown hair during training, but had since shorn it down to crew-cut level; it was even shorter than Vega's own black locks. Vega didn't like the way it looked on her, though he was willing to bet it helped with the not-sweating thing.

Another person who wasn't sweating was the sergeant standing in the far corner of the room, right next to a door. *Figure he's here to make sure we don't steal nothing.*

Even with the crap AC, it was cooler in here than it was outside. It was the latest in a series of increasingly brutal summers, which most people blamed on the Tiberium infestation. Either that, or a Nod plot. And, of course, some folks thought Tiberium *was* a Nod plot. Either way, Vega just knew it was hot and humid.

He'd reported here after being told to leave his duffel bag behind. The staff sergeant who'd told him that had said that the duffel would be sent to his barracks while he reported to the division second in command.

"So what you in for?"

Vega turned to look at the person behind him. The speaker was a short, stocky guy, hair cut in a popular style these days: bushy at the temples, razed almost to the skin on the top and back. He had coffee-colored skin, and eyes that were almost black. " 'Scuse me?"

"I asked what you in for? Me, I pulled assault. Figure this beat the shite outta pen, yah?"

As soon as he said "outta pen," Vega realized that this was someone who chose enlisting in the Global Defense Initiative United Peacekeepers in lieu of jail time. Dad had told him that GDI had been stepping up efforts to recruit in that direction due to the downswing in recruitment since TWII ended.

"I'm not in for anything," Vega said. "I joined up voluntarily."

The assault charge's dark eyes narrowed. "Fotze, sib, you spoofin' me? Why anyone wanna do this cracked-up shite on purpose?"

"It's a legacy, I guess." Vega shrugged. "See, my dad—"

"Ten-*hut*!" That was the sergeant in the corner.

Everyone rose to their feet and stood at attention, in

almost perfect unison, even the guy behind Vega. A middle-aged white guy walked into the room. He was wearing the same black undershirt as the rest of them, but also had on a hat with a major's oak leaf on the front. His nose was a bit larger than the norm, and a dark mustache flecked with bits of gray sat on his upper lip.

In a clipped British accent, the major said, "As you were."

They all sat down. Vega still sat up straight, as did most of those in the room. Vega couldn't see behind him to see how the assault charge was seated, but he was willing to bet that he was hunched over.

The major stood at the podium at the front of the room. "I'm Major Hastings, SIC of the 22nd Infantry Division of the GDIUP." Hastings, Vega noticed, pronounced it as five letters rather than "Giddy-Up," which was how Dad had always said it. "I'll make this brief, as I honestly have better things to do than chat with you lot. First of all, those of you who joined thinking that because we're not formally at war with Nod or anyone else, that this will be a cushy assignment, I suggest you turn around and go back to wherever you came from. The 22nd is an elite division, and those who slack off will not last particularly long. If you get yourself killed, I don't mind much, although the paperwork's a nuisance. However, you might take some talented soldiers with you, and I prefer to avoid that."

Hastings then started to pace the front of the room, making eye contact with everyone there in turn.

"Secondly, you should be clear that the P in GDIUP stands for 'peacekeepers.' What this means in real terms is that you are here to keep the peace. We are the world's protectors, and that is the master we serve—*not* GDI, though they do administrate."

That surprised Vega. He had never really thought of there being any real distinction there, and was surprised to hear a major, the second in command of an elite division, making it.

"Thirdly, we have a chain of command here in the Keepers. If you have an issue, take it up with your sergeant, then with your company commander, then your battalion commander, then with me."

Someone muttered, "And then with God, right?"

"Battle Commander McNeil, actually. He commands the 22nd, which means he has all the responsibility. I merely have the power, which I generally only use on soldiers who interrupt me."

Vega heard a gulp from the same direction as the God comment, but he didn't break discipline to look.

"Also if you have an issue that needs to be raised with a deity, I suggest you go straight to that deity, as none of us are likely to be able to help you." Hastings then walked back to the podium and touched something on it. A holo lit up over it with a list of names, that were backward from Vega's perspective. "Now then, a final check to make sure everyone here should be here and that everyone who should be here is. Signal in some manner when I call your name. Abernathy, Leeshai."

"Here."

"You'll be reporting to Lieutenant Lemish of Company 2. Acovone, Mario."

As each name was called and responded to, Hastings would tell that person which lieutenant (which he pronounced "left-tenant") to report to, then touch the holo of that name, causing it to disappear from the list. He worked his way down the list until there were only two left.

"Vega, Ricardo."

"Here, sir."

"You'll be reporting to Lieutenant Opahle of Company 7, but hang back a minute when we're done, will you?"

"Yes, sir!" Vega had no idea what *that* was about, but he had a pretty good guess: It would have to do with Dad. It always did. While there were some benefits to being the son of a war hero, there were plenty of drawbacks, usually involving older officers who'd served with him who wanted to give him one of two speeches: the "I served with your father, and you've got a lot to live up to" speech or the "I served with your father so if you ever need a favor" speech. He preferred the second, given a choice—it was always nice when superior officers were willing to help you out—but he'd just as soon have avoided it altogether and got on with being a soldier. He wanted to be Private Ricardo Vega not Javier Vega's son.

Vega was just grateful that nobody else had been called for Company 7. He would have hated to hold up other soldiers reporting to their unit because Hastings wanted to reminisce about the good old days.

Hastings touched the holo, leaving one name. "Zipes, Mustapho."

"Yah." That was the assault charge behind him.

"You're also Lieutenant Opahle. Wait outside with her while I speak to Private Vega. That's all."

The sergeant in the corner bellowed, "Ten-*hut*!"

Everyone stood to attention.

"Dismissed," Hastings said.

Everyone exited through the rear door. Zipes leaned over as he got up and said, "Take your time, sib. I ain't in no rush."

Vega snorted, but ignored him. Instead he walked to

the front of the room, saluted—which Hastings quickly returned—and remained at attention.

"That'll be all, Sergeant," Hastings said after all the new recruits save for Vega had cleared the room.

The sergeant saluted and exited via the same door Hastings had come in through.

"So, you're Javier Vega's son, are you?"

"Yes, sir!"

"I have one question for you, Private. Why did you join the Keepers?"

"Always wanted to be a soldier, sir!"

"Mhm." Hastings folded his arms. "Bluntly, Private, did you join because Daddy told you to?"

Okay, this wasn't the speech I was expecting. "No, sir!"

"No undue pressure from the *pater familias* to follow in the family tradition?"

"No, sir!"

"You're not joining against his wishes, are you?"

"No, sir!"

"Because that's *all* I need, is getting links from all of your father's old friends asking me to take it easy on the lad, or to try to convince you to resign as a favor to the old man."

"No, sir! My father has always encouraged me to do whatever I want, sir!"

Hastings nodded. "Very well. You won't get any special treatment, Private—in either direction. Being Javier Vega's son will neither hurt you nor hinder you with me." He hesitated. "If it does with someone else—if you *do* get special treatment or you are treated worse because of it—I wish to know about it. This is one circumstance under which I'm willing to skip a few links on the chain of command, particularly if the problems are happening somewhere on that chain."

Vega hesitated. "Sir, with respect, I can't do that."

"Really?" Suddenly the poor AC seemed not to matter, as with that one word the temperature in the room dropped several degrees.

However, Vega chose to take that as a request to explain himself. "Sir, forgoing the chain of command *would* constitute my receiving special treatment because of who my father is."

Hastings actually smirked at that. "Not bad. All right, then, have it your way. You're dismissed."

"Sir!" Vega saluted, turned on his heel, and headed for the back door.

"Private!"

Vega stopped, turned around, and stood at attention.

"You'll be happy to know that I've neither met your father nor served with him, so you'll be spared tiresome reminisces about the olden days from me. However, I cannot guarantee that from anyone else under my command—or, for that matter, the one person over it, especially since BC McNeil *did* serve with your father—so I apologize in advance for the tedium."

"Thank you, sir!"

"Don't keep Lieutenant Opahle waiting, Private. And welcome to the 22nd."

"Thank you, sir!"

Only after he turned around and left did Vega let himself smile. *This might not be so bad.* The one thing that had caused him to resist the temptation to join the Keepers was that he was setting himself up for endless comparisons to, and stories about, his father, most of which he'd already heard several thousand times, whenever one of Dad's old friends—and he seemed to have an infinite supply of them—came by to visit.

But the one good thing Vega got out of the repetitions of war stories about Javier Vega was the sense that the Keepers did good work, and he wanted very much to be a part of that.

When he got outside, he appreciated what little work the bad AC was able to accomplish, because it was appallingly hot and humid out here. Various military aircraft flew overhead, their sonic booms echoing throughout the sky, and he could see several groups of soldiers in their black fatigues running drills or exercises.

He looked for the familiar face and funky hair of Mustapho Zipes, who was standing next to a woman wearing lieutenant's bars on her fatigues, which were just visible above her rolled-up sleeves. This was presumably Lieutenant Opahle. She was intimidatingly tall, bronze-skinned from exposure to the sun, with short blond hair—except for a thin braid that ran down from her left temple to the middle of her ear, then looped up and was fastened to where the braid began. It was a variation on another popular style. Normally, it would have hung loose, but Giddy-Up uniform code meant she had to restrain the braid as much as possible. It was, Vega knew, a sign of how much had changed over the years. In his father's day, they would've made the lieutenant cut the braid off.

Vega walked up to her and saluted. "Private Vega reporting for duty, ma'am."

Opahle returned the salute. "Stand easy, Private. Hastings done with his pep talk?"

"Yes, ma'am," Vega said with a nod.

"He only does that for people he thinks might give him trouble. You gonna give him trouble, Private?"

"No, ma'am."

"Then why'd the major think that?"

Holding in a sigh, Vega said, "My father is Javier Vega, ma'am. Major Hastings expressed a concern that I was joining due to familial pressure."

"And did you?"

"No, ma'am."

"Was Hastings convinced?"

"I believe so, ma'am."

Opahle finally smiled. Her white teeth stood in contrast to her tanned skin. "Good. If he's convinced, so'm I. Don't prove us wrong."

"That's my plan, ma'am."

"Good. Private Zipes here is going to Unit Alpha, and you're Unit Epsilon. Let's move."

She led them to a motor pool, where a fleet of Pitbulls awaited. Opahle led them to a Pitbull CC6 that had the roof up, since they were on a base and therefore unlikely to be attacked. If they were, the CC6 would be of some use as a light combat vehicle, especially since it had a rocket launcher mounted on the back. It ran completely on electricity, with motors in each of the four wheels, a handy bit of redundancy. That was something that had surprised Vega to learn during Basic, since in his father's day, during TWII, the Pitbulls were all gas/electric hybrids.

The Pitbull registered Opahle's dog tags as she got in, and started right up. If the vehicle were not on military property, it would take a DNA scan of the driver to allow it to start, but while on Fort Dix, the dog tags were enough. Zipes hopped in the back seat, so Vega took the shotgun seat next to the lieutenant.

"We'll drop you off first, Vega," Opahle said as she steered the Pitbull down the base's main access road.

"Epsilon's on their morning run. You can catch the tail end of it."

"Yes, ma'am." Vega smiled.

"Something amusing?"

"No, ma'am, just looking forward to running. I was on the track team in college." That had been the one condition Javier Vega had put on his son: If he wanted to join Giddy-Up, he had to get a college degree first. Vega now had a bachelor's in history from Fordham University, which probably wouldn't do him a whole lot of good as a private, but might be handy as he worked his way up the ranks. If he was ever in a position of authority in the military, a knowledge and understanding of history would be invaluable.

And he'd joined the track team, too, because he loved to run. He was only sorry he couldn't come in at the beginning of Epsilon's run.

"My guys ain't runnin'?" Zipes asked, then quickly added: "Uh, ma'am."

"Alpha had late duty last night, so they're just having breakfast. I'll take you to the mess after we drop off Vega here." She grinned. "Trust me, you'll thank me being late for breakfast."

Zipes chuckled. "Been eatin' my momma's shite cookin' for twenty-two years, ma'am. Ain't nothin' Giddy-Up can gimme worse. 'Sides, was gonna be eatin' pen food."

"Jailbird, huh?" Opahle said as she turned down a dirt road. "So you went through Basic twice."

"Yes, ma'am. Top'a the class both times."

Vega hadn't known that was required, but then Hastings had said that the 22nd was an elite division, so Zipes probably had to go through "thug Basic," which meant taking it twice.

"What were you in for, Private?" Opahle asked.

"Assault, ma'am," Zipes said. "Some tibehead was hittin' on my lay."

"Out of curiosity, did she appreciate it?"

Zipes actually sank lower into the backseat of the Pitbull as it bounced over rocks and uneven ground. *That's another improvement,* Vega thought. *The old CC2s Dad rode had lousy suspension.* But Vega was sitting comfortably in the front seat without moving, even as the vehicle did an imitation of a basketball.

It took Zipes a second or two to answer Opahle's question. "Nah, she didn't, the bint. Called me a Noddie and signed off. Figured I didn't have shite to go back to, s'when the judge gave me Plan B, I took it. She gonna call me a Noddie, I prove 'er wrong by killin' me a few."

"Sergeant Gnaizda's gonna *love* you."

Vega wondered what that meant, but before he could even figure out a way to ask, he caught sight of a bunch of people all dressed the same as he running in formation toward a hill. *Oh good. Got here in time to go uphill. Give me a chance to show my shite soon as we start.*

The soldiers were in ten rows of two soldiers, except for the last row, which had only one. There was a twentieth, but he was out of formation: a pale man with curly blond hair sticking out of his cap, which had three stripes on it. The sergeant was leading the soldiers in a chant:

"I don't know but I've been told!"

All nineteen soldiers replied in perfect unison: "I DON'T KNOW BUT I BEEN TOLD!"

The sergeant: "Noddies, they got no soul!"

"NODDIES, THEY GOT NO SOUL!"

"Ti-rock, that is what they crave!"

"TI-ROCK, THAT IS WHAT THEY CRAVE!"

"But from us they will not be saved!"

"BUT FROM US THEY WILL NOT BE SAVED!"

"*Sound* off!"

"ONE, TWO!"

"*Sound* off!"

"THREE, FOUR!"

At the first "sound off," the sergeant noticed the approaching Pitbull, and he stopped moving forward, but still continued to pump his legs in step. Without missing a beat, all the soldiers did likewise.

"Unit—*halt!*" At those words from the sergeant, they all stopped jogging in place and stood at attention.

Opahle pulled up right next to the sergeant, who saluted. She returned the salute and asked, "How's it goin', Goody?"

Goody shrugged. "Not too bad."

"Glad to hear it. Private Vega, this is Sergeant Goodier. Goody, this is your newest recruit. Feel free to treat him like shite."

"Always do, ma'am."

"Damn right."

Vega hopped out of the Pitbull and saluted Goodier. "Private Ricardo Vega, reporting for duty, Sergeant."

Goodier didn't return the salute right away, but instead looked Vega up and down. Finally, he returned the salute, and asked, "Heard you were a track star, Private."

"I ran track in college, yes, sir."

"And set new Fordham records for the six hundred meter and eight hundred meter."

Vega couldn't shrug because he was at attention, but his records weren't something he liked to gloat about. "Yes, sir, I did."

"Fine, then you can join the run."

Now Vega smiled. "I was hoping you'd say that, sir."

"I figured. Get in the back line with Brodeur."

"Yes, *sir*!" Vega jogged back and went in line with the private who was alone in the back line, whom he assumed to be Brodeur. The pale redhead had devices in his ears that looked a lot like hearing aids. They were linked to a pair of glasses. *That can't be it. Giddy-Up wouldn't put someone hard of hearing in a combat unit.*

Opahle drove off, Zipes still sitting in the back. *I don't think he's gonna last long,* Vega thought as he stood at attention next to Brodeur.

Goodier started jogging in place, and everyone else did likewise—except Vega, who started half a step later. He'd been waiting for some kind of aural clue, like a chime or an order.

Then the sergeant turned around and started running up the hill. Each of the rows of two went in sequence, everyone running in perfect time. Through the corner of his left eye, Vega looked at Brodeur's legs, making sure to match them as they started.

Given a choice, Vega would rather have run all-out up the hill. But that would've been easy. The challenge was keeping in formation and at the slow pace while fighting gravity on slanted ground. Vega noticed that two of the soldiers fell out of step, but also corrected it by the next step. To his surprise, Goodier said nothing, gave no rebukes, which made him somewhat out of character for a sergeant, based on Basic and Dad's stories.

About halfway up the hill, Vega noticed a flash of light in the sky. He looked up, and then quickly looked straight ahead again. Several other soldiers did likewise, and got it under control just as fast. Right now, he was in formation. You didn't break that.

Goodier seemed to notice the flash also, but his response was to lead another chant, this one based on an old rock song, "Doo Wah Diddy." *Didn't they do this in some old movie?* Vega thought as they ran up the hill and chanted in time.

Vega also noticed that Brodeur's voice sounded funny. It was hard to make it out with all twenty of them chanting "Doo wah diddy diddy dum diddy do" in response to Goodier saying, "There she was just a-walkin' down the street," but Vega could've sworn Brodeur was talking like a deaf guy.

What kinda crackarse outfit have I signed up for?

As they got to the top of the hill, Vega started to feel the familiar ache in his legs from a good run, and he smiled.

Suddenly, Goodier stopped running and tapped his ear. Everyone came to a halt, and Vega did likewise half a second later, stumbling backward to stay in line with Brodeur. A couple of others did something similar. This stop wasn't planned.

"Unit, fall in back to main base. We got something."

"Something, huh? Wonder what that means," the guy in front of Vega said.

The guy next to him, in front of Brodeur, said, "I'm hopin' we get to burn some Nods."

Goodier said, "About face."

Vega pivoted and turned around. He was now in front.

"Double time—march!"

Still Vega kept his eye on Brodeur, since every sergeant had a different notion of what constituted "double" time. For some, it was literally twice the usual jog, for others it was more, for others it *was* the usual jog, but you were supposed to lift your legs higher.

For Goodier, apparently, it really was twice as fast as you were running. Vega noticed a look of approval on Goodier's face as he kept pace with Brodeur.

They arrived back at the main part of Dix in short order, and there were several other groups of soldiers—some in fatigues, some in full gear, some halfway between those—heading for a building that was labeled AUDITORIUM. Probably this was the only space in the entire fort that could hold an entire division. Overhead, three aircraft zoomed by, shattering the sound barrier.

Goodier said, when they were about ten meters from the front, "No sense in trying to keep us together. Just find your seats. Vega, find a buddy so you don't get lost."

Several of the soldiers snickered at that, and Vega good-naturedly did as well. "Yes, sir," he said. Then he turned to Brodeur. If there was a deaf guy in the unit, Vega wanted to know about it. Speaking slowly, he said, "You mind being my buddy?"

"You don't have to talk to me like I'm stupid." Brodeur then grinned. "Save it for Momoa." The two of them walked toward the door, mingling with the others.

One of the larger soldiers in Epsilon said, "Crack off sideways, Brodeur."

Talking normally, and deliberately not looking at Brodeur as they filed through the door, Vega said, "I'm gonna go out on a limb and say that's Momoa?"

"Yeah, that's Angry Puppy. Feel free to scorch him as much as possible. He's cute when he's mad."

Inside, Vega found himself at the top of a big amphitheater. The room was a big circle, with a stage in the center. A tall man with a battle commander's stars on his cap stood alone on that stage, holding an animated conversation. *That's probably McNeil, getting some kind of report.*

Brodeur pointed at two empty seats. "Over here." The more Brodeur spoke, the more Vega was getting used to his distorted speech. He sounded like someone whose throat was covered in sandpaper. Vega simply had never met many deaf people in his life, and the few he had met mostly used sign language and interpreters.

"Okay," Vega asked as they climbed over three other soldiers to take the two seats Brodeur had found, "how can you tell what I'm saying?"

Grinning, Brodeur tapped the side of his glasses. "Experimental unit." Once they were seated, he removed the spectacles and handed them to Vega. "Look inside the left lens."

Peering down to do just that, Vega saw the words LOOK INSIDE THE LEFT LENS scrolling up the transparency. "Not bad."

NOT BAD the lens then read.

Vega handed the specs back. "I'm kinda surprised to see you in a combat unit, though."

"It's a pilot program. Not just the specs, but all of my equipment is geared toward making hearing unnecessary in the field."

"I guess when the guns're blazin', we're all deaf, huh?"

Brodeur smiled. "Exactly."

From somewhere, a loudpseaker bellowed, *"Ten-HUT!"*

Vega shot to his feet, as did Brodeur, and every other soldier in the amphitheater. Some were a little slower than others, and Vega wondered if there'd be any consequences. Of course, if they weren't in his unit, he'd probably never know.

Looking down at the stage, Vega could see McNeil, whose lip movements corresponded to the words being said over the speakers: "At ease, everyone. Be seated."

Everyone sat back down.

"I'm not gonna waste time here, people, because there isn't time to waste. Some of you may have noticed a flash in the sky a little while ago. That was the *Philadelphia* being destroyed by Nod terrorists."

A commotion ran through the amphitheater. Vega found himself unable to swallow, suddenly. *They were having that summit. All the Directors were up there . . .*

"Ten-HUT!"

Everyone stopped talking and again got to their feet.

"I said I wasn't wasting time, and that includes waiting for you greenies to get over it. We've got work to do, people, and we can't afford to mourn. Nod took out Goddard, and that left the *Philadelphia* vulnerable. The Directors are all dead, as is General Harkin, and dozens of other top-ranked GDI personnel. General Granger's still alive, and still in charge of our military forces, and he's ordered the 22nd to B-11. Nod has attacked San Diego, and we need to get them the hell out of our territory." McNeil looked around the entire amphitheater for a second, and then said, "I'm afraid, people, that the Third Tiberium War has officially begun. We didn't start it this time, but we're for shite's sake gonna end it. Get to your barracks and suit up. We leave for B-11 in twenty minutes. You'll get the full briefing on the *Huron*. Dismissed!"

All around them, soldiers climbed over the chairs and moved toward the exits at the top of the amphitheater. Vega looked helplessly at Brodeur, who mouthed the words, *Come with me.*

Brodeur and Vega land-sharked their way through the crowds, eventually finding their way to the front door. Once they got outside—*has it gotten colder out here, or is it just me?* Vega wondered—Brodeur pointed left, and they jogged that way.

Vega asked, "The *Huron*, that's one of the transports?"

Nodding, Brodeur said, "Yeah, they're all named for lakes."

I knew that, thanks, Vega almost said out loud, but decided it would be rude. Brodeur was just trying to help.

Soon, they came upon a barracks house. The door to the barracks was open, and several familiar-looking faces from the run were entering. Vega ran in to see two rows of five bunk beds, two footlockers at the front of each bunk. Several of those footlockers were being opened.

Before he could ask which bunk was his, Goodier appeared out of nowhere. "Come with me, Private."

The sergeant led Vega to a bunk. He noticed that several of the soldiers were now putting on their body armor, wrist units, holsters, and boots. Vega also noticed that his duffel was on one of the lower bunks. *Thank God. I hate upper bunks . . .*

"Suit up, Private. We don't have time to break you in."

"I don't need breaking in, sir."

The guy at the next bunk said, "Good, I like it better when the greenies're already broken."

Several others laughed.

"Make fun of the greenie later, Dish." To the room, Goodier then said, "Come on, guys and gals, we've got a transport to catch."

Vega let the footlocker scan his dog tags, and it immediately opened. He was pleased to see that the vest unit of the body armor already had VEGA stenciled on the right breast.

"Hey, Goody!" someone called out from the other side of the bunk. It sounded like a female voice to Vega. "How'd the Noddies blow up the *Philly* anyhow? I thought they were a 'low' threat."

The one Goodier called "Dish" laughed and said,

"C'mon, Gallagher, whaddaya expect from In-Oops? Those guys couldn't find their arses with both hands."

Vega slid his wrist unit on. "Yeah," he said, "but Kane's dead, so they may not have the same fight in 'em."

"The hell do you know about it?" asked Dish.

Goodier said, "More than you, probably, Dish. Guys and gals, this is our newest recruit, Private Vega. He's no ordinary greenie. His daddy's Javier Vega, and if you don't know who that is, then let me just tell you that he's one of the finest Giddy-Ups that ever there was."

Several whoops, jeers, and "la-de-dahs," came from the various troops, and Vega closed his eyes and counted to ten in Spanish, wishing like *hell* the sergeant had kept his mouth shut.

The woman who asked about the low threat came around so that she was visible. She was a coffee-skinned woman with dark curly hair tied up messily on top of her head. "You gotta be kiddin' me." She turned toward Goodier. "Goody, I thought we weren't getting anymore neps."

At that, Vega stiffened. "Excuse me?"

Turning back around, she said, "Look, Private, I'm sure your father was a great soldier, a credit to Giddy-Up, but this is the 22nd. We can't afford to carry neps around."

After fastening his wrist unit completely on, he got right in the woman's face. "I'm *not* a nep. I enlisted on my own merits, and I scored a 98 on the test *and* was at the top of my class in Basic."

Before she could reply, Goodier said, "Excuse me, Private Vega, Private Gallagher, but could you postpone your war for a bit so we can fight the one that's actually been declared? If you're not suited up in three, you're getting left behind."

"Yes, *sir*," Gallagher said, then went back to her footlocker to put the rest of her equipment on.

Vega affixed the HUD unit to his left eye and left ear, looking at Gallagher the whole time. He knew he was going to have to prove himself as the son of a hero, but he found he really didn't like Gallagher's automatic assumption that he *had* to be useless.

He turned to Dish. "She always this much fun at parties?"

"Nah, she's usually worse." His fellow soldier was now fully suited up. His vest said BOWLES. He held out a hand and said, "Alessio Bowles."

Returning the handshake, Vega said, "Ricardo Vega."

"They all call me Dish."

"They all call me Vega."

Goodier bellowed, "Fall in!"

They all ran out to waiting Pitbulls. Vega squeezed into the back of one with Brodeur, someone else, and Bowles.

Suddenly, it hit him with the force of a railgun slug: *We're at war.* He knew he'd have to fight, but he hadn't expected an all-out war, and certainly not on his first day as a private.

The Philadelphia *was destroyed.* Vega had studied history. He understood the impact of the attack had more to do with symbolism than with actually causing damage to the enemy. GDI had protocols in place, and a new Council of Directors was probably already on the job. There was no information on the *Philadelphia* that wasn't backed up in six other places, and there were other space stations that could take on whatever work *Philadelphia* did that was particular to its being in orbit.

No, it was the act of hitting GDI's largest symbol of its perceived superiority that was important to Nod.

The funny thing—funny in the most morbid sense—was that Dad was supposed to have gone to the Energy Summit as a military advisor. Probably he was really only supposed to go to be a war hero in front of the cams, to remind people of GDI's successes.

But his prosthetic had been acting wiggly, and the docs didn't want to risk him taking a suborbital journey, so he didn't go. That decision saved his life.

I need to link him. God knew when he'd have time, now, but suddenly Vega felt a very strong urge to talk to his father.

Maybe I'll have the chance to on the Huron. He smiled, then.

"What's so funny, kid?" Bowles asked.

"Oh, just thinking that I've never seen one of the new transports before. Read about 'em in Basic, but haven't actually been on one."

Bowles shrugged. "S'a plane is all."

From the shotgun seat in the front of the Pitbull, a big guy—after a second, Vega placed him as "Angry Puppy" Momoa—said, "Ignore him, Private. The *Huron*'s a thing of absolute beauty."

"Get the wipers ready," Gallagher said. "Pup's gonna jack all over the windshield again."

"More chance'a that than doin' it 'cause *you're* here," Momoa said.

"Please, these compliments will make my head spin."

Bowles said, "So'll the *Huron,* if Johanssen's piloting."

"I thought they took Johanssen off rotation," the guy next to Vega, whose vest read GOLDEN, said. "After that shite with the Orca."

"Nah, they just grounded him for a week," Momoa said. "That was two weeks ago. It'll be him."

"Fotze." Golden looked at Vega. "You don't happen to have any motion sickness pills on you, do you?"

"Uh . . ." Vega wasn't sure what to say to that for some reason.

Bowles leaned over. "Golden there's our resident hypochondriac."

"I am *not* a hypochondriac," Golden said, "I'm just always sick!"

Vega chuckled, then reached into his pants pocket, which was just above his still-empty holster. (He assumed he'd be issued his weapons on the *Huron* during the two-hour flight to the other side of the continent.) He pulled out an ornate pill case that Dad had given him for his last birthday, and opened it to reveal the six compartments, each containing three pills.

He reached in and grabbed a yellow one and handed it to Golden. "Here. I heard this'll keep you from getting queasy."

"Seriously?" Golden's eyes lit up like saucers. He eagerly took the pill. "You're the best, Private—" He looked down at Vega's chest. "—uh, Vega. I owe you one."

"Forget it."

The Pitbull continued down toward the Dix airfield. It was an odd beginning, but giving Golden one of his pills gave Vega a good feeling, like he'd made his first steps toward fitting in with Unit Epsilon and with the 22nd.

Of course what really mattered was combat, but they'd have their taste of that soon enough.

Then I'll show Gallagher how much of a soldier I really am.

THREE

The first thing Annabella Wu did when the alarm went off was the same thing she always did: she reached for the slot in the wall next to the bed, where a mug of tea had been provided by the House. She didn't even open her eyes before taking a sip of the necessary beverage, mostly by virtue of knowing that she wasn't capable of so complex a gesture without at least a little caffeine, especially because she hadn't slept the night before.

Many of the world's coffee bean growers had been hit hard by Tiberium, and some were also loyal to the Brotherhood of Nod, so coffee had become a rarity. When Annabella programmed her ration chip, she decided to forgo coffee for tea, which not only was cheaper, but could be made into an iced variety that Annabella liked drinking during the day. She always kept a bottle of it in her pack, and it helped keep her hydrated. She usually went for an herbal variety for the iced version, which kept her throat smooth and clean, necessary in her line of work. Sticking with tea also freed up more space on the chip for other luxuries she preferred not to do without. She had told her fellow W3N reporter, Jasmine Martinez, not to focus so much of her chip on coffee, but she didn't listen. Switching to tea had also served Annabella in good stead this year, when the bad crop meant no coffee in B-2, even if it was on your chip.

Thinking about Jasmine made Annabella think about the *Philadelphia,* and that just left her depressed. *I can't believe she's dead.* Annabella had never even *liked* Jasmine that much—she was a little too arrogant for Annabella's taste, always concerned with how a story would make her look—but that didn't mean she'd wished ill on her fellow reporter.

And that made Annabella in turn think about all the other people who were on that station, some of them her colleagues, some of them Directors, who, for all intents and purposes, ruled the free world. According to a story she read before going to bed last night, most of the head aides to the now-deceased Directors had been promoted to their bosses' positions, with former GDI Treasury Commissioner Redmond Boyle taking over from Lia Kinsburg as Acting Director. The cynical part of Annabella figured this had been done mainly because Boyle would be able to keep GDI's public face affable. Once the flames died down, they'd hire a *real* Director.

All those people dead. She knew, of course, that people had died before, thanks to Tiberium and the wars that it had provoked with Nod, but this, this wasn't like anything she'd experienced. Besides, Nod wasn't supposed to be a threat anymore!

Annabella took two more sips of tea, the hot liquid burning away the cobwebs in her brain, and she actually opened her eyes.

All she saw was her flat, which wasn't much to look at. Aside from the bathroom, she could, of course, see all of it, since it was just one room. The kitch was set into one half a wall, the sink piled high with dirty tea mugs that she really needed to get around to running through the dishwasher one of these days. There was no window, which wasn't that big a deal, since the only thing it would look out on was the other tall buildings full of hundreds of flats that characterized most urban residential areas in Blue Zones these days. At least that was how it was done in B-2. Annabella had never actually left B-2, so she had no idea how the other Blues did it.

Not that Annabella cared all that much about her living accommodations. Her work kept her out of the house all day and much of the night. This flat was just a place to sleep and, very occasionally, to eat. She knew that some of the higher-ups in GDI and folks like Penny, her boss, actually got more than one room per person/couple in the household, and while part of her hoped to some day rank that high, she also knew it didn't matter much. She wasn't overburdened with a ton of personal items, and most of those were beauty aids designed to preserve her most important feature, her face. The only way she'd need another room was if she had a child, and that wasn't likely to happen any time soon.

I'd settle for a move to a place with a window that actually showed something, like one of the buildings near Van Cortlandt Park or Wave Hill, she thought as she gripped her mug with both hands and climbed out of bed, kicking the covers off her naked body. While residential areas were now stuffed with dwellings, parkland was still preserved, partly for recreation—one of Annabella's recent stories was about how important park playgrounds were for kids—mainly because trees had become a critical resource. Tiberium had consumed so much of the Earth's plant life that what remained was carefully guarded and preserved.

I can't believe they're all dead.

Padding into the bathroom, she sipped some more tea

and went through her morning ritual. First she checked over her entire body, to make sure she wasn't gaining weight in any unfortunate places, to make sure she didn't have any blemishes on her face or hands (the only parts of her body that were directly exposed on cam) that needed to be covered, and, most critically of all, to make sure she had no sign of Tiberium poisoning. While the first two checks were particular to Annabella's line of work as someone who reported the news to people and who therefore needed to look her best, looking for signs of being a ti-die was something that had been drilled into everyone in the world for all of Annabella's lifetime. She still remembered the sheer panic when she was a teenager over a patch of skin turning green, only to discover that it was simply a gold allergy, a reaction to a piece of jewelry given her by her boyfriend. Said boyfriend broke up with her a week later, her panic attack having gotten him all wiggly.

Sadly, that's how most of my relationships wind up, Annabella thought. Not that she had much time for any kind of social life. She was determined to get the best clickrate of any of the W3N reporters, and that required a lot of hard work, including sometimes actually finding her own stories. Sometimes that backfired—it was only worth finding a story if it was one Penny actually *liked,* and she'd actually gotten on her boss's spamlist for a while by finding one she didn't like—but it was worth it for the gems. Like that one on the playgrounds: the click-rate on that one was much higher than it usually was for a piece of filler like that.

The mirror showed her a 1.7-meter-tall woman with short, slightly curly red hair, olive skin that had had any blemishes lasered, round Italianate cheeks, and slightly slanted Asian eyes, all befitting her rather mixed heritage. Satisfied that she was still cam-ready and still healthy, she performed her morning ablutions, swallowed the seven pills that everyone had to take to stave off the toxins of everyday life, and then swallowed the thyroid and allergy pills particular to her. That was followed by a quick shower, then going out into the flat to check her mail. A holo sprung up in the middle of the flat in response to the instruction she gave to the House by tapping onto the wall. Annabella had tried a voice-activated House, but it kept crashing. The VAs required perfect diction, and Annabella's was generally better than most, but the only times she used the House were first thing in the morning and when coming home from work, which was not when she was at her most coherent. After a month, she sent the VA back and went back to inputting by hand.

Mail shells scrolled by, and Annabella touched the ones that looked like they were worth reading, which only wound up being less than one percent of it. Some she moved to the "get to some other time" folder, which was pretty overloaded at this point, and most she just trashed. Then she remembered that she hadn't emptied the trash in a while, so she did that, then read the actual worthwhile ones, which wound up not being all that worthwhile, either. She watched a couple of the news stories she'd been sent while she got dressed, but nothing much had changed since she went to bed last night. Several military units had been dispatched to fight off Nod attacks on Blue Zones, including one attack on D.C. here in B-2, and there were some skirmishes in Yellows also, but all this had been expected. She also got a casualty report from GDI, which listed those GDI employees and relatives of some who'd been injured or killed by Nod. Annabella scanned it and was grateful to see no familiar names beyond the ones she already knew from the *Philadelphia*.

There was also an important mail from Penny, which said, simply, "Link me when you've had your tea. I've got a story."

Touching the menu portion of the holo, she then called up her speed-link and hit Penny's name. Of course her boss was already in. Penny Sookdeo used her flat even less often than Annabella did hers. In fact, the joke among the reporters and techs was that she *didn't* have a flat, and just lived in her office. That wasn't really true, as the overnight shift had a different supervisor, although legend around W3N had it that Penny and the night supervisor were supposed to share an office, with Penny using it during the day and the other supervisor—at present, a weaselly little man named Timothy Mak—using it at night. However, Penny was there so far into the night shift that it became impractical, especially since she wouldn't let the night boss into her office until she actually left for the night, which was often more than halfway into that shift. Mak did complain pretty regularly about how small his office was, too . . .

Penny's angular face framed by salt-and-pepper hair—cut in a bob that was very popular among adults when Annabella was five, but which nobody these days wore—shortly appeared in the center of the flat. *"You actually finish your tea yet?"*

"I'm awake, Penny. What's up?"

"You're holding the mug in your hand with a death grip. That means you haven't finished it yet."

Making a show of putting the mug down in the sink, she held her hands palms-up and said, "I'm awake, I've had my tea, I've showered, I've dressed. The only reason why I'm not on my way to the office right now to finish editing the Margolin piece is because you sent me an urgent mail to link you, so here I am. What's on?"

"You're heading down to Georgia tomorrow."

Annabella blinked. "Am I being punished for something?"

"Not at all. I want you to spend a few days down in Atlanta. That's really the nerve center for the southern portion of Y-6, and I want you to do a lengthy piece on how they're surviving down there. I need you to do another playground story, but on a much bigger scale."

"Playgroun—Penny, there's a *war* on, and you've got me doing shite work."

"It isn't shite work. It comes straight from Boyle. He wants the public to see that regular people are fighting the good fight against Tiberium, particularly in Y-6. Too many Yellows are under Nod control, and right now Boyle wants to show how successful we've been there." Penny sighed. *"Look, this has been one of Boyle's pet projects for ages. His last three memos have mentioned it, but since the Treasury Commissioner has no actual authority over W3N, I was able to ignore him. Now he's in charge, which means when he says 'jump,' we ask for a direction, a trajectory, and what to do when we land."*

Annabella smirked. "You've been wanting to use that line for a while, haven't you, Penny?"

Grinning, Penny said, *"Actually, you're the fourth person I've used it on today."* The grin fell. *"We don't do this right, I get on the new Director's scanners, and I really really don't want that, and neither do you."*

"Okay." Then she realized something. "How come it's not until tomorrow?"

"Was wondering if you'd catch that." Penny scowled. *"Finished the tea, my arse. I bet half the mug's still in it."*

Now Annabella was tapping her foot. "You're wrong." In fact, only a quarter of the mug was still full. "Why am I not going today if it's so high up in Boyle's queue?"

"Travel restrictions until D.C.'s secure. Besides, I still need you to finish editing the Margolin piece, and Jasmine's service is tonight. I figured you'd want to be there."

She hadn't, actually, but no sense telling Penny that. "Who's covering D.C.? Cassandra?"

Penny nodded. *"And before you say anything, you don't get to cover combat until you've been on the job—"*

"—for three years, I know, I've only heard you say it several billion times, Penny. I wasn't angling for it. I was just curious who you sent."

"Right." Penny sounded like she didn't believe it. Annabella couldn't blame her. War reporting was the Holy Grail, in many ways, since those stories always got the best clickrates. Annabella was still nine months away from that three-year cutoff.

"Anything else?"

"Not that can't wait until you get your arse in here, so get your arse in here. Oh, but before you do that?"

"Yes?"

"You might want to put your shirt on right side in."

Since she figured she'd be editing today, Annabella had put on a simple plain long-sleeved shirt. If she had to be on cam unexpectedly, she had a change of clothes at W3N's Manhattan office. Looking down at her arms, she saw that the seams were showing.

Angrily pulling the shirt over her head to expose the tank top she wore underneath it, she muttered, "I finished *most* of the tea."

"Next time finish it before you talk to me. Or better yet, don't. I can use the laugh this early in the morning."

"You don't fool me, Penny. You haven't laughed since 2021."

"So now's a good time to start. By the way, I hope you're planning on wearing more than that in Y-6. If you're outside, wear two layers, and—"

"Penny, isn't there a brochure or something that they give you when you go Yellow?"

"Yeah. It's in your box already, along with all the contacts down there for the story."

"Fine, I'll read it when I get in and pack accordingly tonight."

"All right. I'll see you in twenty minutes."

Penny's face faded from the middle of the flat. Annabella went back to the bathroom, checked to make sure she hadn't put on any *other* clothes wrong, then headed out the door, which automatically locked with the flat empty. Then she pulled out her Hand and put on the imager. Had she a mirror on her, she would now see a different face in it. While she wasn't the most recognizable face on W3N—that had to be Cassandra Blair, though it would probably be poor Jasmine for the next few weeks—she was on enough that people tended to recognize her in public, and that made her commutes difficult. While it had been a long time since it was common practice to kill the bearer of bad tidings, the tradition of blaming and yelling at the people who bore them remained quite active. It was standard for anyone who went before a cam on W3N to have an imager that would alter their features enough to keep them from being recognized. Imagers used to be used by Nod terrorists in the early part of the century as disguises. Now, with full bioscans being ubiquitous, a mere physical disguise was useless as a terrorist tool, but it was very handy for celebrities, even minor ones like Annabella.

She walked down to Riverdale Avenue and waited in the very long line for the bus. Given the time of morning and the length of the line, one would arrive at any second. While she waited, she did another mail check on her Hand, but there was just junk.

Then she realized that if she was leaving the city, she needed to tell Uncle Freddie and Aunt Monica. Her mother's brother and sister-in-law had raised Annabella after her parents died in a construction accident. Artemis Fiorello and Conchata Wu were building contractors, and they had gotten the gig to put up the GDI buildings that were needed at the border walls on the edges of B-2. While the walls themselves were constructed by the military's Corps of Engineers, they had subcontracted the various office buildings they needed to Annabella's parents. Unfortunately, a minor fault line that hadn't existed before Tiberium had developed in Ohio, and an unexpected earthquake felled the shack where her parents had their temporary office, killing them and several members of their crew.

The ironic part was that, until then, nobody had ever considered Tiberium's effects on plate tectonics, and Annabella's parents' deaths had served as a spur to do more research on the subject. Hundreds of lives had been saved by GDI's research and fault-line detectors in the last twenty years.

Annabella only wished it could have been done at a lower price.

But high prices were the norm these days. Annabella knew intellectually that once people used to own cars, that in fact many households had two, but now only the very rich, the very important, and the ones who required them for their work had their own automobiles. Most people didn't travel very far, and if they did, they used public transportation, which was why the bus line was so long.

Tapping her earpiece, Annabella linked to her aunt and uncle. She usually had dinner with them once a week, and that once would have been two days hence. It would have been nice to do it more often, but her schedule barely allowed for the once.

Immediately, Aunt Monica's voice said, *"Bella, you okay?"*

"I'm fine, *zia*," Annabella said quickly. "Everything's just fine, no different than it was the four times we talked yesterday. I just wanted to let you know that I'm gonna be out of town for a few days starting tomorrow, so I'm gonna miss dinner Friday."

"Oh, okay. That's too bad. I was gonna make the ziti vindaloo you like."

Rolling her eyes, Annabella said, "Well, I'm sorry I'm missing it." Monica *always* said she was making ziti vindaloo when Annabella couldn't make it for whatever reason. Annabella was convinced that her aunt didn't actually know how to make it, but didn't want to admit it.

"Tell *zio* he'll have to show me the vid he found next time." Freddie had picked up a zapchip reader and was going through an old box of zapchips that he hadn't been able to look at since people stopped using zaps around 2038. In fact, for Annabella's first birthday after her parents died, Monica and Freddie got her a "zapper," which was a great gift for a grieving ten-year-old, since only the rich kids had them.

"He's gonna wear out the reader, he watches them so many times. They're just stupid vids he took on trips, but he's gotta look at all of them. One thing you'll like, though, he got that trip we took to the zoo before they took the monorail down."

Annabella smiled at the memory. The Bronx Zoo was only sometimes open to the public these days, as its importance as a wildlife preserve superseded its use as public recreation. Tiberium had done as much in fifty years as human indifference had in fifty decades to kill off whole animal species, and GDI had been instrumental in keeping as many preserved as possible. The zoos in the Bronx, San Diego, and Sydney had become critical to saving many of the Earth's animal populations from extinction via Tiberium.

A bus wended its way down Riverdale Avenue. Annabella noted that it was one of the old hybrids, which only came out during major commuting hours, since the fleet didn't have enough fully electric ones to handle the traffic.

"I gotta go, *zia,* the bus is here." She actually could have kept talking, but she feared Monica going off on a tangent about what they did when Annabella was a little girl, and the one benefit to missing Monica's home cooking, which she loved, was that she also missed her aunt's veering into nostalgia, which always made Annabella's teeth hurt. She'd gotten plenty of that yesterday when Monica linked four times to make sure Annabella was okay after the *Philadelphia* exploded, as if Annabella had actually been on board.

"Okay, Bella. Call us if you need anything, and we'll talk when you get back."

"Bye, *zia.*"

The bus scanned her as she got on and deducted the fare from her credit. She was far enough down the line that a seat was a forlorn hope, so she gripped one of the poles along with several dozen other people. She was just grateful that mass transit was running—but then, without it, the city would shut down, and that couldn't happen. Besides, if the city was attacked, the subways were actually one of the safer places to be.

Two other people on the pole were holding a conversation, a tall bearded man wearing a worn-out blue cap with an interlocking NY on it that, if Annabella recalled correctly, represented a local baseball team (Annabella never paid much attention to sports), and a short, round woman with a large mole on her cheek that Annabella couldn't believe she hadn't had removed, since it was a four-minute, thirty-credit procedure.

Beard asked, "You hear from your brother?"

Mole shook her head in reply. "Ain't like they gonna let nobody link while the Nods're around."

"Fotze, least the tibeheads could letcha talk, find out if he's *alive*."

Shrugging, Mole said, "I keep watchin' W3N, hopin' they do a casualty report, but they ain't sayin' nothin'. I figured since he works there, they mighta said somethin', but I guess the janitors don't count for shite."

"Yeah, like they give a crack whose family's dead. Just tryin'a keep everything all pretty. I ficken *hate* those W3N tibeheads."

Suddenly, Annabella was extremely grateful for the imager. She also realized she might be able to help. "Excuse me," she said to Mole, "but what's your brother's name?"

"Why the hell *you* care?" Mole asked.

"I work for GDI," Annabella said, which was a lie, but better that than to identify herself as a "W3N tibehead," "and they send us a list of GDI employees who've been killed."

Mole blinked. "Seriously? Tommy never told me they did that."

"Well, they do. I can check."

Beard squinted at her from under his cap. "You sound familiar, lay. I know you?"

"I doubt it."

"His name," Mole said, "is Tommy Stephane."

Annabella linked her Hand to the mailbox at home. She never trashed casualty lists, because they might be valuable for research. Scrolling down, she saw nobody named Stephane at all. "He isn't on the list."

Mole closed her eyes and let out a long breath. "Thank the Goddess." She opened her eyes and put her free hand on Annabella's arm. "And thank *you*."

"That doesn't guarantee anything," Annabella said quickly, realizing that she may have gotten this woman's hopes up for nothing. "That just means he hasn't been reported injured or dead. It's pretty crazy down there right now, and—"

"It's okay," Mole said, "at least I know there's a chance. That's better than nothing."

"Not to me," Beard said. "Me, I'd wanna know for sure or not at all, not this halfway shite."

Annabella shrugged. "Best I can do."

"Oh, hey, no, that's okay. Ain't *your* fault. You just tryin' to help, and that's spicy, but that's just 'cause those W3N tibeheads can't do shite. Hacks me off, y'know?"

Opening her mouth to respond, Annabella thought better of it. She'd only be on the bus a few minutes more. It was turning on to 231st Street and heading to the subway.

Indeed, they arrived at Broadway a few minutes later. The New York subways had been totally revamped in 2033. With the residential areas of the city more concentrated—mostly around existing subway construction—the subways were also overhauled, made faster and more efficient, if not more comfortable. They also made fewer stops, so that, for example, the 1 train now only had one stop in the northwest Bronx instead of the four it used to have. While it made for a more crowded waiting experience, it also meant that a trip that would've taken an hour when Annabella was a kid now took twenty minutes, and that was with the bus ride.

As she squeezed on to the platform with everyone else commuting to Manhattan—which was still the center of activity in this region, all the more so because it was in one of the largest Blues—Annabella thought about her new assignment. She'd never actually *been* to a Yellow. She assumed there was some kind of procedure she would have to go through, decon and such. Penny didn't mention it, but it was probably in that material she'd sent. Annabella could have accessed it from here, but she decided to wait until she got to the office, so she could see the full holo rather than the flatscreen translation she'd get on her Hand.

The train arrived, and at least three different people stepped on her foot as they moved. She almost didn't have to provide the forward motion herself. She could just go limp and be carried on the wave of people.

Unlike the buses—or the subways before '33—the trains had no seats, except for ones reserved for those who had physical limitations, and they could only use them if they were authorized. (Annabella remembered coming home late one night to see two teenagers try to hack past the scanner to use the seats, only to be arrested at the next stop by a shield who had been alerted and was waiting for the train to pull in.) Instead, people all crowded around one of the many poles.

It was an awful way to live, really. Uncle Freddie had often talked about the good old days before Tiberium, when people had flats bigger than one room per person or couple, when people owned cars, when not everyone had to take seven pills a day just to at least have a chance of not being poisoned by the very air, and when there were more than two nations in the world. Technically, there still were separate nations, but their power and influence was very local and all but irrelevant in the grand scheme of things. These days, you lived under GDI or you lived under Nod.

As bad as this life is, Annabella thought as the train lurched and a well-muscled man fell against her, *at least I'm not ruled by terrorists.*

FOUR

Golden was on his fourth barf bag when "Angry Puppy" Momoa leaned over to Vega and asked, "What'd you give him?"

Before Vega could answer, Bowles said, "When he gave it, he said that the pill would keep him from getting queasy."

Brodeur then put in, "That's not what he said."

Vega nodded. "Brodeur's right. What I said was that I *heard* they'd keep you from getting queasy." He grinned. "Guess I heard wrong."

Unit Epsilon was sitting on a long metal bench, one of five in this chamber on the *Huron*. They had taken off twenty minutes earlier, not two seconds after the entire 22nd and all their equipment—including several Orcas and tanks—got on board. The ride had been a lot smoother than he had been expecting after the scorching the others did about the pilot.

Most of them were laughing right now. Momoa, who was sitting next to Vega, slapped him a little harder on the back than Vega liked—it actually stung, even through the battlesuit—and said, "Not bad, greenie!" The big man's shoulders were so wide, Vega actually had to lean to the left a little to avoid being hit by them whenever he moved. He wasn't wearing his shoulder pads, and his black undershirt was sleeveless, exposing massive, well-muscled arms.

Golden finally finished off his barf bag, and looked murderously at Vega, though the effect was diluted by the bloodshot eyes and the greenish tinge to his skin. "You're ficken *dead,* greenie."

"Don't worry," Gallagher said, "I'll hold him down for you."

"Calm down," Vega said, "you'll be okay in about three minutes. Trust me."

"*Trust* you?" Gallagher said. "I oughta ficken *kill* you!"

"Oh, step *down,* Gallagher," Bowles said. "Golden's had that in his queue for months."

"Yeah, the greenie did good. Made Golden green. A greenie green." Momoa then laughed at his own witticism, as did several others.

"Ficken hilarious, Pup," Gallagher said, moving her dirty look to Momoa.

On the other side of him from Momoa, Brodeur said in a low voice, "That was smart."

Vega deadpanned, "I have absolutely no idea what you mean."

"You Vega?"

Turning at the new voice, Vega saw a short woman with a large nose and penetrating brown eyes standing in front of him and Momoa. She had two stripes on her fatigue sleeves, and wasn't wearing armor. That meant she was probably clerical, since nobody on the *Huron* would be out of armor unless they were support staff. Besides, she was holding a box, and infantry didn't usually make deliveries.

Momoa smiled up at the woman, and Vega noticed that it was a much nicer smile than the one he'd had on in

Vega's short acquaintance with him. "How you doing today, Corporal Silverstein?"

"Better as long as I breathe through my mouth in your presence, Private Momoa." She looked back at Vega. "You didn't answer my question."

Making a show of looking down at his chest, Vega said, "If I'm not, someone needs to requisition me a new battlesuit."

Silverstein rolled her eyes. "Great, another smart-arse."

"Beats being a dumb-arse, my dad always says."

"Oh," Gallagher said, "*that's* why he's a war hero. He invented all the stupid clichés."

With a rattling *thud*, Silverstein dropped the box unceremoniously in front of Vega. "This is your stuff. If there's a problem with any of it, come to *me*. Do *not* go to the quartermaster. They will crack it *right* up, understand me? You go to QC, I *won't* be held responsible."

"Problem, come to you, got it."

"Good." She looked at Momoa. "Oh, and I heard back on your req."

Momoa actually leaned forward on the bench, and his eyes got as wide as the moon. "And?"

"They said no, just like I *told* you they would. The GD3s haven't been approved for regular use."

"Yeah, like *he's* regular," Bowles said.

"Be that as it may," Silverstein said, "you can't have one for at least another month. Sorry."

She didn't sound particularly sorry as she walked away. Momoa growled.

Of Brodeur, Vega asked, "Company clerk?"

"Yes, that was Memo."

"She's called 'Memo'?" Vega chuckled.

Bowles said quickly, "*Not* to her face. She hates it."

He frowned. "Least I think she does. Either way, I sure as shite ain't findin' out the hard way. *Never* hack off the clerk. That's our motto."

Having had respect for the support staff drilled into his head by his father, Vega silently agreed. However, he was curious about other things. "I didn't know the GD3s were ready yet."

With a sigh, Bowles said, "Apparently they aren't. Looks like you don't get your BAG, Pup."

Frowning, Vega asked, "Huh?"

Brodeur explained: "Big-Arse Gun. Pup isn't happy unless he has the biggest weapon on the market."

Momoa pounded the bench with a meaty fist. "*Fotze!* I really *wanted* that one, too! This one's supposed to have a grenade launcher!"

"Yeah," Bowles said wistfully, "imagine what a Noddie would look like after one of those spicies blew his head off."

Golden said, "C'mon, Pup, you'll be fine with the GD2 you got on your chest."

"Not the *same*." Momoa almost snarled the words.

Rolling his eyes, Golden said, "You'll live." Then he smiled. "Probably."

"Hey," Bowles said, "you sound almost lifelike."

"Yeah, honestly, I feel better than I have in ages. Hey, kid, thanks."

Vega chuckled. "No problem. And my name's Vega, not 'kid.' " He'd been spending his whole life as "JV's kid," and he would've been perfectly happy to never hear that particular three-letter word for the rest of his life.

Momoa looked thoughtful, an expression that in his case showed tremendous effort. "We could call you 'Puke.' "

Gallagher immediately said, "Works for me."

Before Vega had the chance to nip that nickname in the bud as fast as humanly possible, Sergeant Goodier—who was sitting all the way at the end of the bench—stood up. The section of the *Huron* they were in was a medium-sized cabin that only had these benches, five rows of them, for the five units that made up Company 7 of Battalion 4 of the 22nd. The bench Vega was on was the fourth of five, fitting for Unit Epsilon. For some reason, Alpha and Beta were sitting with their backs to the bulkhead, facing the middle of the room, and also facing Gamma and Epsilon.

Goody wasn't the only one to rise. All five sergeants got to their feet.

"Everybody listen up!" said the Alpha sergeant, a flat-nosed woman with a shaved head. Vega could only tell she was female because of her high-pitched voice and her rather large chest. "We're about to get our marching orders."

A holo appeared in the center of the room right over their heads. The Gamma guys all had to crane their necks to look right up at the holo, while everyone else just had to look up. *That's why we're all facing the middle*, Vega realized, though it still sucked for the Gamma guys.

Whoever the guy on the holo was, he had captain's bars on his cap—only his head was visible—so he was probably the battalion commander, Ryon Henry. The captain had dark skin, with darker freckles under his eyes, and serious brown eyes. Although the cap obscured most of his head, he appeared to be bald. Presumably, he'd just finished meeting with the other six battalion leaders, Major Hastings, and Battle Commander McNeil to work out the battle plan.

"Pals 'n' gals, we got us a mission. The Nod have

taken San Diego, and our job is to take it back. They've taken over the naval base and are using the convention center as their C&C." Next to Henry, an image appeared of the San Diego Convention Center, which was a massive, lengthy structure of more than two million square feet, according to the statistics that scrolled alongside the image. "*Local forces've been taken out, though we got reports of stragglers, particularly some shields. Can't count on that, so it's just us.*"

"Like usual," Bowles muttered.

Henry continued: "*Bat 4's job is to take out the C&C. Bats 1 and 2'll be taking the naval base, and Bat 3's gonna be air support for both ops.*"

Vega nodded. The soldiers of Battalion 3 were the ones who'd be operating the Orcas and Cranes. Battalion 1 was the tank group, with Battalions 2 and 4 being infantry. Sending the tanks to the naval base made the most sense, with support from infantry. From the sounds of it, taking the convention center would require surgical strikes, so that meant infantry also.

"*We could just bomb the shite outta the convention center, but there's a wrinkle. See, there's a GDI crany who got himself captured by the Nod, and In-Ops says he's in the SDCC. This crany's name is Dr. Joseph Takeda, and he's very valuable to GDI, which means that if we* don't *succeed in putting his arse on the* Huron *in one piece, we'll be scrubbing latrines for the rest of this war.*"

"Ah, fotze," Gallagher muttered. "I hate this political crap. Probably just some gent who gave the Council some creds and a foot massage."

"If he is a scientist," Vega said, putting his head in the lion's mouth, "they're gonna need him, especially with all the ones like Mobius they lost on the *Philly.*"

Gallagher shot Vega a look that seemed to say, *What the hell do you know about it?* But she said nothing as Henry proceeded to outline the plan of attack.

"In-Ops has got Takeda being held in one of the tiny second-floor meeting rooms, which is pretty much impossible to get to without wading through half a dozen guards. While Bat 3 distracts 'em with air strikes—all of which will miss—Companies 1 and 2 will come in from the Marina, while 3, 4, and 5 come in by the southeast entrance, with 6 and 7 taking the northwest entrance." As Henry spoke, the holo next to him rotated to show an aerial view of the SDCC, with representations of soldiers from Battalion 4 all moving into position from the places Henry indicated. Vega focused his attention on his own team, which would be coming in on the right of the holo, coming in from the parking lot up a flight of stairs to the convention center's second level.

The holo of the SDCC zoomed in, focusing on the first-floor exhibit hall, which was only slightly smaller than the entire massive center. Companies 2, 4, and 6 were coming in there from their assorted entry points, making Vega wonder where his own company was supposed to go. *"In-Ops also says they might be holding prisoners in the exhibition hall. As far as GDI is concerned, those people are casualties of war."*

Everyone tensed at that. It would be one thing if they were all soldiers or local law or whatever, but if there were civilians in there . . .

Then Vega thought, *Yeah, well, there were civilians on the Philadelphia, too.*

"Prisoners would be nice, but we can live without 'em. The only person who's just got to come out of the SDCC alive is Doc Takeda." The SDCC image then zoomed out to the aerial view again, then zoomed in to the second

floor, which, in contrast to the exhibit hall, was a lattice-work of hallways and meeting rooms, broken up by two big outdoor pavilions under what looked like tents. Companies 1, 3, 5, and 7 were shown moving along that floor, each coming from a different direction. *"Only thing we know for sure—check that, the only thing In-Ops says they know for sure—is that Takeda's somewhere on the second floor."*

Henry's expression hadn't changed all that much during the briefing, but he looked dubious when mentioning Intelligence and Operations. Vega recalled something his father always said about In-Ops and their reliability, or lack of same: "On very rare occasions, if everything goes perfectly and they actually pay attention, In-Ops might be able to determine whether or not Tiberium is green."

"EVA's sending all of this to your HUDs. We make landfall in eighty minutes—seventy if Johanssen gets his arse in gear. Henry out."

Vega levered the HUD eyepiece, which was currently up over his forehead, down in front of his left eye. As soon as he did, he saw a menu that included the battle plan on it. Touching the keys on the wrist unit, he called up the plan Captain Henry had just outlined.

"S'matter, Puke, you ain't gonna open your present?" That was Gallagher.

Pausing the playback, Vega asked, "Huh? And don't call me that."

In a slow voice, as if talking to an idiot, Gallagher said, "Memo gave you a present, and you're checking the HUD?" She pointed down at the box at Vega's feet.

Following Gallagher's finger, Vega looked down at the box as if he'd never seen it before. "Fotze," he muttered, and flipped up the HUD, which reset it, and bent over to open the box.

It flipped open at his touch to reveal several items: A GD2 rifle, shoulder and thigh armor, a .50-caliber pistol, several boxes of ammo, and a helmet.

He inspected the equipment. The GD2 was magnetized and attached to the front of his battlesuit, the rifle's handle at his right shoulder, muzzle pointed down and to the left. He checked the ammo, put the GD2 spares in his top- and bottom-right pouches, and top-left pouch. The spare .50-caliber rounds went into the lower-left pouch.

As he did that, he noticed something odd. The rounds were heavier than he expected.

Momoa noticed him noticing that. "That's a Nighthawk you got there, not an Eagle. Fires forty 'stead'a thirty."

"Nice." The only pistol Vega had ever fired was his father's old .40-caliber.

He then looked up. "No first aid?"

That got a laugh from Momoa. Brodeur said, "Welcome to the 22nd. We've got the new battlesuits."

"Wait," Vega said, "they got the microfibers working?" He'd read that the next generation of infantry battlesuit would have microfibers that would handle field first aid automatically, by constricting around wounds to bind them, applying antibiotics as needed. They were also supposed to augment musculature.

"Yup," Brodeur said. "We always get the new toys."

"Except for the ficken GD3s," Momoa muttered.

Bowles laughed. "We'll get 'em."

"But not for this op. That just hacks me off."

Vega then pulled out the helmet to make sure it fit— Vega had a larger than normal head, and he'd gone through most of his life being issued headgear that was too small—and he was pleasantly surprised to see that it did. As he settled it on his shoulders, the inner part of the helmet lit up with a large display screen, as well as a few smaller ones. He used his wrist unit to run through the checklist, and everything seemed to be in working order.

But then, as he hit the last item, the wrist unit stopped working. He tapped it several times, but nothing happened.

His first instinct was to go to Silverstein, but then he remembered what his father always said about "percussive maintenance." So he whacked the side of it with the heel of his right palm.

It worked fine after that.

By the time he was done checking his equipment, they were less than ten minutes from their arrival. He looked up to see Bowles, Momoa, and Brodeur all staring at him. "What?"

Bowles shook his head. "Ain't never seen nobody plow through a checklist like that, 'cept for Gallagher."

"Oh *please*," Gallagher said.

"May wanna check the circuitry, too, make sure it's all programmed right," Bowles said.

"Crack off," Brodeur said. "He's being thorough."

"*Five minutes to target,*" said a voice from over the speakers.

As that voice spoke, Opahle entered the room. The Alpha sergeant screamed, "Ten-*hut*!"

"As you were," Opahle said with a wave of her hand.

Gallagher said, "Hey, Loo, how we gonna get to the convention center without Nod shooting us down? We're kind of a big target."

"We could leave Pup behind, then we'd be smaller," Bowles whispered. Golden snickered, while Momoa glared.

Opahle either didn't hear or ignored Bowles's comment. Vega's money was on the latter. "The *Huron*'ll drop us on Harbor Drive about half a click out from the SDCC. Then we boot it."

Vega grinned, even as those around him groaned.

"Fotze, we gotta take a *jog* into combat?" someone from Beta said.

"We're running *outside*?" someone else, this from Alpha, said.

Another Alpha said, "It's a Blue, you tibehead; we'll be fine."

"Yeah, but the Nod took it. Maybe they brought tirock in."

That caused Vega to shudder. The notion that the Brotherhood would introduce Tiberium to the Blues was one that filled him with dread. The Blues were the last bastion against ti-rot.

"It's our job to stop that happening," Opahle finally said. "But we can't just fly over their C&C with a big plane, so we get dropped off down the street, and we run." She smiled. "Time to see if we're up to spec."

Turning to Brodeur, Vega shot him a questioning look.

"Those straps on your back and thighs and such?"

Vega nodded. "Yeah, what about 'em?"

Brodeur then reached down and touched the back of Vega's left thigh. "Touch it there."

Vega did so. While it wouldn't respond to Brodeur's biometrics, it did to Vega's, and the black strips across his back, shoulders, upper arms, and thighs all bulged.

"I don't feel any different."

"You won't," Brodeur said, "until you start to exert yourself. You'll notice the difference because everything takes less effort."

"Spicy."

Then Vega flipped down the HUD over his left eye and checked something. Sure enough, the engagement plan for their company (and only their company) was available, and it had them landing on Harbor Drive where it intersected with Pacific Highway, which, according to the map in the HUD, was an extra-wide street, just barely large enough at the intersection to accommodate the *Huron*. From there, they'd run down Harbor to the SDCC.

Companies 6 and 7 actually had the easiest time of it, since their entrance was closest to the landing point. Vega actually found that to be disappointing.

Then he checked the distance from the intersection to the northwest entrance of the convention center, and was amused to see that it was six hundred meters. *Maybe I'll get the chance to break my record...*

FIVE

Annabella Wu sat in Penn Station's VIP waiting area, a luxury afforded her as a W3N employee. Each seat had an InstaFood slot that provided almost-cold drinks and over-waved food, which Annabella had learned years ago to avoid. She had brought her usual bottle of iced tea, as well as some snacks she'd scrounged from the W3N offices before heading down here.

"Now boarding: the YZ100 to Atlanta on Track 7. Repeat, YZ100 to Atlanta now boarding on Track 7."

Annabella was one of about a dozen people who rose—much fewer than had gotten on the four other trains that had boarded since her arrival. But then, those others were all staying within B-2. The YZ100 was the one train per day that went straight from New York in B-2 to Atlanta in Y-6, and it was much less well populated than the usual trains. With fewer cars in use, trains had become the most popular mode of intercity travel.

However, traveling between zones didn't happen particularly often, and those who did had very good reason for doing so. That was why there was only one train per day between B-2 and Y-6.

When Annabella took her luggage down the lift down to the track, she saw that the YZ100 was also smaller than usual. Most intercity trains these days were at least a dozen cars long, but the train she was taking today consisted only of two. She got a bioscan as she stepped on the platform, verifying that she had a reserved seat on the train, and she entered the back car, choosing a window seat and stowing her luggage overhead.

She shifted in her seat. Having dressed for Yellow, she was uncomfortable. While she hadn't bothered with the gloves and hat—those could wait until she actually disembarked in Atlanta—she was wearing two long-sleeved shirts, two-ply denim jeans, a thick pair of socks, and hiking boots. Her hair was also completely tied up in such a way that the brimmed hat she brought would hide it altogether.

Pulling out her Hand, she read over, for the ninth time, the cross-Zone procedures. When they reached the border with B-2, the entire train would go through a brief decontamination procedure—as opposed to the trip back in four days' time, when she'd go through a much longer decon.

It only took a couple of hours to get to the B-2 border. Annabella spent that time catching up on journals she'd neglected over the past few months. *If this trip's worth it for anything, it's the two uninterrupted hours of reading time,* she thought wryly, as she caught up on the worlds of entertainment and literature that she'd been ignoring. She also played music on her Hand, mostly the usual inspirational jazz that one generally found on the radio. It was good background noise.

At the border, they went into a tunnel. Annabella caught sight of a few people in military uniforms, but mostly it was dark.

The decon was surprisingly harmless. Everyone had to stand up and then what felt like hot air was blown on them for a few minutes. Then the train went dark, and they were instructed to stand still.

Finally, when the procedure was finished, the lights came up and they were allowed to sit. According to the literature she'd read the previous day, the scans were automated and supervised by nearby military personnel. Of course, her creds would be checked instantly, and if there were any problem, she was sure she'd know about it by now. By the same token, if there were a problem, she likely would not have been allowed to board the train in the first place.

On the way down, Annabella had glanced at the scenery. The train went through some rural areas, including a great deal of heavily guarded farmland. Tiberium had consumed a great deal of arable land—including the central portion of North America, which was now a Red Zone—so the farms that remained were critical. That was why they were surrounded by state-of-the-art security, including dozens and dozens of armed GDI troops. There was the usual haze in the air that indicated midsummer.

After the decon, though, the scenery changed with an abruptness that Annabella had been intellectually prepared for, yet was still shocked by.

The haze in the air was now a miasma. The farms weren't guarded—the few that existed—and a lot of empty land was tinged with the crystalline green of Tiberium. In B-2, they'd gone through Philadelphia, Baltimore, D.C.—which had been liberated by GDI the previous night—and Virginia Beach, and they all looked like cities. Many of them had suffered considerable damage from Nod attacks, but they looked more or less intact.

Going through Charlotte, she got a much bleaker picture.

Blue cities had modern architecture, in some cases (particularly in Philadelphia and Baltimore) with a few older buildings dating back to the twentieth century mixed in. In Charlotte, however, she saw only a few modern buildings, and many broken-down, burned-out older ones. Windows were shattered, and some structures were wracked with Tiberium infestation.

The biggest difference between Y-6 and B-2, though, was the people. She didn't see any. That wasn't completely true: There was a smattering of folks here and there, but they stood out because, even in the urban environment of Charlotte, there weren't enough to make a crowd.

Of course, it wasn't a total surprise. Even in Blues, outdoor travel was restricted between eleven and fifteen, and it was only a little before fourteen now. But she really got a feeling of emptiness that she never got in New York, not even at lunchtime.

An hour later, the train pulled into Turner Station in Atlanta. The terminal had been built in the 2030s in honor of one of Atlanta's favorite sons, who had died of Tiberium poisoning in 2021. Atlanta's previous train station wasn't really able to handle the load of people who suddenly needed it.

Pulling her duffel down from the overhead, Annabella slowly walked on to the platform, the duffel wheeling itself along behind her, matching her movements.

She immediately recognized the face of the person who was supposed to meet her: Salvatore Patel, an aide to Mayor Liebnitz.

Holding out her hand, Annabella said, "Mr. Patel, I'm Annabella Wu."

Patel—a short man with dark hair and an olive complexion—looked confused at the outstretched hand, but did not accept it. "Uh, yes, Ms. Wu. Welcome to Atlanta. You'll need to put your gloves on," he said nervously. Annabella noticed his hands were gloved.

Shaking her head, Annabella said, "Oh, of course, sorry." She knelt down at her duffel and pulled the gloves and hat out of the front compartment. "Old habits and all that."

"What were you just doing, Ms. Wu?" Then Patel's face brightened. "Oh, wait, that was supposed to be a handshake, wasn't it? I'm sorry. I should've known."

Annabella blinked in surprise. "You don't shake hands?" The habit was so ingrained that it didn't even occur to Annabella that somebody *wouldn't* do so upon meeting a person for the first time.

"Why would we?" Patel sounded not just confused, but revolted at the very notion. He started walking toward the platform exit, Annabella and her duffel following. He said, "In any case, I'm to take you to your hotel, get you checked in, and then you're to have dinner with Mayor Liebnitz and his staff. Tomorrow—well, that will be up to you."

They reached the lift. "Up to *me*?"

Patel chuckled. "Well, you *are* the reporter. It's your story."

Annabella thought a moment. "I think I'll make that decision after I've spoken to His Honor some."

"Who?"

"Er, Mayor Liebnitz."

"Oh, is that some sort of honorific? Interesting. We don't generally stand on that kind of ceremony around here."

They entered the lift, which took them to the main level of the station. Annabella was starting to wonder if this wasn't so much a news story on the Yellow Zones as it was one about first contact with an alien species.

At dinner that night, Annabella was stunned to hear Mayor Liebnitz ask the question, "So what-all's your story about, Ms. Wu?"

Swallowing her food, Annabella asked, "Didn't Director Boyle tell you?"

Liebnitz chuckled. "Ms. Wu, you can rest assured that ain't no Director of GDI gonna be havin' words with no Yellow Zone mayors." Liebnitz's southern accent was fairly strong, so that the word was pronounced "yella." "All I was told was that some reporter'd be comin' down and I was to show her every courtesy."

Giving the mayor her brightest smile, and deliberately ignoring what Patel had told her at the train station, Annabella said, "Well, Your Honor, I must say that the courtesy so far has been first-rate."

The hotel Patel had taken her to was a standard chain hotel, though her room was actually larger than her flat in New York, complete with a king-sized bed, which alone made the whole trip worthwhile to Annabella. Patel had waited for her in the lobby while she unpacked and changed into clothes she hadn't been sitting in for four hours. She felt silly wearing two layers of clothes in midsummer, especially given the high temperatures outside that her Hand was reporting. On the other hand, they didn't seem to be in any danger of *going* outside.

They had come to the hotel in a shuttle bus that went from the train station to most of Atlanta's major hotels. Annabella had activated her spec-cam when they were waiting for the bus, wanting to record her movements throughout Atlanta in the hopes of seeing how they differed from how she got around New York. The most obvious was that at no point did the bus ever open its doors while in the open air. The arrival point at Turner Station was in an underground location, and rather than drop people off at the hotel's front entrance, which was what buses would do in B-2, they instead went into underground garages that were sealed off from the outside by titanium gates.

The check-in procedure had actually been handled by a person, which had surprised Annabella. She knew that was how things used to be in the old days, but she had always assumed check-ins to be automated everywhere in the world. She hadn't even been scanned, though her ID info had been in the hotel computer. *Good thing I wasn't wearing the imager,* she thought with a small smile.

Of all the questions the clerk had asked, the one that had surprised Annabella the most was, "I see you're T-negative."

"I don't know what that means."

The clerk had looked at her funny, and then said, "No Tiberium infestation. That means you'll be staying on the upper floors."

What had especially thrown Annabella for a loop was being handed a small piece of plastic when she was finished. "Er, what is this?" she had asked.

The clerk looked at her strangely. As if talking to a small child, she had said, "It's a key. You use it to get in the room."

"I'm sorry, I just—we don't have these where I'm from. The doors have bioscanners."

"That's sweet," the clerk said with a wholly insincere smile and a withering expression, and Annabella had decided right there that she hated personal check-in service.

After she had settled in her room—and after spending

five minutes trying to figure out how to use the stupid key, since she refused to ask for help after the treatment she got from the clerk—Patel had led her back to the garage. This time they were met not by a bus, but by a large truck, which Patel said belonged to the mayor's office. Annabella climbed in and was taken to a large mansion on the outskirts of town. At first, Annabella had been afraid that she was being taken to a Tiberium-infested wreck, as the truck had slowed down as it approached one. It turned out that the mayor's residence was the place across the street. Annabella had found that a little peculiar. The wreck, she noticed as they pulled in, had several devices surrounding it. While she wasn't sure what they were, she assumed them to be designed to keep the Tiberium at bay. She'd look it up on her Hand later, but in the meantime, she recorded it.

The mansion looked old-fashioned to Annabella's admittedly untrained eye, and she suspected that it had originally been built after the U.S. Civil War in the nineteenth century, during which much of the city had been burned by Union forces. She had to qualify it with "originally" because the huge garage that was attached to the side of the house like a holster was most assuredly not part of the original structure. Where the house screamed "antebellum," the garage was very obviously of GDI design. Standing at various points around the mansion were fully-armored GDI troops, armed with intimidatingly large weapons.

Stepping out of the truck, Annabella was brought to a lavish dining room. A huge crystal chandelier hung from the ceiling, a table seating about a dozen sitting under it covered in a yellow lace tablecloth. Peering down, Annabella saw that the legs looked like wood. She was sure to get that on cam. She couldn't remember the last time she had seen real wood.

The food was fairly standard Cuban-Chinese, not too lavish, but fairly tasty. To Annabella's surprise, Liebnitz served it himself. The mayor was a giant bear of a man, though he was suprisingly skinny for someone with shoulders as wide as he had. His dark head was covered with patches of white hair, and his jowls abutted the top of his old-fashioned collared shirt.

In response to Annabella's calling him "Your Honor," Liebnitz chuckled, a reaction that made those jowls shake. "We don't b'lieve in all that formal hogwash, Ms. Wu. 'Round here, folks just call me Moné."

"Well, in that case, Moné, I'm Annabella."

Holding up his glass of wine, Liebnitz tilted it slightly toward her in acknowledgment.

Another of the mayor's staff, a woman whose taut skin was that of a young woman but whose crow's-feet suggested she might be somewhat older, said, "You didn't actually answer the question, Ms. Wu. Why *are* you here?"

Smiling sweetly, Annabella said, "That wasn't the question, actually. The question was what my story is about. The answer to both questions is the same. W3N wants me to do a story on what life is like in a Yellow."

A pale man sitting opposite Patel regarded Annabella as if she were insane. "What's that supposed to mean? Our life is our life."

Annabella dipped some of her lo mein in garlic and citrus sauce and popped it into her mouth before answering. "Yes, but the people in the Blues don't really know about your lives. I certainly don't. Imagine my surprise earlier when a person actually had to physically check me into my hotel, and then I had to use a key to get in my room."

"That ain't how y'all do things in the Blues, then?" Liebnitz asked.

"It's all automatic."

"Well, that's a little out of our budgetary range 'round here."

"Okay." Annabella swallowed some more lo mein before going on. "Also, a lot of the Yellows are in Nod hands, even these days. I don't know for sure, but my guess is that W3N wants to show how you guys fight against Tiberium and on GDI's side."

The woman muttered, "It's not Tiberium we're fighting."

"Excuse me?" Annabella asked.

"Nothing," the woman said quickly. "I assume you're recording right now?"

"Yes, of course. I was told that I could—"

"It's fine, Annabella. Terise is just being her usual pain-in-the-side self," Liebnitz said quickly with a look at Terise. "Nobody here ain't got nothin' to hide."

Feeling the need to change the subject, Annabella asked, "Moné, is this the mayoral residence?"

Liebnitz chuckled. "I suppose you could call it that. I mean, this is where my wife and I sleep, 'long with the other families."

That surprised Annabella. "What other families?"

"This is a big house, Annabella, and so far it ain't a health risk, even with that disaster 'cross the street. We can't afford to let it go to waste."

"So how many live here?"

"Right now, we got fifteen families livin' here."

Annabella blinked. "Where are they?"

Liebnitz gave another jowl-shaking chuckle. "Most of 'em are upstairs or off elsewhere, workin' or somesuch."

"Is that normal?"

"I guess." Liebnitz shrugged.

Annabella noticed that the others around the table looked nervous—except for Terise, who looked out-and-out angry. In fact, they'd mostly been nervous since she walked in. She wondered if they thought she had some other agenda. Or maybe they didn't like cams. After a moment, she asked, "You mentioned the disaster across the street. Tell me about that."

After taking a sip of his wine, Liebnitz sat back in his chair. "I believe I shall, Annabella. See, that's probably the best example of what life's like hereabouts."

Annabella looked straight at Liebnitz, wanting to make sure she got every word he said and had a straight shot on him. Given the discomfort of the staff, she felt throwing the drone out was a bad idea, so she decided to stick with the spec-cam for the time being. Any excess movements she'd cover with the footage she planned to get of the house in question.

"That place had a dozen families livin' there, kinda like this one. Couple kids were wrestlin', the way kids'll do, and sure enough, one of 'em managed to break a window. Now normally, when that sorta thing happens, there's a shade that automatically comes down to protect the house. Unfortunately—well, let's just say that the equipment wasn't as state-of-the-art as PTZ'd lead you to believe."

"PTZ?" Annabella assumed it was the company that installed the equipment in question, but she wanted to be sure.

Smiling sheepishly, Liebnitz said, "Sorry, figured there weren't nobody didn't know who PTZ was."

"We usually just call 'em 'putz' around here," said the man sitting next to Patel.

Liebnitz said, "It's Pérez-Toscano-Zelenetzky. They got the GDI contract for all the construction work that's supposed to keep out the green death."

Annabella didn't bother asking what "green death" meant. *That one's pretty self-evident.*

"So PTZ didn't do such a hot job with the shutter system in that house and it didn't come down. One of the kids, well, he went and panicked. Now, let me be clear, Annabella. We don't skimp on tellin' folks how to deal with the green death 'round here. There's pamphlets, there's stuff all over the WorldNet, and all the schools go over it least once a week, sometimes more, particularly this time'a year when folks're more likely to do somethin' stupid like go outside."

Annabella's eyebrows raised. "But?"

Smiling sardonically, Liebnitz said, "But folks will talk. And they will pass off the most ridiculous nonsense you ever wanted to hear as fact. See, anybody who's been in any kinda marketin' or advertisin' job'll tell you that there ain't no such thing as a hundred percent penetration. And by that I mean that there's no way to tell *everybody* somethin'. There's always gonna be somebody who don't know. Now, somethin' anybody who's been a scientist'll tell you is that nature abhors a vacuum." Liebnitz paused to sip his wine.

Annabella said, "So they fill that vacuum with the most ridiculous nonsense?"

Pointing at her approvingly, Liebnitz said, "Exactly. Now, the boy who broke the window, he saw that the shutters didn't come down and, like any sensible child, doesn't wanna die. He's heard stories 'bout the green death and he don't want that happenin' to him, his family, or the other folks in the house. He's also heard his gramma tell him 'bout how the best way to get ridda the JJD—that's what they used to call it in the old days 'round here," he quickly added at Annabella's confused look, "used to stand for 'jade jaws o' death'—anyhow, she said best way to get ridda the JJD was to use paint thinner."

At that, Annabella winced. Back in 2020, GDI had put out the *Living with Tiberium* handbook. It had been regularly updated over the past twenty-seven years; the most recent iteration of it was released right after the end of TWII in 2035. One of the many things that handbook did was debunk a lot of the "home remedies" for Tiberium that had cropped up. One of the big ones was paint thinner. Unfortunately, paint thinner was one of the substances that Tiberium particularly feasted on.

"Now that boy's brother, he said to get some wet towels and use 'em to plug up the hole. The boy, he didn't just get 'em wet, he dumped 'em in paint thinner, figurin' that'd keep the JJD out like his gramma said."

"So it didn't work?" Annabella said.

"No, ma'am." Liebnitz shook his head. "Things was fine until later that night when an ion storm blew through, and that was all she wrote. The green death feasted on that towel like it was a four-courser. Three of the people in the house got T-burn, and three more got the rot. Had to abandon the house."

Shaking her head, Annabella said, "That's terrible."

Terise rolled her eyes. "That's *normal*. It's what we have to face every day here. Didn't you *know* that?"

How should I? Annabella thought but managed not to say. Instead, she asked the mayor, "Moné, is there any way I can visit those people who got—got the rot?"

"Weren't you planning on a hospital tour as part of your visit?" one of the staffers asked.

"Probably. I honestly didn't have it that carefully planned out. I wanted to see how things were, play it by ear and see what came up. I've found the stories tend to work better that way, if they grow organically instead of being planned. Besides, the idea is to find things out. Can't do that if I know ahead of time what I want to do."

Finishing off his wine, Liebnitz said, "That strikes me as kinda wasteful."

"What do you mean?"

"Well, what if you're led down a dead end? Or to something you don't want or that isn't part of your story?"

Annabella shrugged. "That's fairly standard. You always record more than you actually need. I think of everything I've ever gotten on cam, I've used less than one percent of it in actual story content. That's what the editing process is for."

"Besides," Terise said snidely, "it also has to go through GDI oversight."

"They look over my content, of course. That's standard. But it's not oversight. They make suggestions, but they don't control what we do."

"Really?" Terise sounded dubious.

"Really," Annabella said forcefully. "You *have* heard of freedom of the press, haven't you?"

"Goddess bless, you really *do* believe that, don't you?"

"You'll have to excuse Terise," Liebnitz said quickly before Annabella could reply. "She's been in a bad mood since 'bout 2029 or so."

That caused Terise to blush. "I'm sorry, Moné, but—"

"It's all right," Annabella said. She thought, and then

decided to confide something personal, figuring it might help them get past her as a W3N reporter and think of her as a person instead. "I'm pretty used to it. Whenever I walk around back home, I have to use an imager."

Patel asked, "What's that?"

Another man asked, "Ain't that them things that Nod used for disguises back in the day?"

Annabella said, "Exactly. It's a device that alters how your face appears. Basically, it superimposes a holo over your actual face so you look like someone else. The Brotherhood used it to fool video surveillance, back when that was all some people had for security."

Liebnitz chuckled again. "It amazes me that folks didn't get robbed blind in the old days, just dependin' on sight like that."

"Yeah, I couldn't believe it either when my boss told me about it. But now it's great for me."

"Why do *you* need it?" Terise asked harshly.

"Because people know my face. They see me in their flats and in their offices, and they associate me with the stories I do. And if it's a story they don't like, they blame me." They also associated her with stories they did like, which had its own brand of harassment, but Annabella suspected this particular audience wouldn't appreciate that much. "So I have to use the imager when I go out in public so people won't recognize me."

"I would've thought you'd *want* to be recognized," Terise said.

Refusing to be baited, Annabella said, "I also like to go to and from work in peace. Or go shopping or have a meal without being bothered."

"Seems to me," Terise said, "if you're gonna be in the public eye, you should accept being 'bothered' as part of your job."

"And when I'm working, I'm okay with that. I never use the imager when I'm working, Terise."

At the woman's expression, Annabella realized she'd made a tactical error by using Terise's given name. But she also didn't have another name to use. Besides, the mayor was the most important person in the room, and *he* was okay with being called Moné, so why should this woman get her bowels in an uproar?

And so Annabella plowed on: "When I'm off duty, as it were, I prefer to keep my anonymity, same as anyone else."

"But you aren't the same as anyone else, are you?" Terise asked, her tone now actively hostile. "You're a W3N reporter, a public figure. You think any of us try to hide who we are from the public? Fotze, you think any of us ever get to *be* 'off duty'?"

Everyone at the table tensed at Terise's use of profanity while on cam. While W3N had no real restrictions of that sort, it was one of those things that one generally didn't do. Indeed, Annabella could count on the fingers of two hands the number of times someone had cursed on cam, and all of them were people who were particularly emotional at the time.

And that includes Terise here, she thought.

Liebnitz had been content to let Terise carry on, but the use of "fotze" on camera got him on his feet. "All right, Terise, that's enough of that. Annabella's a guest in our city, and I ain't about to start treatin' guests like that, you hear?"

To her credit, Terise looked and sounded contrite and sincere when she said, "I'm sorry, Moné." Sounding less of both, she then said, "I'm sorry, Ms. Wu. That was rude of me."

"It's fine," Annabella said. "You were speaking from

the heart. I appreciate the honesty." Turning to Liebnitz, who was sitting back down, she asked, "Moné, do you think it's possible for tomorrow, besides the hospital visit, if I could just, I don't know, follow you around for a day? Get a sense of what things are like from what you do on a normal day, and then see if there are any tangents I want to pursue from there."

"That'll be fine, Annabella." Turning to Patel, he said, "Sal, you wanna handle that? Get Annabella clearances to be wherever we'll be tomorrow."

"Of course," Patel said.

Eating the last of the lo mein, Annabella wondered just what she had gotten herself into.

SIX

Corporal Hugh Isembi tried not to scratch his arm. He'd gotten a new ti-too—a Tiberium-laced tattoo—when he got the promotion to corporal, and it still occasionally itched.

He was lying on his stomach in a ventilation shaft over one of the hallways in the San Diego Convention Center, one of the new T7 rifles in the crook of his arm. Isembi had never been to this hemisphere before, and he was grateful that he was able to do so in the service of the Brotherhood of Nod.

Alongside Private Voyskunsky, he was there to defend against attacks from GDI heathens.

Isembi had volunteered for this mission when it was first revealed to him. Besides the fact that he'd always wanted to visit California—Isembi loved the ocean, but had never seen the Pacific—he approved of anything that cut into GDI's so-called "blue zones."

The very notion made Isembi almost physically ill. Earth had been given the gift of Tiberium, and how did GDI respond? By quarantining themselves, building walls against it, and trying to come up with ways to stop it. No wonder so many of their people died from exposure to it. It was divine retribution for rejecting the gift.

"I hope these things work," Voyskunsky muttered next to him.

"What are you talking about?" Isembi asked.

Voyskunsky looked down at his own T7. "The ray-guns."

Archly, Isembi said, "You mean the Tiberium-enhanced energy weapons?"

"Yeah, the ray-gun," Voyskunsky said, shaking his helmeted head. "You scan the specs on these things? The power curve's through the stratosphere."

Confused, Isembi said, "Of course it is. How else would it be able to fire streams of energy?"

"What I'm worried about is whether or not it'll stay in one piece." Again, Voyskunsky looked down at the weapon. "There's a lot of power in there, and that's a very small piece of metal holding it all in. I'm worried about it blowing up in my face."

"If it does, at least we'll have died fighting the enemies of the Brotherhood."

Voyskunsky smiled. "I have no problem dying while fighting the enemies of the Brotherhood, Corporal, it's dying while lying in a ventilation shaft doing nothing that concerns me."

"We serve the Brotherhood. What else matters?" Isembi asked.

"Save me from fanatics," Voyskunsky muttered.

Isembi was starting to grow angry, and wondered how Voyskunsky had managed to make it into Kane's glorious army. "Private—"

"No disrespect intended, Corporal," Voyskunsky said. "I believe in what we're doing, believe me. I just don't like the idea of dying pointlessly. I know I'm going to die. We all are. I'd rather do it taking down some of those GDI fascists, not because the equipment failed."

Isembi supposed he saw the private's point, but refused to acknowledge it out loud. Voyskunsky needed to learn to respect his superiors. "These weapons will allow us to destroy our enemies once and for all. That is why we could muster these invasion forces."

"You sure?" Voyskunsky asked.

"Of course I'm sure." Isembi shook his head. "If we limited ourselves to outmoded projectile weapons, this invasion force would be taken out in an instant. But we have the strength of Tiberium on our side."

"I hope it's enough," Voyskunsky said. "Besides, they could just bomb us from the air."

Isembi smiled under his helmet. "They won't. Don't you know who it is in the room under this shaft?"

Chuckling, Voyskunsky said, "You may not believe this, Corporal, but I am a good soldier. I go where I am told and don't ask questions."

"No, you merely make comments."

"Of course. The Brotherhood believes in its members expressing themselves freely, does it not?"

Opening his mouth to argue the point, Isembi bit back his planned retort, and yanked the subject back to what they were guarding. "In the meeting room under us, they're interrogating a GDI scientist we captured when we took this city."

"So? The GDI is rather overburdened with scientists. I doubt they'll miss another."

Derisively, Isembi said, "This gentleman is what passes for an 'expert' on Tiberium among the GDI. Their other 'experts' were destroyed when the *Philadelphia* was cleansed."

"Oh, *please*. The station wasn't 'cleansed.' It was blown up. And rather nicely, I might add. I always hated the design of that place."

Isembi tensed again. "The point is the man below us is a valuable resource. The reason we're here is to stop the inevitable GDI thugs from trying to rescue the good Dr. Takeda."

"Good. So if this thing *does* blow up when I try to fire it, at least I'll take them out, too."

Sighing, Isembi made a mental note to write up Voyskunsky to Captain al-Rashan when this mission was over.

Voyskunsky then muttered something in his native Russian, a language Isembi did not speak. "What was that, Private?"

"I was just saying that I hope you're right about the numbers, Corporal."

"What do you mean?" Isembi asked.

"Even with the Very Large Gun of Doom here," he said, again indicating the T7, "I don't think we have enough forces here to seriously hold the city against GDI. We were damned lucky to even take the city."

"It wasn't luck," Isembi said. "GDI has grown weak, thinking us to be even weaker. Their pathetic intelligence was unable to even notice our gathering strength in secret, even as they let their own defenses lie fallow. We were able to take San Diego because the forces defending it were reduced to almost nothing."

"Yes, but it won't be like that for long," Voyskunsky said. "Besides, do you really think we could take *all* these Blue Zones? Perhaps I'm wrong—it certainly wouldn't be the first time—but if you ask me, we're not here to take San Diego, but to annoy GDI and strike fear into their hearts."

I'm definitely putting him on report, Isembi thought, but said nothing out loud. He was tired of hearing Voyskunsky's voice.

Besides, it didn't matter. Tiberium would save humanity, bring them out of the dark ages of fossil fuel dependence and petty borders and wars. It had already done more to unite the world than anything else, although they weren't there yet. Still, the world had, in essence, become two nations, where once there were hundreds. When the Brotherhood finally destroyed GDI, there would be one world, under Tiberium, using its unlimited potential to bring humanity to the next level.

Isembi hoped he would live to see it. If not, at least he got to see the Pacific Ocean. Having been born and raised in Kenya, he had seen the Atlantic plenty of times and also the Indian Ocean during his training in Bhopal.

When the VT32 troop transport had taken Isembi and the rest of his unit to San Diego, they had flown over the Pacific, and Isembi had spent every spare moment scanning the portholes. The two oceans he'd seen had their charms, but they were as nothing compared to the massive blue majesty of the Pacific, dotted only occasionally with small islands.

Even if I die today, at least I saw that.

After that, they flew over San Diego, which was a pristine, if lifeless, city. Unaugmented by Tiberium, it was a great deal of drab concrete and glass, with plant life and then desert as you proceeded outward from the city itself. *Typical GDI,* Isembi had thought at the time. *They put their "blue zones" behind walls, like ships in bottles, hoping to preserve a past that no longer exists.*

Refreshed by the memory, which managed to wash the bad taste of Voyskunsky's snide commentary out of his brain, Isembi shifted his weight slightly.

The ti-too started itching again. He put his hand to his arm unconsciously, then pulled it back.

"I'm impressed," Voyskunsky said. "The last corporal

they teamed me up with couldn't stop scratching his ti-too."

Looking over at the exposed part of Voyskunsky's arm, Isembi shook his head. "I notice you don't have one."

Voyskunsky visibly shuddered. "I'm allergic to needles. Besides, I don't fancy the idea of Tiberium actually in my skin."

Coming to a decision to speak up instead of just thinking it repeatedly, Isembi said, "You realize that with every word you speak, you increase my determination to put you on report."

"For what, exactly, Corporal? I'm a loyal acolyte, willing to lay down my life for the Brotherhood—*especially* if it means taking those fascists down a peg. I don't agree with everything the Brotherhood stands for, but I believe that we're in the right and GDI is very much in the wrong. I don't love the Brotherhood as much as you, sir, and I apologize for that, but you can rest assured that I hate GDI more than you ever could."

Up until now, Voyskunsky's tone had been one of light snideness, an almost amused contempt that made Isembi's teeth hurt. But when speaking of his hatred, Isembi could actually see the private's body tense under his armor.

Isembi decided to postpone his final decision on whether to put the private on report depending on how he acquitted himself against GDI. Assuming they did attack the convention center, at any rate. The captain seemed pretty sure that GDI would stop at nothing to rescue Takeda. Isembi was looking forward to destroying enemy combatants in the Brotherhood's name.

Vega decided that if he could wear this battlesuit all the time, he'd never stop running.

He'd run for six hundred meters dozens—no, hundreds—of times since he was a young teenager, including plenty of times competitively while wearing Fordham maroon, and he'd never felt as exhilarated as he did at the end of this particular run, because *he wasn't tired*. Those black straps Brodeur had shown him did the trick, augmenting his already well-toned leg muscles. Whatever extra effort was required to do the run with the weight of the battlesuit, the GD2, the Nighthawk, the spare ammo, and the helmet was more than made up for by the enhancing effect of the battlesuit.

By the time they reached the upward-curving driveway that led to one of the many hotels that serviced the convention center, it was just Companies 6 and 7. Harbor Drive was a wide street, originally designed to carry the heavy vehicular traffic that used to be common in this region. Skyscrapers rose all around them, before giving way to clear skies. This was earthquake country, after all, a condition that had worsened since ti-rock, and you didn't find too many tall buildings outside of downtown regions, and those were all reinforced like crazy.

Lieutenants Anderson and Lemish had peeled off to the right with 1 and 2 a little bit earlier to head down to the Marina and come in the back way. Just before reaching the hotel, Lieutenants d'Agostino, Giughan, and Demitrijian took 3, 4, and 5 off to the left to go around to the far side of the convention center.

Captain Henry had stayed with 6 and 7, which meant he'd be in charge of Vega's part of the op. Chain of command in the 22nd was that the ranks went by company number, so Anderson and d'Agostino would be in charge of their portions. If something happened to Henry, Lieutenant Lipinski would take over, and only if something happened to her would command go to Opahle.

Vega noticed that no medics accompanied them, which showed a confidence in the battlesuit's first aid capability that he dearly hoped was justified.

A report came over Vega's helmet. *"Perimeter's all clear to target."* That was good news. It meant that Nod couldn't hit them until they reached the SDCC. It also meant that, in the middle of downtown San Diego, normally a pretty bustling metropolis, there was *nobody* on the streets.

Of course, this was primarily a business district, with no residences beyond the hotels, so it was likely that between the *Philadelphia*'s destruction and the Nod takeover, everything was closed, but it still felt eerie to Vega.

The driveway to the hotel was two-pronged and curved up a hill. Between the two prongs was plenty of vegetation, so Henry brought them to a halt on the far side of the vegetation from the SDCC. They had to wait until the other companies were in place before they could begin their attack.

Henry nodded to Lipinski and Opahle, and the two lieutenants each tapped two sniper teams. The eight of them—one sniper and one spotter per team—ran the rest of the way up the driveway and into the hotel's front entrance; from there, they'd head to the upper floors to get the SDCC in general and any sentries in particular in their sights. None of the snipers were from Vega's unit, so he didn't know them, but he had seen the four in his company talk about the hotel and its layout on the way over after Henry had given them their marching orders.

While they waited, Vega did a quick check of his helmet systems. The cam was working fine, and transmitting to whichever GDI satellite was over B-11 right now, which meant there'd be a full record of what each soldier did. Vega knew that might prove useful, both as a historical document and also for any possible courts-martial, as cams gave much more convincing testimony than battle-shocked soldiers.

The night vision, however, wasn't working.

"My IF's out," he said after banging the side of the helmet once and getting the same result.

Momoa shook his head. "Shite. Guess you need Geek the Greek."

"You pinged?" A corporal walked over to Vega. He was wearing the standard battlesuit, but was armed only with a pistol, and had no helmet. Putting out a hand, he said, "Jason Popadopoulos, Tech Corps. They call me 'Geek the Greek' because most of these tibeheads can't pronounce 'Popadopoulos.' Lemme see the helmet."

After returning Popadopoulos's handshake, Vega undid the seals and removed the helmet. Before Vega could actually hand it to him, Popadopoulos took it.

"Ah, see, the veeblefetzer's not hooked up right to the frammistan, so I'm gonna need a potrezebie to get the thing back together."

"C'mon, Geek," Momoa said, "you ain't even looked at it yet."

"He also made all that up," Vega said with a smile. At Popadopoulos's surprised look, Vega added, "My roommate in college had a huge collection of old *Mad* magazines."

Reaching into one of his pouches, Popadopoulos grinned and took out a tool and applied it to the inside of the helmet.

"That the potrezebie?" Vega asked.

"Screwdriver, actually. Connection's loose." With a final grunt, he pulled out the screwdriver and put it back in the pouch. "There you go. Bring it back to me when the op's over. The helmets for peaches your size, they get misaligned at the drop of a tweezer, so it'll probably be a mess by the time this is done. A system goes out, just—"

"Conk it on the side, I know."

"Good man. Anything else?"

Before Vega could say anything, Momoa said, "You mean veeblefetzers ain't *real*? What the crack, sib? The hell you been fixin' all this time?" Everybody else was trying very hard not to laugh, since they were only a few meters away from a Nod-held convention center, but Momoa's look of anguish didn't make it easy.

Looking at Popadopoulos, Vega said, "Sorry I ruined your joke."

"Worry not, I'll find a new one. With the good Private Momoa, it's like shooting fish in a shot glass."

Somebody from Alpha said, "Hey, Geek, the ficken GD2's jammin' again."

With a look at Vega, Popadopoulos said, "Jam-proof, my right toe. Ficken engineers. Be right there, Bennett!"

Just as the tech jogged off, Henry put his hand to his ear. The captain said, "Companies 1 and 2 in position. Vega, get your helmet on."

Vega had been about to do that anyhow, so it was an easy order to follow. He clicked the helmet into place. As soon as he did, he heard chatter over the speakers.

"Sniper 1 in place."

"Sniper 2 in position."

"Sniper 4 ready to go."

Then Opahle's voice, which Vega heard both on the helmet and right in front of him: "Sniper 3, what the hell?"

"Sorry, ma'am, the ficken ammo won't load."

Popadopoulos ran over to Opahle. "Want me to—?"

"No," Opahle said. "Emmanuelli, I swear to God, Buddha, Allah, Yahweh, and my Great Aunt Fanny that if you don't learn how to load a GLS 70 in under thirty seconds, I am going to make it my life's work to make sure you are assigned to—"

"*Sniper 3 is a go!*" a different voice said very quickly. Vega figured that Emmanuelli didn't want to know where she'd be assigned if she hacked the lieutenant off.

"Faur, did you have to load the ammo again?"

"*No, ma'am.*"

"Are you lying to me, Faur?"

"*Yes, ma'am.*"

"The three of us are having a conversation when this is over. Actually, it'll be a monologue, and I promise lots of profanity. Out." She turned to Henry. "Sorry about that, Captain."

"We'll talk about it later," Henry said dismissively. Then he put his hand to his ear. "Companies 3, 4, and 5 in position."

Vega pulled his GD2 off his chest and stood at the ready. They were waiting for Bat 3 to provide air strikes, and then they'd move in.

"Sniper 1," Henry said, "what do we have?"

"*Patrols on each entrance. Four at each door.*"

"What about the roof?"

"*Nada, sir.*"

At that, Henry actually smiled. It wasn't an expression his face was suited for, and Vega found himself wishing he hadn't.

Momoa said, "Stupid tibeheads don't have snipers? Spicy!"

"If they don't have any good shots," Gallagher said, "it's not worth it. A bad sniper's worse than no sniper."

Vega said, "Yeah, but if they don't have one, they've probably made up for it in some other—"

An explosion screamed through the air to the right

and above them. Vega looked up instinctively to see that the top floors of the hotel had exploded in a fiery conflagration, then he ducked as he saw glass and steel raining down from the sky.

"Fotze!" That was Momoa. Several shards of glass had sliced through his exposed arms.

"All companies, go, go, go, go!" Henry screamed, and immediately, Companies 6 and 7 ran toward the SDCC. Waiting for the air strikes was no longer an option.

Lipinski took the lead, along with two of her people with railguns. They quickly took up position on the other side of the foliage and started shooting. The remaining members of 6 and 7 all ran toward the SDCC, the front-most shooting at the walkway in front of the entrances, where the guards that Sniper 1 had mentioned were stationed.

Vega tried very hard not to think about the fact that Sniper 1—and all the other snipers, including Faur and Emmanuelli—were dead.

"Ficken Nods." Bowles was running alongside Vega, so he could hear the private's voice over the reports of their weapons. "They're gonna ficken *die* for this shite!"

The railguns made short work of the closest patrol, but the next one down was able to turn and fire.

Green beams of energy spat forth from the muzzle of the Nod soldiers' guns. One beam struck Lipinski right in the left shoulder, burning right through and causing her left arm to fall to the ground. The lieutenant did likewise a second later.

"Crack me sideways, where the hell'd they get?—" Bowles's question was cut off by Momoa running forward and, bleeding arms and all, cutting all four members of the second patrol down with his GD2.

With Lipinski down, Henry had a decision to make

once they entered the SDCC, Vega knew. Vega suspected that Henry went with this group because he wanted to be the one to rescue Takeda—not surprising, really, since that was the primary objective of this portion of the op. That meant he would be accompanying Company 7 upstairs.

Now, though, Company 6's commander was down. With Lipinski out of action, Henry needed to step up and lead 6 into the exhibit hall. *But would he?*

While Vega thought on that, sonic booms overhead were followed in short order by small explosions. *Bat 3 closes the file after it's been hacked,* Vega thought uncharitably, then admonished himself. *Ain't their fault Nod boobied the hotel.* Vega also heard a railgun being fired from inside the SDCC, and Vega found himself hoping the tiberheads were bad shots.

Companies 6 and 7 ran inside the glass doors in proper formation, three at a time, rotating in and out, everyone covering everyone else. Vega tried not to notice the corpses of fellow GDI soldiers, their bodies horribly violated by the Nod energy weapons. Most of them had holes burned straight through them, some large enough that Vega could see clear through to the pavement they were lying on.

How the hell'd they manage that, anyhow? Vega's father had told him that GDI had been trying to make energy weapons for years, but they could never get the power consumption down. In order to be effective, they needed a huge energy source, one that wouldn't require more power than was cost-effective for mass production to issue to soldiers. Tiberium was the only energy-producing substance that could do it, but nobody could figure out how to use it as a power source but keep it from infesting the weapon itself, and plenty of people didn't even want to on general principles, seeing ti-rock solely as a blight on the planet. As far as Vega knew, GDI wasn't anywhere near to solving that conundrum. *Looks like Kane and his off-nets managed it.*

Kane. On the *Huron,* they'd played the news reports about the *Philadelphia*'s destruction—Vega figured it was to get everyone riled up, not that they needed it— including Kane's message. The surprise was that Kane was still alive, since everyone thought they'd gotten him in Kenya twelve years ago. Vega's father had never entirely believed it—"They didn't find a body, son," he'd said, "and that tibehead's got more lives than three cats"—and, as usual, Dad was right.

As they moved to secure the section they were in, Vega wondered why there was so much broken glass on the floor here. The doors themselves were intact.

Once both companies were inside and secure—Vega figured the other GDI companies were engaging the other Nod patrols—Henry turned to Opahle. "Lieutenant, get Takeda."

Opahle looked surprised that Henry had given up that part of the op, then nodded. "Yes, *sir.*"

Vega's respect for Henry went up a level. He did what was best for the battalion, not what was best for him.

"Company 6, let's move!" Henry called out, then looked at Opahle. "Don't crack this up, Lieutenant."

"Wouldn't dream of it, sir." She turned to her soldiers. "Company 7, let's go. Kim, Momoa, McAvoy, take point."

In order to get to the second level, where Takeda was supposedly being held, they needed to run up the escalator. The three that Opahle sent first, Vega noticed, were the three largest people in the company. Vega figured they'd draw any fire by being large targets.

Vega suddenly found it hard to breathe. Running six hundred meters had had no effect on him whatsoever, but seeing all those bodies, knowing that the snipers had also been killed . . .

Get it together, greenie, he admonished himself.

He looked up—

—and saw the Noddie hiding under the escalator who was drawing a bead on the three taking point. Vega raised his GD2 to fire.

Before he could pull the trigger, the soldier was riddled with bullets. Looking across, Vega saw that Gallagher had taken him down.

"Nice shot, Gallagher," Goodier said.

"Fotze," Vega muttered. *That should have been my shot, not that stupid bint's.*

Momoa started shooting when they were three-quarters of the way up, firing in several directions at once.

"The hell, Pup?" either Kim or McAvoy said. Vega couldn't see either of their chestplates.

Shrugging his massive shoulders, Momoa said, "Just figured I'd be sure. Ain't like one of *us* is up there."

"Looks like you got one," either McAvoy or Kim said.

When Vega got to the top of the escalator, along with Gallagher, Brodeur, and Bowles, he saw that there was a Nod soldier slumped over a railgun that was pointed at the large window—or, more accurately, in the large hole in the window. *That's where the broken glass came from. And all that railgun fire.*

"Nice job, Pup," Opahle said. "Let's do it by the plan, people."

Even as the lieutenant spoke those words, one of the smaller windows inside Vega's helmet came to life with the same schematic they'd seen on the holo earlier, and which he'd looked at again after the briefing.

Then it went out.

Vega tried to bring it back up, then hit the side of his helmet for good measure. Still nothing.

"Shite," he muttered.

Goodier led them down one of the wide corridors on the second level. The other units went in other directions. Vega stuck by Brodeur and followed his lead. So far, at least, the 22nd seemed to follow standard op procedure, but in the middle of an op was *not* the time to find out that Goodier, Opahle, Henry, Hastings, or Mc-Neil had some cracked-up variant on SOP that nobody bothered to tell him in the admittedly three and a half seconds he'd been with the division. Plus, his HUD was wiggly, and there wasn't time for Geek the Greek's potrezebie to fix it.

As they went down the corridor, Vega felt almost overwhelmed by gray. The walls were a light gray, the carpet was a darker gray, and the ceiling and meeting-room doors were something in between those. He supposed that they didn't need to be all that colorful, but Vega wondered why they didn't at least make an effort.

In sequence, Unit Epsilon checked each of the meeting rooms in the corridor, only to find them empty of all save chairs and a podium.

Golden and two others Vega didn't know were next up for the final room on the end. Just as Golden was approaching the door, the other two covering him, Vega's helmet switched to night vision.

He was about to conk the helmet on the side again, when he noticed something odd: a heat sig in the ceiling that wasn't where one of the lights was. It was just a small circle.

Like the muzzle of an energy weapon. Vega immediately fired at the sig.

As soon as Isembi saw the GDI troops enter the hallway, he signaled Captain al-Rashan. "GDI troops on approach." The scope on the T7 was able to scan through the vent to the room beyond, providing him with an image of black human-shaped forms amidst the gray of the room itself.

"The booby's armed and ready," al-Rashan said. *"Don't fire on them until you see the whites of their eyes."*

"They're wearing helmets," Isembi said, confused.

Al-Rashan laughed. *"It's an old saying, Corporal. It means don't fire until they get very, very close. They won't know you're up there, so take advantage."*

"Yes, sir." Their body armor was proof against their infrared scans, and so were the T7s.

"The other infantry are standing by behind the door here, and will engage once the booby's gone off. Out."

Voyskunsky said, "If it makes you feel any better, sir, I didn't get it, either."

"It doesn't," Isembi said sourly.

The GDI troops methodically checked each door. Isembi had to almost physically restrain himself from depressing the T7's trigger.

Two of the heathens moved toward the meeting room where al-Rashan was interrogating Takeda. *Excellent.* He took aim at the group of soldiers that had checked a different room, since there were about half a dozen clustered there. Voyskunsky, he knew, was a crack shot—that was why he'd been assigned to this post in the first place, so he said, "Target the ones in the back."

"Yes, sir," Voyskunsky said with a relish Isembi

wouldn't have credited him with when they first met. But the private obviously hated GDI, and that was something Isembi could use.

As he took aim and started to depress the trigger, Isembi thought he saw something through the scope: One of the GDI troops seemed to be looking directly at him—or at the very least had his head angled toward the ceiling.

Just as Isembi fired his weapon, the trooper lifted his own rifle and fired right at Isembi.

A burst of heat slammed into Vega's chest, sending him careening backward into several of his fellow soldiers. Clambering quickly to his feet, he saw three things at once: the door that Golden and the other two were going into had exploded outward, probably boobied; two Nod soldiers fell to the floor from the hole in the ceiling that Vega's weapons fire had made; and Golden landed on the other side of the hallway, screaming.

Vega ran over to Golden. The private was bleeding from dozens of wounds, his battlesuit shredded. In both his ears and his helmet speakers, he heard Golden say, "Can't—breathe!"

Instinctively, Vega tried to remove Golden's helmet, but he couldn't get it to budge. *Of course not, tibehead, only Golden, a medic, or someone of higher rank can take it off.*

Vega felt a blast of heat by his neck, and then noticed the green energy beam that was cutting into the wall in front of him.

Whirling around, he prepared to fire, only to see Gallagher gunning down the Noddie who was aiming his energy weapon at him.

"Watch your arse, greenie!" Gallagher said. "How's Golden?"

"He can't breathe! Goody!" The sergeant was the only person here who could get Golden's helmet off.

Only then did Vega focus on the rest of the corridor. Half a dozen Nod soldiers had engaged them, walking through the now-destroyed meeting-room door, which meant that Nod was outnumbered even with the casualties Company 7 had taken, but Nod was *much* better armed.

It also meant Nod was waiting for them.

Vega looked up, then, and fired at the same hole he'd made.

"We already *got* them, Puke," Gallagher said, pointing at the two bodies on the floor. "Come *on*!"

She ran toward the meeting room. Vega was wondering what she was thinking, but the Noddies who'd run out of there were now engaging the rest of their unit, and the doorway was actually clear. So he followed, Bowles running up alongside him. "Let's get these arseholes."

Gallagher, however, had stopped just inside the door, and Vega and Bowles did likewise.

Vega saw why immediately: on the stage, which was raised about a meter off the floor, stood three Nod soldiers, all wearing the dark fatigues and boots, beige vests, and stylized red helmets that all the soldiers they'd seen today wore. All three held energy weapons. Two were aimed at the door.

The third energy weapon was aimed at the fourth person on the stage, who Vega recognized from the material he'd gone over after the briefing: Takeda. The middle-aged scientist differed from the photo in his file mostly by virtue of his dark hair flying out in all directions and the multiple cuts and contusions on his face.

Still, Vega couldn't mistake the bulbous nose or the thin mustache. The scientist looked dazed, his eyes unfocused.

He's probably been tortured, Vega thought. *Well, this is totally cracked up.*

The one holding the gun on Takeda, who had a captain's rank insignia on his uniform, as well as the distinctive ti-rock-laced tattoo, said, "Lay down your weapons, heathens, or Dr. Takeda dies."

"Crack that," Bowles said, and fired.

Vega's heart went into his throat, but Bowles wasn't firing at the Nod soldiers. He was firing at the stage, which went right out from under all four of them. Green energy streamed into the ceiling.

Gallagher then fired at the two who were farthest away from Takeda. Bowles was about to fire on the other when Vega said, "Dish!" even as he took out his pistol and dropped his GD2 to the floor.

That seemed to do the trick, as Bowles suddenly remembered Henry's words on the subject of Takeda's importance.

The one on Takeda hadn't dropped his weapon, and was now cranking it up to shoot Takeda, who cried out in either agony or fright.

Vega paused for a millisecond to aim and then shot the captain between the eyes.

Blood splattered out in all directions, including all over Dr. Takeda.

Bowles ran over to the Noddies. Vega assumed he was making sure they were dead. Vega, for his part, went to Dr. Takeda, pausing only to holster his Nighthawk, then bent over to retrieve his GD2. "Sorry about that, sir," he said as he stuck the GD2 to his chest. "I'm Private Vega with the 22nd. We're here to get you out of here. Can you walk?"

"Private Vega," Takeda said, "if it means getting out of here and back to a safe, secure GDI location, or even a nice GDI military plane, then I assure you, I can *run*."

Gallagher was looking at Vega like he had grown a second head. "Where'd you learn to shoot like that, Puke?"

"It's a talent, Gallagher, not something you learn. And stop calling me that."

"Crack off."

Bowles was now standing over the two corpses. At first, he was just staring at them.

Then, out of nowhere, he started kicking one of them over and over again.

Gallagher rolled her eyes. "Dish, for shite's sake, will you cut that out?"

Turning around, Bowles said, "Whatever." Then shot all three in the face.

Takeda said to Vega, "I think that man has some aggression issues to work out."

"Good guess," Vega said. He touched the side of his helmet. "Sergeant Goo—"

Goodier's voice sounded on Vega's helmet before he could finish. *"We've secured the hallway, but we're the only ones doing that well. We've got to get over to—"*

Vega interrupted. "This is Vega. Sir, we have Takeda."

There was a pause. Vega walked toward the door, guiding Takeda along.

"Say again, Vega."

He came out the door with Takeda. "I have Takeda, sir."

Everyone was staring at him. Gallagher and Bowles came up behind them.

Goodier said, "Private Vega, what do you drink?"

"Sir?"

"If you want to get toasted, what do you drink?"

"Uh, German beer, when I can get it. Tequila when I can't."

Turning to the others, Goodier said, "Let's move out! Simonton, Kelerchian, grab the wounded. Any Noddies left breathing?"

Momoa kicked the two who were under the hole Vega had blown in the ceiling that had gotten this whole shooting match started. "These two."

"Grab 'em," Goodier said.

"What for?" Momoa asked.

Bowles added, "Yeah, Goody, the hell we need *their* arse for? We *got* the target."

"You questioning a superior officer, Private?" Goodier asked. Vega noted that his tone hadn't modulated from its usual polite conversational one, which belied the seriousness of his words.

"Of course not, sir."

"Then help Pup grab the ficken prisoners."

"Yes, sir."

The sergeant then raised his voice. "Let's go, people. Out, out, out!" He touched the side of his helmet. "This is Goodier." Vega heard his voice on his helmet speaker as well. "Unit Epsilon has secured Takeda, plus two prisoners, proceeding to the egress."

Now Vega heard Henry's voice, with a lot of weapons fire behind him. *"All units, fall back to first position. Say again, all units fall back to first position! Bat 3, prepare final strike on SDCC."*

That surprised Vega at first, but then he remembered what Henry had said in the briefing. Takeda was the only reason why they hadn't bombed the SDCC from the air. With him getting out . . .

Vega was still guiding Takeda, who was living up to his promise to run. Goodier ran alongside, and asked, "Are you all right, Doctor?"

"This blood isn't mine, Sergeant," Takeda said. "Thanks to Private Vega, I believe that I will someday be fine, yes."

"Good." Looking at Vega as they reached the top of the escalator, Goodier said, "Private, you're gonna be swimming in tequila by sunup."

In truth, Vega had been hoping for the German beer, as he only drank tequila with his father, but he knew how hard that was to come by these days.

Gallagher and Kim both took out six more Nod soldiers on the way to the escalator, and they stepped over a lot more GDI corpses than Vega was entirely happy with. He and Takeda were bringing up the rear.

A flash of heat that was becoming very familiar sailed by Vega's head, and he whirled around to see a green energy beam cut through the heads of both Kelerchian and the private he was carrying. Unlike the weapon Vega had used to shoot the captain, these weapons didn't leave holes that spewed blood.

Snarling in anger, Vega turned back around, yanking the GD2 off his chest, and fired in the direction of the beam.

But he fired at empty air. Gallagher had already taken out the sniper.

"You gotta move faster than that, Puke," Gallagher said. "Let's pump feet."

"Don't call me that."

As they ran down the escalator that Battalion 3 would be bombing to microscopic dust in a few minutes, Vega found he couldn't get the images of the dead and wounded GDI soldiers out of his head: Golden, unable to breathe; Lieutenant Lipinski, her arm blown off; Kelerchian's head vaporized.

But the images of the Nod soldiers they'd taken down didn't bother him at all. In fact, Vega found himself wishing he'd joined Bowles in kicking their corpses.

Henry's voice echoed in his helmet. *"Battalion 4, fall back to landing zone, double time. Move it, move it, move it!"*

Vega looked at Takeda, whose weight he was supporting with help now from Goodier. "I think we're gonna test that running theory, sir."

"Be happy to," Takeda said gamely. To Goodier, he said, "Sergeant, may I take it as read that now that I am no longer a presence in that structure, it is GDI's intention to raze it to the ground, along with as many of Kane's lunatics as they can take?"

"I can't speak to that, sir," Goodier said flatly. Then he yelled out, "Private Brodeur!"

Brodeur flagged in his jogging so that the three of them caught up to him. "Yes, sir?"

"Your helmet, Private."

"Er, yes, sir." Brodeur undid his helmet and handed it to Goodier.

"Thank you, Private. Stay with us." Brodeur, who now looked as confused as Vega felt, nodded, and kept pace with the three of them.

Goodier put the helmet on Takeda's head. "You'll want to be wearing this, sir."

Because its designated soldier wasn't wearing it, the helmet's external speakers weren't working, so it was only Takeda's muffled voice that came out when he said, "I can't see."

"Private Vega and I will be your eyes, sir. Trust me, you'll need this."

Vega still didn't get it, but he knew better than to say anything.

When they were about three-quarters of the way to the landing zone, Goodier, Opahle, Henry, and Sergeant Gnaizda of Unit Alpha all cried, *"Hit the deck!"*

Everyone went down immediately, except for Vega, Goodier, Brodeur, and Takeda. Vega and Takeda only took an extra half a second, as the private needed to help the scientist more gently to a prone position on the Harbor Drive pavement. Goodier grabbed Brodeur, and guided him down as well.

The explosion that followed was deafening, and Vega was suddenly grateful for the muffling effect of his own helmet to protect his—

To protect my ears! Suddenly, the sergeant's actions made sense. Four hundred meters from the destruction of the SDCC, the noise could cause ear damage to anyone not protected by GDI military helmets, which was why Goodier gave Brodeur's helmet to Takeda, since the deaf private didn't have to worry about the noise.

It was Opahle only who said, *"Everybody up, up, up, up! Double-time it to the* Huron, *now!"*

Vega got up and saw that downtown San Diego was already covered in a cloud of dust and smoke. He tried switching to night vision, but most of the dust was hot enough from the weapons fire for that to not be much of an improvement.

He then noticed that Takeda was still lying on the ground. Bending over, Vega guided the scientist to his feet. "Come on, Dr. Takeda. Let's get you home."

* * *

Corporal Isembi had been trying to get his mouth to work for several minutes now, but couldn't manage much more than an incoherent moan. His display was telling him that his body armor had suffered considerable damage from projectile weapons fire, but the auto-repair circuits were engaged, and would be fully functional in seven minutes. Unfortunately, it took him several minutes to read that information, because the words were swimming in his vision.

I must have a concussion or something. How did that damned heathen see me? Whoever that soldier was who fired on him and Voyskunsky, he was able to see the two of them. *Has GDI improved its tech?*

Isembi felt uncomfortable, like he was draped over a sharp rock. After a second, he was able to activate his display enough to show him that he was being carried on the shoulder of a GDI thug who was running down a dust-choked San Diego street with Isembi over his shoulder.

I'm a prisoner.

A quick scan showed that they'd gotten Voyskunsky, too, and also rescued Takeda. *We have failed.*

The auto-suicide function had yet to be repaired, but Isembi had every intention of using it when it was.

"Are those prisoners?" said a voice.

Expanding the scan, Isembi saw that the thug carrying him was talking to a man of battle commander rank.

"Yes, *sir*!" said the one carrying him.

"Put the private in the brig, but bring the corporal up front. I want him to see what we did to them."

Isembi saw that he and Voyskunsky were being brought into a troop transport. The Brotherhood knew of these planes, but had no useful intelligence on their interiors. He set his scanners to take in as much as they could. He wasn't sure if he'd be able to transmit to any Brotherhood receptors, but he'd do whatever he could before he was finally able to take his own life. As he watched Voyskunsky being carried off, presumably to the brig as ordered, Isembi prayed to Kane that the private would be wise enough to do likewise.

"Sir," said another officer, "you may wish to remove their armor first."

At that, Isembi started to panic.

"Looks pretty shot up to me, Hastings, but you're probably right. Private, remove that armor."

"Yessir."

With a rather sudden motion, the private threw Isembi to the deck, causing Isembi's stomach to lurch. The armor, at least, protected him from the impact.

A systems query showed that the suicide option was not yet online. *Not that it matters,* Isembi thought smugly. *It isn't as if these fools can bypass the security on the armor.* With any luck, this brute would try to rip it off, which would result in his arm being blown off and Isembi being completely safe.

"Hang on, Pup," said another voice. "That's gotta be boobied. Gimme a sec."

"Knock yourself out, Geek," the one called Pup said. "I'm okay without touchin' 'em."

Isembi scanned each of the GDI thugs in the room. The one called "Geek" was a corporal named Popadopoulos—according to the patch on his vest, anyhow—and wore different armor from the others. He was probably a noncombatant. The one called Pup was a larger-than-usual specimen named Momoa, still a private. The other two nearby were a battle commander—his suit's database identified him as BC Michael McNeil, which jibed with the MCNEIL stencilled on his vest—and a major, who had been called Hastings, and was probably one of McNeil's seconds.

Then the display went offline.

Panicking, Isembi tried to activate it. Nothing happened. He tried, on instinct, to move his arm, and found that he couldn't. The display had gone dark, and his field of vision was now limited to the ceiling of the deck.

"What did you do?" he cried aloud.

"Knocked out your systems," Popadopoulos said, and Isembi could just *hear* the heathen's smug grin. "Right now, sib, you're just wearin' dead weight. Pup, you wanna do the honors?"

Momoa loomed over him now, with a vicious smile on his face. "Gladly."

Soon, Isembi became aware of what life was like for a banana. The large private gripped the armor at the shoulder and started to pull down, peeling off each piece. Sparks flew as wiring was severed by the heathen's powerful grip. After his helmet was removed, Isembi had a wider field of vision, and the first thing he noticed was another GDI private with the name BOWLES on his vest holding a gun right at his knees. The implication was clear to Isembi: If he moved, he would be crippled with a shot to the knee.

As Momoa tossed each piece aside, Popadopoulos collected them, muttering about how much he was looking forward to getting his hands on Nod tech.

Isembi seethed. He had been denied a noble death on the battlefield, and now the heathens were keeping him from taking his own life to avoid being sullied by their filth. If he tried to escape, they would just maim him, not allowing him to die.

Within minutes, Isembi was down to his underclothing, at which point Momoa hauled him violently to his feet, almost dislocating Isembi's shoulders.

McNeil looked up and down Isembi's near-naked form, then shook his head. "Just an ordinary person without the armor, isn't he?"

"Not with that gobshite on his arm, sir," Bowles said in a bitter tone. "That makes him one'a *them,* sir. Permission to take out his kneecaps."

"Denied, Private," McNeil said sharply. "The corporal here is our prisoner, and that means he'll be treated properly. Some may consider the Geneva Convention a pleasant anachronism, but in the *civilized* world, we treat our prisoners like human beings."

Our prisoners are all heathens, and deserve to be treated like all infidels, Isembi thought, but refused to say aloud. He had nothing to say to these people.

"Bring him," McNeil said, walking forward.

The large private pushed Isembi forward down a corridor and on to what looked like a flight deck. Isembi tried to remember everything he saw, from the layout of the controls to the arrangement of the chairs, in case he found himself in a position to bring back intelligence to the Brotherhood. It was a long shot, but he would *not* be derelict in his duty to Kane and to the cause.

Feeling pressure on his feet, as if they were being pushed into the deck, was the only reason why Isembi was able to ascertain that they were taking off. Isembi hadn't realized GDI tech had advanced this far, and was impressed despite himself.

"Point him over here, Private," McNeil said to Momoa, who turned Isembi around and twisted his head so he was facing one of the windows. Isembi considered resisting, but that would serve only to damage his neck. Besides, he might be able to see the ocean.

What he did see was even better.

The pristine city he had seen a day ago when they arrived was barely recognizable. Buildings were damaged, some gutted. Where the convention center had stood was a smoking, fiery pit. Beyond that, a once-proud naval base, which had served as the first line of defense for the west coast of the United States, was now a crater, steam rising off the ocean, a gash in the coastline.

"This is what's left of your mighty Nod forces, Corporal," McNeil said. "You keep thinking you can beat us, but you can't. We'll crush you."

Isembi just smiled. GDI may have regained control of San Diego, but it was not untouched. Scars marred their precious Blue Zone, and that meant the Brotherhood had truly won this day, even if GDI didn't realize it.

The bottle had been shattered, the ship broken.

SEVEN

After spending a morning observing Mayor Moné Liebnitz at work, Annabella Wu found herself grateful that she carried a cam. The day so far had been so stultifyingly dull that she found herself unable to remember the specifics of anything that had happened.

This wasn't a total surprise to her—the mundanity of day-to-day politics was something she had learned during her early days at W3N, covering town hall meetings and the like—but today was a sharp reminder of it.

The office where he did his work was a bit of a disappointment, though. Annabella had been to the offices of the mayors of five different cities in B-2, from the restrained elegance of Gracie Mansion in New York, which had housed the mayor's office since New York's City Hall was demolished in '32, to the old-fashioned splendor of Baltimore's mayoral sanctum, to the magnificent modern architecture of Camden's Pasha Hall.

So she had been rather taken aback to find that Liebnitz worked in a small, cramped twentieth-floor office barely thirty square feet, with an industrial desk, uncomfortable chairs, and not enough space.

While the cam dutifully reported every dull meeting and face-to-face and link that Liebnitz went through in the name of keeping civic order, Annabella found herself looking out the window. Most of the streets she could see were disturbingly empty. Aside from evenly posted GDI military troops, almost nobody walked around. Those who did were almost all very young or very disheveled. The former were mostly kids who were outside playing. Annabella saw at least three different games, including several kids playing hopscotch, something she hadn't seen since she herself was a kid, a circle of children, plus one adult, playing *bocce* ball with what looked like a bean bag, and a game of basketball in a parking lot.

The latter, she realized, were ti-bos. Annabella had heard of "Tiberium hobos" being all over even the GDI-controlled Yellows, but hadn't believed it. After all, one of GDI's tenets was that everyone who contributed would have a home. Certainly there were no issues of homelessness in the Blues.

She made a note on her Hand to interview some of the ti-bos, while noting that there were a lot more vehicles on the street than she was expecting. Of course, New York had almost none, but even the more rural areas back home were usually limited to large trucks and such. Apparently in these parts, some people did actually have their own cars. Of course, Atlanta's mass transit system wasn't on par with New York's, but still it was a peculiar disconnect for Annabella.

Liebnitz interrupted her sightseeing. " 'Scuse me, Annabella?"

"Yes, Your Honor?"

Laughing, Liebnitz said, "I toldja not to call me that, didn't I?"

"Yes, sir, but I'm a slow learner." Annabella deliberately said that to bait Terise, who was one of about six people in the cramped office with them, but the aide didn't rise to it.

"Well, I've got lunch comin', and I wanted to go to Laubenthal Memorial, pay my respects to the folks across the street. You said you wanted to see 'em, so off we go."

"Good." She pulled the drone back in, figuring her spec-cam would do for the nonce, and followed the mayor, his aides, and his security detail—who had been stationed outside the office—to the lift, which took them down to the garage.

A truck similar to the one that had taken her to and from the mansion the previous night was waiting for them outside the lift door, and everyone piled in. The driver, a large-nosed older man, said, "Back for more abuse, Ms. Wu?"

Annabella smiled. "That's why they pay me the big creds, Mike."

Terise shot Annabella a stunned look. That gave Annabella a certain self-satisfaction. *Yes, the Blue bint can remember the name of the hired help.*

They drove down one of several streets in this town called "Peachtree," and then turned on to another street, thus giving Annabella a close-up view of the *bocce* ball game.

"Y'see a lotta that," Liebnitz said without prompting. "It's a game that you can play anywhere and can stop anytime."

Before Annabella could ask why being able to stop at any time was a factor, a siren pealed through the air at deafening levels. Putting her hands to her ears, she asked, "What the *hell?*—"

Nobody responded until the siren died down, at which point Liebnitz said, "Ion storm. Mike?"

"On it," Mike said. He started steering the car into a U-turn, and headed for the nearest parking garage.

Annabella found her eyes falling on the kids playing

bocce, who were still playing their game. "How far out is the storm?"

"When the siren goes off? 'Bout ten minutes. Satellite picks 'er up, and the siren's to tell everyone to get inside."

She looked back at the kids, who still hadn't moved, as Mike pulled the truck into a line that had already formed at the parking lot. "Your Honor, those kids're still out there. Shouldn't they go inside?"

"Yeah, they should." Liebnitz's words were heavy. "But they're kids. They think they're indestructible. S'why the ti-wards're full of 'em."

When they arrived at the door, a holo activated over the dashboard with the image of a helmeted GDI soldier. *"Mayor Liebnitz, glad to see you're okay."*

"Thanks, Captain. Listen, there're some kids playin' *bocce* about a block back. Get 'em inside for me, willya?"

"If we can spare anyone, sir, we'll be happy to—"

"Make *sure* you can spare someone. Those're *kids* out there, and—"

"With respect, sir," the captain said, and Annabella found herself frustrated with the fact that she couldn't read his expression through the helmet, or even tell if he was a he, *"they've been informed of what to do if that siren goes. We can't be held responsible if they choose not to follow those instructions."*

While Annabella thought back on what Liebnitz had said the night before about one hundred percent penetration, the mayor himself said, "Oh, I think you can be held responsible, and I intend to if I don't see those kids in the garage with us by the time that storm hits, am I clear, Captain?"

"We'll do our best, sir. Go on through."

"Right," Mike said, and he steered the truck into the garage.

Annabella was very grateful that she never turned her spec-cam off. That was a recording that might do her some good.

"That was very good of you," she said to Liebnitz as Mike, directed by another armored military person, pulled into a parking spot.

Liebnitz made a noise like a bursting pipe. "It was nothin'."

"Hardly. You tried to—"

Terise finally spoke up. "What he means is, it was absolutely nothing. Moné has no authority over GDI military, and there's precisely no way to back up his threat. I wouldn't worry about it, though. The kids are probably just waiting until the last minute to go inside. My kids do that all the time."

Somehow, Annabella had a hard time imagining Terise as a loving mother. Since they were at leisure until the storm passed, she called up Terise Plashko's file on her Hand. Sure enough, she was a widow with four children. Her late husband had died of Tiberium poisoning.

Ouch.

Looking at Liebnitz and avoiding looking at Terise, she asked, "How long do the storms last?"

"Depends," Liebnitz said. "We didn't get an advance on this one, so it'll probably be a quickie. The ones that last a couple, three hours, we usually know they're comin'. But this—prolly no more'n an hour."

Nodding, Annabella decided that, since she had a captive audience, she'd ask about something that had been bothering her since she got back to her hotel room. "One thing confused me at dinner last night."

"Only one?" Terise asked.

Annabella ignored her. "My first day at work after the *Philadelphia* was destroyed, it was all anybody could talk about. One of our reporters was on board, and we had a service, and everybody was wondering about the attack and the war and if they knew anyone who was hit when Nod attacked all those Blues, so I was kinda surprised that nobody talked about it last night."

"Why should we?" Patel asked.

"What do you mean, why should you?" Annabella asked right back, having expected the vehement response to come from Terise. "Nod's being back in business affects all of us."

"How, exactly?" Liebnitz asked. "They ain't attacked us here. We got problems of our own, in case you hadn't noticed."

"I realize that, but Nod's attack affects the whole world."

"That's the whole world's problem." Liebnitz sighed. "I know that sounds kinda harsh, Annabella, but right now, I'm just tryin' to keep our people alive. We *been* fightin' a war."

"Against Tiberium?"

Liebnitz nodded. "If Nod attacks here, well, we ain't got no shortage'a GDI troops to deal with that. But my concern is for the people of this city."

Whatever other questions Annabella might have had died on her lips.

Instead, Terise asked her a question. "Tell me, Ms. Wu, do you listen to music?"

"Sure."

"What kind?"

"All kinds, I guess. I mean, it's generally whatever's playing on GN. Why?"

"On GN, huh?" Terise chuckled. "Okay. Just curious is all."

At one point, Annabella left the truck to relieve herself. When she stepped out of the bathroom, she noticed that one of the soldiers was watching a flatscreen image of the storm in action.

The garage was soundproof and windowless, so Annabella hadn't heard or seen anything of the storm yet. She wished she had left the drone outside—it was proofed against lightning strikes, so it should've been safe—but, as Uncle Freddie had always said, if wishes were horses, they'd be hip-deep in shite. Since she did have the drone, she sent it over to watch over the soldier's shoulder while she herself did likewise.

The sky had turned a deep purple color, which gave all the buildings an almost dark glow. Lightning-like fingers jumped among every metal object out there—lampposts, traffic lights, air-traffic beacons, WorldNet towers—like a thousand tesla coils released with their own agendas. They sparked and shocked and glowed and danced, shattering pavement and windows. Litter and other detritus blew straight up, and Annabella almost thought the feed was messed up, because wind didn't blow things *up*, it blew things in circular patterns, but no, there was a wad of paper rising as if it were flying, then plummeting back to earth as if it had been batted down by a giant hand.

After about five minutes of this, the soldier turned around. "Never seen one before, have you?"

Annabella shook her head.

"From in here, it's beautiful. Out there, not so much."

Smiling, Annabella said, "I'm sure. Mind if I let the drone record this?"

The soldier shrugged, and Annabella returned to the truck.

An hour after it had commenced, the storm ended. The captain's face showed on the holo saying that they were free to go. They had never actually gotten lunch, which Annabella had been hoping for, as her stomach was starting to rumble, but she figured it was more important to ride out the storm.

Liebnitz asked the soldier, "Captain, those kids?"

"I detailed a couple of soldiers to bring them in, but they were gone. Left their *bocce* ball behind and everything."

"They weren't using a ball," Annabella said.

"Yeah, it was a beanbag of some kind," the captain said quickly. "The point is they obviously found shelter on their own. I'm sure they're fine." The captain didn't sound all that concerned.

When the truck pulled out of the garage, Annabella saw the devastating storm's aftermath: The streets were pockmarked with smoking potholes, and the sky still had a purple tinge. Mike expertly drove around the craters, and Annabella asked, "Is the damage usually this bad?"

"No, it's usually worse, but we got a whole section'a the budget for civil repairs like this." He smiled. "The pavement companies do good business hereabouts."

Annabella's stomach rumbled as the truck pulled into Laubenthal Memorial Hospital's underground parking garage. Only Liebnitz and Patel got out with Annabella. At the reporter's questioning glance, Liebnitz said, "Ain't good to have half'a creation trampin' through the corridors. Just keepin' it to the three of us is best."

There was a military post and a boxy structure at the lift entrance and an armored soldier said, "Step into the decon unit please."

In turn, Liebnitz and Patel walked into the box, which sealed them in, a red light going on. After about seven seconds, the red light turned green, and the box opened up. The mayor and his aide each put on a yellow coverall while Annabella stepped into the box, which went completely dark when it closed. *Good thing I'm not claustrophobic,* she thought as she felt hot air blowing all over her, just like on the train down.

When the box opened, the soldier was waiting for her. "I'm sorry, ma'am, but we can't allow your equipment in the hospital."

"Excuse me?"

"Your equipment—your glasses and the item in your belt."

"Those are my cams. I'm a reporter. I—"

"I know who you are, ma'am. That came up in your scan. I've also checked with GDI, and they confirmed why you're here, but I'm afraid that your clearance to record for your story doesn't extend to the inside of this hospital. You're allowed in, and can report what you see and hear, but recording will simply not be allowed."

Sighing, Annabella removed her glasses and instructed the drone to fly out and into her hand. She then gave both cams to the soldier. Luckily, the unit automatically backed up to W3N's satellite, so everything she'd recorded was safe. *Hell, knowing Penny, she's probably linked most of it already to check up on me without actually checking up on me.* And if these goons damaged it, Penny would send her new equipment in a matter of hours.

It still rankled, though. Nobody wanted to see second-hand reports. It was images that got the clickrates, not people talking.

Still, it wasn't as if she had a choice, so she did what

she was told, clambering into the yellow jumpsuit and then putting on the hood that fastened to the jumpsuit's neck.

To her surprise, it was nice and cool in the jumpsuit. She had expected to be boiling inside the thing, but it had been created with comfort as much in mind as protecting the wearer from the "green death," as well as its attendant radiation, which was all over this hospital.

The lift took them up to the fourth floor, which Liebnitz said was the ti-ward.

As soon as the doors slid apart, though, Annabella found her ears assaulted by a scream that made the ion storm siren sound like a whimper.

"Code green! Code green!" someone in a green jumpsuit was shouting as she ran toward a man who was doubled over in agony. He had been the source of the scream.

Three more people in green and one in purple ran to the man. He was not wearing a jumpsuit, which Annabella assumed meant that he was a patient. The one in purple was holding a wand, and ran it over the man, whose screams somehow managed to get *louder*, so much so that Annabella was wishing they had forgone a cooling system for her suit in favor of sound bafflers.

"Ipecac, *stat*!" the one in purple said. Another person in green ran over with two pills, which the one in purple literally dropped into the open mouth of the screaming patient.

The screams stopped for half a second while the man swallowed, but started right up again. Not once did he open his eyes.

Then his entire body convulsed, arms outstretched, and the screams became a gurgle. Spittle flew from his mouth, and veins started to bulge on his forehead.

And then he went limp and collapsed to the floor.

On the one hand, Annabella wished she had had her cam with her to record this. On the other hand, she knew she would have no trouble remembering every detail.

"Fotze," the one in purple said, "we were too late. Stomach has completely ruptured. What the hell happened?"

Now that she wasn't focused on his screaming, Annabella noticed that the man's clothes were shabby and filthy, his sweat-soaked skin was streaked with dirt and grime, and what little hair he had was wild and unkempt. A *ti-bo*.

One of the ones in green said, "Came in complaining of stomach pain. Probably ate green."

"Probably."

"Annabella?"

Turning at the sound of her name, she saw that Patel was standing next to her. Liebnitz had walked over to the main desk. "Hm?"

"They're ready to take us to the room now."

"Oh, right. Uh, sorry, I"—she shook her head—"I've never seen anything like that."

"Then you're lucky," was all Patel said in reply.

Trying to shake off the horror of what she'd just seen, Annabella followed Patel and the mayor as they were led down a corridor by a person in green. Patel explained that the jumpsuits were color-coded: doctors in purple, nurses in green, medtechs in orange, and visitors in yellow. Everyone save the patients was wearing them.

To the nurse, Annabella asked, "Do people do what that ti-bo did regularly?"

"Do what?" the nurse asked.

"Ingest Tiberium."

"Probably not on purpose. But when you don't know

where the next meal's comin' from, you take what you can get and figure it's worth the risk."

"Nothing's worth that risk," Annabella said quietly.

"If you're starvin', you might think different. Here you are."

They had passed several doors, and the nurse now stood in front of one, which slid open at his presence.

Annabella had, of course, seen holos of ti-dies—everyone had, whether they wanted to or not. Those holos, more than anything else, served to caution people about the dangers of Tiberium, with their images of crystallized skin and tumors and such. So she thought she was prepared to see Tiberium poisoning in person.

She was wrong.

For starters, the holos never gave you the smell. The odor of diseased flesh permeated the room even through the suit's cooling system, making her wonder how stomach-churningly wretched it must be without it. The inside of her nose burned with the tinge of ammonia, fighting a losing battle with the Tiberium to keep the place as uninfected as possible.

There were four people in the room, and while the mayor went to talk to a young woman in the far right corner, it was the one on the near-left bed that caught Annabella's attention.

The boy in that bed was young, no more than thirteen. His face was blotched with tumors, one of which was leaking a white ichor down his left cheek. The right side of his face was mottled with green, and his right arm was pockmarked at the biceps and completely transformed at the forearm into a faceted green stump.

Annabella found herself eternally grateful that they hadn't stopped for lunch, as bile lurched to the top of her throat. She swallowed fiercely to try to keep it down and was only partially successful, so she swallowed again, determined not to throw up while inside a biohazard suit.

Turning to one of the doctors, Annabella asked, "How long does he have?"

The doctor hesitated. "Not long. He was only infected about thirty-six hours ago, but it's already in his bloodstream. That's why his arm looks like that. Honestly, it's only a matter of time before the infection moves to his heart or lungs. As soon as that happens . . ." He didn't need to finish that sentence.

For the third time, Annabella swallowed down bile. It only just barely worked.

Annabella went through the rest of the day in a fog thicker than anything produced by Tiberium in the air. The GDI troops had given her back her equipment with no fuss when they left Laubenthal Memorial and their jumpsuits had been tossed into disposal units where they'd be destroyed. She'd attended meetings, observed civic responsibility in action, watched public speeches, and the entire time, the only thing she could see was a dying thirteen-year-old boy, the only thing she could smell was the rot of the boy's flesh, the only thing she could hear was the beeping of the hospital equipment.

The day ended somewhere around twenty-one. Terise had had to say Annabella's name three times before she replied. "I'm sorry, what?"

"I asked if you have any plans for this evening."

"Oh. Uh . . ." Her plans mostly consisted of taking advantage of the hotel's bath. She hadn't had a proper bath in so long she wasn't even sure she remembered how to take one. "Nothing specific, why?"

"I want to show you something. I'll pick you up in your hotel garage in an hour?"

"Uh, okay, sure."

She said her goodbyes to Liebnitz, who said it was a pleasure having her there today, and Annabella managed not to say, *That's because I was a total zombie most of the day, except for the part where I almost barfed in my hospital jumpsuit.*

In silence Patel drove her back to the hotel in a small utility vehicle. Once she took the lift to her room—and after she spent five minutes trying to remember what pocket she'd put the stupid key in, and another three remembering how to use the thing properly—she checked her mail, put most of it aside or trashed it, and then linked to Penny.

"How's it going?"

"It's going to be a good story, I think," was all Annabella trusted herself to say.

"I took a quick scan of what you shot so far. Not bad. Why's there a one-hour gap?"

Annabella stripped off each of her layers of clothing. The truck and the buildings she entered all had been air-conditioned, but she still felt like she'd been suffocating. The innermost layer was clammy with her sweat.

"They wouldn't let me take my cams into Laubenthal. And, trust me, you didn't want me to record what was in there."

Angrily, Penny said, *"Why the hell not?"*

Normally that tone in Penny's voice would have Annabella running scared, but not today. "Because I've seen other people record what I saw there, and a holo *won't* do it."

The subsequent silence extended long enough that

Annabella tapped her earpiece to make sure she was still linked. "Penny?"

"Fine. You've got two more days there."

"Okay." *I don't know if I can take two more days of this.* "The people here are very helpful. I think they want folks in the Blues to know how they live."

"That's why you're doing the piece, Annabella."

She peeled off the last of her clothes, and reveled in the goose-bump-inducing feel of the room's air-conditioning on her sweat-soaked skin. "One of them's actually invited me out for something tonight. She didn't say what, but I think it's a peace offering. Her name's Terise Plashko, and she's been riding my arse pretty hard the whole time."

"Gee, and I sent you down because of your friendly face."

That got a chuckle out of Annabella, which almost floored her. She hadn't even cracked a smile since the siren went off for the ion storm, if not before.

Which reminded her: "I wasn't able to record the ion storm. We were underground and I wasn't able to get a drone out in time"—a lie, as she actually hadn't thought of it, but why tell Penny that?—"but if there's another one, I'll work hard to get it."

"Don't worry about that so much. We've got enough ti-storms to last us a while. I want more people stuff. I really wish you'd gotten a cam into the hospital."

"No, you really don't," Annabella said emphatically.

Terise was unusually subdued when she met Annabella in the parking lot. "This is our car," she said as she approached it. The medium-sized silver sedan was of a type Annabella had last seen a few years ago when covering a story in upstate New York.

The doors didn't unlock at Terise's approach. She had

to wave a wand in the direction of the car. "Isn't that a little unsecure?" Annabella asked.

"It's what we could get," Terise said as she climbed into the driver's seat. "Anything new enough to have bioscans is way out of our price range, even with four incomes."

"Your family?" Annabella asked as she folded herself into the front seat. The truck had had much more room.

Terise nodded and pushed the button to start the car up. They drove out of the garage in silence, although the guard at the door gave her sedan a dirty look that somehow managed to be conveyed even through the GDI helmet. *Now* that's *disdain,* Annabella thought.

They drove on in silence for a bit, finally arriving at a small structure with an outdoor parking lot, the first Annabella had seen.

When Terise stopped the car, she reached into the backseat. "You'll need to put these on before we get out of the car." She leaned forward and handed Annabella a plastic bag. Unzipping it, Annabella discovered it contained a hood and gloves, which would cover Annabella's head and hands, the only parts of her body left exposed by her multilayered wardrobe. "It's only a short walk," Terise said, "but it's not worth the risk."

As she slid the gloves on—they felt tacky and sticky, and she had to tug them at the wrists several times to get her fingers all the way in—Annabella asked, "Why risk it at all?"

Terise was having a much easier time with her own gloves. "You'll see."

Once they were fully protected from any possible Tiberium infestation, they exited the car, Terise pausing to use her wand to lock it, and then both women ran toward the entrance. The front door was only a few meters away, but it seemed to take forever, and the entire time she ran toward it, Annabella kept seeing a ti-die boy in a hospital bed.

When they got inside, Terise removed her hood and gloves; Annabella did likewise, half expecting to have to put them in a bin to be destroyed, as she had at Laubenthal, but Terise just held on to them as she led Annabella to a seat.

The space was small, containing two rows of about ten picnic-style tables. To Annabella's shock, the tables appeared to be made of wood.

However, the feel of the wood was of less interest to her than the smell of the food that wafted throughout. Though she had seen no sign to indicate such outside, it was obvious that this was a restaurant, and what it lacked in size, it made up for in flavor, at least based on the spices her nose was reporting. *It's like dinner at Monica and Freddie's when zia's on a particularly good roll . . .*

At one end of the shack was a doorway to a kitchen area. The other end had a raised platform on which stood four people holding assorted musical instruments. They were either tuning or practicing on the instruments, not really playing anything coherent. Annabella was again surprised to see wood, this time on an old-fashioned piano, something she'd never seen in person before. A blond woman was behind a drum kit, a dark-skinned man was at the piano, and the remaining two men, both pale, one of whom was wearing a pair of dark sunglasses, were holding guitars. Annabella—whose musical knowledge was scattershot—was pretty sure that one was a guitar, and the other a bass.

After a few more moments of this, the one holding the

regular guitar walked to the front of the stage. "Good evening! This one's called 'Walkin' Blues.' "

The quartet then pounded into a driving rhythm that almost shocked Annabella out of her chair. Music had always been a relaxant for her, so this pounding beat was an almost physical shock.

The man with the guitar started singing:

Woke up this morning, felt around for my shoes.
I knew I had to have me the walkin' blues.
When I woke up this morning, I was feelin' around
   for my shoes.
I knew I had to have me those walkin' blues.

The lyrics were nothing to write home about, just talking about walking, but it was the intensity of the guitar, the piano, the bass, the drums, all of which pounded into her rib cage, one, two, three, four, that was like nothing she'd ever heard before.

Somewhere during the song, a person came over and took their order. Annabella had been so entranced by the music that it never occurred to her to question why they didn't just enter their order into the table station. *Obviously,* she thought once she realized what had happened, and that Terise had chosen food for her, *they run their restaurants like they run their hotels.*

The next song wasn't as intense musically, but it made up for it with the lyrics:

There's a man goin' 'round takin' names.
There's a man goin' 'round takin' names.
He's takin' my sister's name,
And he's comin' 'round again,
There's a man goin' 'round takin' names.

At first, Annabella found the lyrics harmless, but realized there was a certain—commentary? seditiousness?—to them.

Turning to Terise, she asked, "Where have you brought me, Terise?"

Terise shrugged. "It's just people making music."

"Yeah, but—the way they're using the music, it's just so—so passionate, so—so *emotional.*"

"Isn't that what music's supposed to be?"

Annabella's instinctive answer of "no" died before it could reach her mouth. The band continued on to several other songs, all of which had the same insistence of the first two. The singer gave the words far more meaning than the jazz singers she was used to on GN radio.

At some point, the person who took their order brought some ribs over. Annabella had had ribs in the past, but not like this, not with this type of sauce. She asked Terise what it was made with—Monica *had* to have this recipe—but apparently it was a closely guarded secret. Terise had seemed to expect a fight on that subject, but Annabella quickly explained about her *zia* and how protective she was of family recipes.

When the set was over, and the ribs all consumed, Annabella turned to Terise. "Thank you, Terise, I—I didn't know music could *do* that."

For the first time, the old Terise came back. "There's a lot you don't know, Ms. Wu."

"Yeah, I'm seeing that. But I'm trying to learn."

"I hope so. Come on, let's get back."

Annabella put the hood and gloves back on—the gloves were even more difficult the second time—and they ran back to Terise's car. Within a few minutes, they were at the hotel parking garage. As she opened the door to get out, Annabella said, "Thanks again, Terise. You didn't have to do this, but I'm really glad you did."

"I didn't do it for you," Terise said tersely, "I did it for your viewers. So whatever epiphany you're having right now better make it into the piece. It's been——" She hesitated.

"Been what?" Annabella prompted.

"We're supposed to be a Blue Zone, did you know that?"

Frowning, Annabella asked, "What're you—"

"The original plans," Terise said, her grip on the steering wheel tightening so much that her knuckles were going white. "When they were first drawing up the zones, B-2 was supposed to extend all the way down the East Coast to Key West."

Annabella blinked. "I—I didn't know that." She also surreptitiously started her spec-cam going. She had the feeling this conversation was something she'd want a record of.

Smiling, Terise said, "It's not something they advertise. Dig around the archives, though, look for the maps from '35 or so, and you'll see it. That's why this Yellow has such a hefty GDI presence. They probably feel guilty."

"Guilty about what? What happened?"

"They screwed up." Terise sighed. "It wasn't really anyone's fault, but—" She let go of the steering wheel. "See, the biggest problem with the entire gulf coast is the hurricanes. They bring the green death in spades. But the reason why hurricanes hit the coast is because they move from warmer to cooler water."

Annabella chuckled. "Thank you, Mr. Schiame."

Terise looked at her quizzically.

"My third-grade science teacher, sorry. Go on."

"GDI set up sonic resonators all around the Florida peninsula and in the Keys, and they used an ion cannon to heat the coastal water."

"Sounds like a good plan. What happened?"

Terise sighed. "There was a canal, part of the Intracoastal Waterway, except it had been built over and forgotten. They went completely off-net in Florida around the turn of the century, the population was just exploding and they just kept *building,* including over some of the canals. They didn't put any resonators there, and the ficken Tiberium managed to get in." Another sigh. "That was the end of it. They had to move the border for B-2 all the way back to Charlotte because they couldn't risk it." She gazed hard at Annabella. "Honestly, Ms. Wu, that's why I don't like you all that much. You've got the life *we* were supposed to have."

Before Annabella could cobble together something to say that didn't sound like a stupid platitude or cliché, Terise said, "Look, I need to get home. Good night."

That's the end of that, Annabella thought.

As soon as the door shut, Terise drove off as fast as her clumsy old sedan would move, leaving Annabella standing in the hotel parking lot with a great deal to think about.

EIGHT

The celebration at the Fort Powell Officers' Club had gone on for several hours.

When the 22nd had lifted off from the intersection of Pacific Highway and Harbor Drive, the holos inside the *Huron* had shown the members of the 22nd what Battalion 3 had done to the San Diego Convention Center: an AC222 Mako fired its cannon at various points, several of which were load-bearing walls and pillars, and then two A50 Orcas dropped a half-dozen missiles on the site.

Once everyone who was still alive from Bat 4 was back on board the *Huron,* they proceeded to the remains of the naval base, which Bats 1 and 2—led by BC McNeil himself—had taken back from Nod control fairly easily, since their C&C was in the convention center, but which Nod then proceeded to blow up in lieu of surrendering. There were very few casualties among the 22nd. Nod took only themselves out, as well as a relatively useful naval base and several prisoners.

The remaining three battalions came on board and handed control of San Diego's military security off to local forces—those who hadn't been interrogated and killed in custody, or blown up with the base.

McNeil ordered the *Huron* to Fort Powell in central California for debriefing, a bit of R&R—"restocking

and resupplying," according to Sergeant Goodier—as well as dealing with their two Nod prisoners.

The hero of the day was Private Ricardo Vega, who was on his third tequila of the night—or maybe it was his fourth, he was starting to lose track—as provided by Sergeant Goodier. Most of Unit Epsilon was present, as were several other people from Company 7. Gallagher didn't bother to show up, which didn't surprise Vega in the least, and of course Golden was still in the infirmary. Vega was sitting at the bar with Momoa on one side, Brodeur on the other, and Silverstein, Popadopoulos, and Zipes standing around in front of him.

"Shite, sib," Zipes was saying, "one day in, and you got the hero juice."

Chuckling, Vega said, "It's nothing, I just got lucky."

Momoa moved to slap Vega on the back for the fourteenth time tonight, but Vega barely had the presence of mind to shift his position so that Momoa missed. Momoa, who was on at least his sixth vodka, didn't seem to notice or care. "Soldierin's all 'bout luck. See, luck is when you come home alive. Bad luck is when you don't."

Silverstein, who was nursing a beer, said, "That's very profound, Momoa."

Nodding, Momoa said, "Thank you, Corporal Silverstein. Comin' from you, tha' meansa lot."

Before Silverstein could explain her use of sarcasm, Vega asked, "Hey, Popadopoulos, what're you doin' here, anyhow?"

Popadopoulos threw back the remainder of his ouzo and placed the glass on the bar. "What, I ain't fit to get toasted with the real soldiers?"

"Nah," Vega said with a grin, "I'm just surprised you

aren't up to your arse in the Nod tech you took off the prisoners."

Bitterly, Popadopoulos said, " 'Cause it ain't nowhere near my arse." He signaled the bartender—a very harried-looking corporal who probably hadn't been expecting this kind of crowd on a Wednesday night—for another ouzo. "Soon's the *Huron* touched dirt, the big dogs in Tech Corps got their grubby mitts on it. I made notes, but they'll just ignore it and do their own thing." He grinned as the bartender handed him another drink. "They'll probably crack it up all to pieces, but what the hell, I did my part."

Holding up his tequila, Vega said, "Well, here's to reverse-engineering, then."

"Hear, hear!" Momoa said. "An' I can't even pronounce tha' word."

Laughing, Vega asked, "Drunk or sober?"

"Either," Silverstein said before Momoa could reply.

Zipes then said, "Somethin' I don't be gettin'."

"What's that, Zipes?" Vega asked.

"This is the Officers' Club, yeah?"

"S'what the sign onna door says," Momoa said, pointing at the front door, even though the sign he was talking about was on the other side of it. He also pointed with the hand holding his vodka glass, and it spilled onto his legs, which he didn't really notice.

Making a show of looking at his sleeve, Zipes said, "Well, I ain't no officer. Neither ain't none'a you. Sergeants over there," he pointed at Goodier and Gnaizda, who were sitting at a table talking with a corporal Vega didn't know, "they officers, maybe, but we ain't. So why we in here?"

Vega shrugged. "My dad always talked about goin' to

the O-club from when he first signed up. I don't think they really give two shites about that anymore."

"Okay, so why's it *called* the O-club?"

No one had an answer to that.

"Cracked if *I* know," Momoa said.

"It's a mystery," Brodeur put in.

Silverstein looked at Vega. "Who's your dad?"

Zipes gave Silverstein a feral grin. "I'm your daddy, lay."

"Get some hair, first," Silverstein said disdainfully.

That got several whoops and jibes at Zipes, who, for his part, looked wounded. "You don't like my cut?"

"Oh, hey, I'm sure it's all the rage in Cell Block 9 where you got it."

Vega laughed. "Do *not* mess with the company clerk, Zipes. That's something else my dad always said."

Before Silverstein could question him further, Goodier started clinking the side of his glass.

The O-club quieted down.

"I'd like to propose a toast."

Vega blushed, as he assumed it to be another toast to his bravery and wonderfulness in rescuing Dr. Takeda from the evil clutches of the Brotherhood of Nod. That had, after all, been the subject of the last three toasts.

Goody had a surprise up his three-striped sleeve, however. "To the men and women of Unit Epsilon, Company 7, Battalion 4 of the 22nd Infantry Division. I was informed shortly before arrival at this house of ill-repute—" Several of the soldiers guffawed at that. "—that our unit had the lowest casualty rate of any unit in Battalion 4's lunatic run through the erstwhile San Diego Convention Center."

Cheers and ragged whoops came up from those present. One private yelled out, "We roll!"

Vega joined in the toast, but it actually caused him to sober up rather quickly. Again, the images of Kelerchian and Golden and Lipinski and all the others flashed before him. The fact that Epsilon had done so well filled Vega with pride, of course, but their being the best meant that everybody else had huge body counts. In fact, over half of Bat 4 was killed in action, with another twenty percent wounded.

He turned around to face the bar, turning his back on Zipes, Silverstein, and Popadopoulos.

Brodeur leaned over to Vega. "You okay?"

"It's nothing, I just—" He threw back the rest of his tequila and then slammed the thick-bottomed glass onto the plastic bar with a hollow *thuck*. "If they were willing to bomb the shite outta the place anyhow, couldn't they have done it before we lost half our guys?"

"So you're saying Takeda should've died?"

Vega found that he had to concentrate to understand Brodeur in this crowded bar, and the tequila was making that difficult. "Say again?"

Brodeur repeated his question.

"Nah, 'course not, it's just—well, what about the civilians in the exhibit hall?"

"There were none. I was talking with one of my buddies in Company 2—the hall was boobied, but there weren't any people. They picked it for C&C 'cause it was easy to defend, probably, especially since I think they figured all the firepower'd be focused on the naval base."

Vega nodded. "Yeah, okay. So no civvies got scorched?"

Shaking his head, Brodeur said, "Nope. Only ones who died were either Nod or fellow travelers."

"Good."

"Ten-*hut*!"

Vega automatically got to his feet. So did several of

those inside, though most of them did a shite job of it. Turning around, Vega saw that Battle Commander McNeil had entered the O-club, alongside Captain Henry, Lieutenant Opahle, and some other officers Vega didn't know.

"Oh, for shite's sake, at ease, will you?" McNeil shook his head. "I'm looking for the man of the hour." His gaze ran across the O-club until he found Vega, and then made a beeline for him.

Like the Red Sea at Moses's urging, the soldiers who stood between the battle commander and where Vega was still standing at the bar parted, allowing McNeil to walk straight to him. Opahle and Henry were right behind, and they seemed to be beaming.

Vega saluted, which McNeil quickly returned, and then stuck out his hand. "The hell with saluting, mister, I want to shake your hand. I can't begin to describe the service you've done GDI today, son. With Dr. Mobius's death on the *Philadelphia,* Joseph Takeda is now our leading expert on ti-rock, and he'd be in Nod's hands right now if it weren't for you."

Having returned the handshake, Vega said, "I was just doing my duty, sir."

"Of course you were, but the difference is, you did it spectacularly well. I served with your father, you know—"

Here it comes, Vega said, barely keeping in a sigh.

"—and today you proved to me that you take after him in all the best ways. If you're even half the soldier JV is, then you're already several orders of magnitude better than the average Giddy-Up." He turned to face the entire room. "And before the rest of you decide to get hacked off at your BC, let me assure you that that is *not* a dig at *any* of you, but a statement as to how great a soldier Javier Vega is. I was proud to serve alongside him in

TWII, and I'm proud to have his son under me now that TWIII has commenced."

McNeil put a hand on Vega's shoulder, causing Vega to wonder if this would make most of the people in this room a friend or an enemy.

"With people like Ricardo Vega fighting on our side, I suspect that TWIII will be a short one indeed." Removing the hand, he continued to address the entire O-club. "All of Battalion 4 did well, especially Company 7 and especially Unit Epsilon. But the war is intensifying. With recent Nod activity on various Blues across the globe, we must be vigilant. That's part of why I'm here tonight, actually. The formal announcement'll be tomorrow morning, but I wanted to let you all know that your actions in saving one of the most important people in GDI, and in liberating one of our precious Blues from Nod control, have not gone unnoticed by the powers that be, in particular the roles played by Private Vega here, as well as Private Gallagher." He looked around the bar. "Is she here?"

"No, sir," Vega said quickly, having signaled the bartender for another tequila.

"Pity. In any case, there are also, sadly, some vacancies that need to be filled, thanks to the noble sacrifice made by your fellow soldiers in San Diego. It therefore pleases me to announce that Captain Henry is moving over to command Battalion 2, with *Captain* Opahle taking over Battalion 4. *Lieutenant* Goodier will take over command of Company 7, with *Lieutenant* Gnaizda taking Company 6."

Apparently, this was the first Goodier or Gnaizda were hearing of this, as the former's jaw literally fell open— something Vega had never seen happen in real life before—and Gnaizda did a spit-take with his rum.

"That leaves two sergeants' positions available in Company 7. I can't think of two people who've earned command of Units Gamma and Epsilon more than *Sergeants* Gallagher and Vega."

Somehow, Vega managed not to drop the tequila the bartender was handing him.

"Holy *shite*!" Momoa's *basso profundo* sliced through the thick air of the O-club, and caused one or two snickers that were quickly cut off.

Vega wasn't sure whose eyes got wider, McNeil's or Momoa's.

In as subdued a voice as he was likely capable of, Momoa said, "I'm sorry, sir."

McNeil, to everyone's relief, broke out in a grin. "Quite all right, Private. I'm sure what you said was from the heart. Or at least the general vicinity."

"Sir?" Vega said. "Ah, there must be some mistake."

"No mistake, son. I know you just joined the unit a few days ago—"

"Sir, please, excuse the interruption, but I just joined the *Keepers* a few days ago. I hadn't even unpacked my duffel when we got the call to go to San Diego. In fact, sir, come to think of it, I *still* haven't unpacked it."

"Good, that'll make it easier for you to move to your new barracks."

"Er, yes, sir."

"The official ceremony will be in the fort's mess hall at breakfast tomorrow. Shortly after that, we'll all be reboarding the *Huron*. This war isn't over yet, not by a long shot."

Now Vega stood at attention. "Yes, sir. We'll be ready, sir."

"That's what I like to hear, son—that's what I like to hear."

With that, the BC turned on his heel and left.

Opahle and Henry both walked up to Vega. Henry clapped him on the shoulder. "Congratulations, Sergeant."

"To you too, Captains," Vega said.

"Don't congratulate me," Henry said, shaking his head. "I just got shunted is all. Opahle here's the one that deserves it."

Goodier walked over. Gnaizda, Vega noticed, was headed for the bathroom. Goodier asked, "Why am I a lieutenant? I don't want to be a lieutenant."

"There's nothing wrong with being a lieutenant, Goody," Opahle said.

"That's easy for you to say, ma'am, you've *been* one. I don't like to give people orders, it makes me break out in hives."

"Y'know," Momoa said, "that explains a lot. Uh, sir."

Henry regarded Momoa. "You know, Private, that mouth of yours is likely to get you in trouble."

"Already has, sir."

The laugh that exploded from the captain's lips struck Vega as an involuntary one. "I bet. Well, I think this calls for a drink."

"You buying, sir?" Momoa asked.

"No, Private, I think, in honor of you bellowing 'holy shite' in front of the battle commander, that honor goes to you."

Momoa winced. "Yes, sir."

Vega leaned over. "You can afford it, right?"

"Well, I *was* planning on sending my poker winnings home to my parents, but—"

"Poker, huh? Is there a unit game?"

Grinning, Momoa said, "A company game. You play?"

"Been known to."

"It's Fridays—least it was. We'll see, with the war and all. But I'll be glad to take your money."

"I'm sure you will be." Vega threw back the tequila and ordered another on Momoa's tab.

I'm a sergeant. It felt wiggly, even though it hadn't formally happened yet. *Maybe it won't. Maybe the BC was drunk, and he'll forget by morning. Besides, Dish was right there with us getting Takeda back, so why promote me and not him?*

That seemed unlikely, though. Smiling as he waited for his tequila, Vega thought, *I can't wait to tell Dad . . .*

Alessio Bowles couldn't sleep.

He'd been all set to go along with the new guy and the rest of the unit to the O-club to celebrate their victory. Gallagher had passed—Bowles had no idea who had lodged that pole up her arse, but she really needed to get it surgically removed—but Bowles had every intention of going along.

First, though, he had to see if any links had been forwarded from Dix. So he went to the barracks they'd been assigned, called up a holo of the unit's mail queue on a display over his bunk, and scanned for his links.

Sure enough, there was one from Stephanie Anisfeld, the private investigator he'd hired two years ago now. Almost putting his entire arm through the holo display, he punched up the link, practically bouncing on the bunk, hoping against hope that this would be it, this would be the one where she told Bowles that she'd found his family.

"Alessio: I hope this finds you well. I'm afraid I have some bad news."

His heart beating faster, Bowles felt a pit open in his

stomach. A shudder ran through his body and he had to keep himself from crying out in anger.

"The lead in Spain didn't scan. There is a Heidi Bowles living in Madrid, and she is a member of Nod, but it's not your mother. She's married to a woman named Penelope Artz. I tracked her down and got several good looks at her. The snaps I took are attached to this link."

Bowles had noticed that there were attachments, but had wanted to read the link first. Now he called them up, and five snaps of a short, pale woman with a round face, blue eyes, and dirty-blond hair appeared around the link, as well as two different IDs that indicated that the person was Heidi Bowles.

Since the Heidi Bowles who gave birth to Private Alessio Bowles twenty-four years earlier was tall, willowy, and had an angular face—never mind the hair and eyes, which Alessio's mother could have altered with the greatest of ease in the seven years since he'd seen her—this couldn't be her. The latest in a series of attempts by Anisfeld to find the mother, father, and siblings who'd abandoned Bowles in order to join the Brotherhood of Nod had failed.

He read the rest of the link.

"I'm really sorry about this, Alessio. I know we'd both gotten our hopes up on this. I'm gonna peep around Madrid a bit more, see if I can shake out any other Nod contacts. With the war on, Nod's recruitments have gone up, so I should be able to find something. I'll keep you posted. Best, Stephanie."

"Fotze!" he shouted.

"What is it, Dish?" came a voice from the door to the barracks. Bowles looked over to see Gallagher entering.

"Sorry," he said more quietly. "It's nothing."

"Let me guess, the PI pixelated again?"

With a long sigh, Bowles nodded in the affirmative. "You know how many creds I've flushed for this?"

"So why do it?"

Bowles leapt off the bunk. "They're my ficken *family*, Gallagher! What'm I supposed to do? Just forget 'em?"

"You ain't them, Dish," Gallagher said gently as she tossed her gear into a footlocker. "They're just four tibeheads who joined Kane's goons, same as a whole lotta other tibeheads 'round the globe."

"They ain't just any ficken tibeheads. They're family."

"Crack family," Gallagher said as she walked over to Bowles's bunk. "They don't mean shite. It's who *you* are that matters." Then she broke into a grin. "Sarge."

Bowles started. "Uh, Gallagher, I thought you weren't goin' to the O-club."

"I didn't."

"Then you're gettin' toasted on the side, 'cause I ain't Goody."

"I know that." She laughed. "I overheard the BC and Hastings talking outside. They said there's two sergeant positions open—I heard my name, and they said it was the guys who rescued Takeda, so you gotta be the other one. The official coronation's tomorrow, but you and me, Dish, we're sergeants."

The pit opened up in Bowles's stomach again, and again his heart beat faster, but he didn't mind so much this time. "You're ficken' me. We got *stripes*?"

"Three of them, sib," she said, still grinning. "This is what happens when you rescue hotshite cranies from the bad guys. Goody and Gnaizda got bumped, so we're takin' over."

"Hang on, there were three of us in the room," Bowles said.

"Yeah, but Puke ain't gonna get promoted after one day. Even Giddy-Up ain't that cracked."

Bowles sighed. "Don't be so sure. I haven't gotten any kinda notice, and I just checked."

Gallagher wandered over to her bunk and activated her holo. "They probably ain't sent 'em, yet." She touched the light for her mail, and started reading the shells. "There it is." Calling it up, she started reading aloud: "Private Tera Gallagher, gobbledy gobbledy, it is our pleasure, gobbledy gobbledy, to promote you to the rank of sergeant, with all the privileges and responsibilities thereof. You and Private Ricardo Vega are to—" Her face fell. "You *gotta* be spoofin' me!"

Quickly, Bowles said, "Don't worry about it, Gallagher."

"Don't *worry* about it? That ficken nep's been in Giddy-Up for two seconds, and he gets stripes when you don't?"

"I *said* don't worry about it," Bowles said sharply. "Look, Vega was right there with us. Shite, he's the one that took out the two prisoners, *and* he's got a daddy who's a war hero. Me, I got a whole family that worships ti-rock and takes orders from Kane. I'm lucky to *be* in Giddy-Up. You think they're gonna give *me* stripes? I wouldn't, I was them."

"Puke didn't 'take out' shite, it was just a lucky shot. And having family connects don't mean—"

"Didn't you just say to me, 'crack family'?" Bowles asked. "And that they don't mean shite?"

"They don't." Gallagher shut down her holo and lay down. "I'm gettin' some sleep."

That pretty much ended the discussion. Shaking his head, Bowles got back into his bunk and started to compose a link.

He started it the same way he started all of them. *"Dear Mom and Dad: Hope you guys are okay."* It took him a moment to catch his breath and compose himself before continuing. *"We just finished a pretty dangerous op. We had to go to San Diego and liberate it from the forces of the Brotherhood of Nod. That's probably bad news for you, because it's possible that today I killed friends of yours. I'm sorry about that, but fighting Nod soldiers is my job now, and I don't regret it. I can only hope that one of the soldiers I killed was one of the ones who corrupted you and lured you to their way of thinking, taking you away from me."*

After another deep breath, he finished it off. *"I love you. Your son, Alessio."*

After a quick read-through, he deleted everything after *"dangerous op."* Then: *"It was a very difficult engagement, but the 22nd came out on top. I love you both. Your son, Alessio."*

Then he stored the link in the same folder where he kept all the other links he'd written over the past seven years.

When Anisfeld finally found his family, he'd send them.

Gallagher started snoring. Everybody else was probably still at the O-club.

Closing the holo, Bowles got up, put on minimal gear, and started walking the fort.

It was dark, with only small lights on the ground to illuminate his path. Powell was located in the middle of the California desert, so there wasn't much to see even in daylight, and on this moonless night, there was even less.

Without realizing it, Bowles's feet took him toward the brig. He'd already been there once, when he and Pup dropped the two Nod prisoners off with the MPs there.

For a while—he wasn't really sure how long, and he didn't really care to check his HUD to be sure—he stood outside the brig, wondering why he had come here.

Yeah, that's a real tough question there, sib, he admonished himself. *You know damn well why you're here.*

The door scanned him and wouldn't open. A face appeared on a holo next to the door. *"Can I help you, Private Bowles?"*

"I was wondering if I could see the prisoners."

The face hesitated. *"You were one of the ones who brought 'em in, yeah?"*

Bowles nodded.

"Yeah, okay, fine, but anyone asks, I was asleep and you hacked the lock."

The door slid open. Bowles thought letting him see the prisoners would be better for the soldier than to be asleep and derelict, but Bowles wasn't going to argue with the results.

Inside, he saw the face he'd seen on the holo, which was attached to a male body that had the name OSBORNE on the vest and corporal's stripes on the arm. He was seated at a small desk with a holo display over it. "Thanks, Corporal."

"I can only give you a minute or two, Private," Osborne said.

"That's fine."

Osborne added, "And don't expect 'em to say much. Couple MPs tried interrogatin' 'em, but they're locked down. The private ain't said a word, and the corporal's just said one thing over and over again. HQ's sending somebody from B-6 who's supposed to be spicy at this kinda shite."

Bowles walked past the corporal's desk to the wall containing several cells that were cut off from the rest of the room by metal bars that Bowles knew were electrified. Most of the cells were empty, but two were occupied by the familiar faces of the Nod soldiers, a corporal and a private. The corporal's rank insignia was tattooed on him, so that was still visible. The corporal was a dark-skinned man with a flat face and a perpetual sneer; the private was paler, with a large nose and steel gray eyes.

He shook his head. "The BC was right. They do look just like people."

The pale one spoke up suddenly. "Of course we're people, you stupid piss pot."

"Oh, that's funny," Bowles said. "*I'm* a piss pot when *you're* the off-nets inking yourselves with ti-rock."

The corporal yelled at the private in a language Bowles didn't know, but the private ignored him. "Tiberium is a reality. It's *part of the planet* now! You keep fighting it, and to what end? You live in walled cities, the military runs roughshod over your entire lives, and you live in a perpetual state of war. Even in peacetime, you are under martial law. Your lives are chaos, yet you cast *us* as the villains when we have *embraced* the new world."

Throughout the private's diatribe, the corporal was yelling at him in the same foreign language.

Shaking his head, Bowles said, "You guys really are a bunch of stupid feckers. Ti-rock is *poison*! It kills people!"

"Alcohol is a poison and it kills people, yet you still drink it. Constantly fighting against a force you cannot defeat is the definition of psychosis. Your way does not work, yet you try to impose it on the world, while we— we have tamed the element, bent it to our will. *That* is our destiny, not running away like small children."

"What a load of gobshite," Bowles said.

"Is it? Tell me, how has GDI saved the world, exactly?"

Before Bowles could answer, the corporal finally spoke in English. "You have never won. At best, you have delayed the inevitable, leaving more corpses in your wake. If you had embraced Tiberium from the beginning, the world would be united—"

"Under Kane? That ain't a world I wanna live in, sib."

The corporal stared right at Bowles with his pitiless brown eyes. "This is only the beginning. Fire will fall from the skies. Disease will waste your bodies. And your souls will cry for forgiveness when Kane unleashes his fury."

Whirling around to the desk, Bowles asked, "That what he said before?"

Osborne nodded. "Uh, Private, I think you'd better go."

"Fine by me." Bowles looked back at the corporal. "Shoulda shot you in the knees when I had the chance."

With that, he left the brig.

The next morning, Vega was linked a message instructing "soon-to-be-Sergeant Vega" to report to Major Hastings's office after breakfast. Vega didn't actually read it until after he took the hangover remedy along with the rest of his morning regimen of pills. Once the medication removed the packing material from behind his eyes and the laser drill from the back of his skull, he read the major's rather surprising link.

Using his HUD, which linked up to Fort Powell's EVA network, Vega was able to find the mess hall fairly easily. All the promotions were handed out by McNeil. While all those in the O-club last night had been kindly disposed toward Vega—after all, they had gone to the

O-club in the first place to celebrate his accomplishment in rescuing Takeda—he looked around the mess hall now to see a bunch of very angry faces.

He knew what they were all thinking, too: *He's been here less than a week, and* he's *a ficken sergeant? What the hell?*

Vega knew he was going to have to prove himself because of his father. He hadn't expected this. But based on the dirty looks he was getting from soldiers who were almost all more experienced than he was and whom he now outranked, this promotion was going to do Vega more harm than good.

The dirtiest look, unsurprisingly, came from Gallagher, who did not seem at all pleased to be getting her stripes alongside the nep.

After the ceremony, and everyone who was getting a new rank got it, Vega went over to where Bowles had been sitting by himself, twirling his scrambled like-eggs with his fork, but not actually eating them. Having already tasted them, Vega couldn't blame him. "Hey, Dish. Missed you last night."

"Yeah, sorry."

"I'm the one who should be sorry." He indicated the three stripes on his arm as he sat down across from Bowles. "You deserve these a lot more than me."

"No, I don't. Anyhow, I was just—just writing home."

Shaking his head, Vega said, "Dish, that wasn't even a good attempt at a lie."

Bowles sighed. "I really was writing a letter. I just didn't link it."

That confused Vega. "Why not?"

Ignoring the question, Bowles went on: "When we first got back here, I got a link that Dix forwarded. The

PI came up empty. That's why I didn't come to the O-club last night."

"PI? Step back a few there, Dish. What do you need a PI for?"

For the first time, Bowles looked up from his like-eggs. "You don't know?"

"Don't know *what*?"

Shaking his head, Bowles said, "Shite, I just figured *somebody* woulda told you. No wonder you think I deserve those stripes."

"I been a little busy since I reported, and you *do* deserve them."

"Not really." Bowles sat up straight. "My family all joined Nod a few years back. Parents, sibs—all of 'em. I had to go through hell and back twice before GDI cleared me to enlist. S'why they gave you and Gallagher the stripes and I've still got the one."

"Oh." Vega shook his head. "That doesn't even make sense."

"Sure it does. Shite, you guys rescued Takeda. I don't know if you know this, but he's got serious mass in GDI. This division's the golden goose now."

"Yeah, but you're as much a part of that as me and Gallagher." He started drumming his fingers on the mess hall table. "Look, it's not like you're the only one with Nod connections. You've been hearing pretty much nonstop about the great Javier Vega, right?"

Bowles actually smiled at that. "Yeah, it's been mentioned once or twice."

"Well, what people *don't* talk about is Dad's brother. My uncle joined Nod, and—" Vega hesitated. He had started telling this story without thinking through the consequences of telling Bowles the ending.

"And what?"

Wincing, Vega said, "They killed him."

To Vega's relief, Bowles's response was more resigned than angry. "Not surprising. I ever find my family, I'll tell 'em about that."

"The point is, I got family in Nod, too."

Bowles popped some like-eggs into his mouth. "Yeah, but you got your Dad to make up for it. I ain't got shite."

Looking at his wrist unit, Vega saw that it was almost time for his appointment with Hastings. "I gotta go see the major."

"What, again? Didn't he keep you after class when you reported to Dix?"

Vega nodded as he rose from the table.

"Watch your arse, Sergeant," Bowles said. "Hastings doesn't usually spend that much time at your pay grade, you peepin' me? That's not a scanner you wanna be a blip on if you can avoid it."

"I'll keep that in mind. And hey, Dish, you ever need to talk."

Bowles nodded. "Thanks. Really, Sergeant, I appreciate it." He then gave Vega a quick salute.

After returning the salute, Vega went to the office that had been temporarily assigned to Hastings until they shipped out that evening. On his way over to the office, Vega saw that, as a sergeant, his wrist unit and HUD now had actual EVA access, and he saw that the 22nd was heading to B-5 the next day.

After waiting for a good fifteen minutes, the door slid open to reveal the major's mustached face. "Sergeant Vega, thank you for coming. Please, enter."

Vega got up and saluted. Hastings returned the salute, then stood out of Vega's way so he could enter the office.

It was a fairly typical, drab office, one that many officers had used as they came through here. Vega was sure it would go to some other major as soon as the 22nd vacated.

"Have a seat, Sergeant," Hastings said.

Sitting down in the guest chair, Vega said, "Thank you, sir."

Hastings plopped himself into his own chair and regarded Vega with penetrating eyes for several seconds. Vega wanted desperately to look away, but he had the feeling that the major would interpret that as a sign of weakness, and there was something about Hastings's attitude that gave Vega the impression that he had done something wrong.

Finally, he spoke: "I wonder, Sergeant Vega, if you recall the conversation we had at Dix when you reported."

"I do, sir, yes."

"Including the bits about your not receiving special treatment due to your father?"

"Yes, sir." Vega was starting to get a feeling for where this was going.

"I mention this because I want you to know how vehemently I fought with BC McNeil over your promotion. He assumed that it was due to your comparative lack of experience, and he launched into a rather tiresome speech on the subject of desperate times and desperate measures and extralinear thinking and apples falling from trees and other clichés that were all rather beside the point. You see, Sergeant, I have no issue with a deserving soldier receiving a promotion regardless of his level of experience or his, for lack of a better word, pedigree."

Since Hastings was being brutally honest, and since he was scorching a superior officer behind that officer's back, Vega was willing to risk interrupting. "You're saying I'm not a deserving soldier, sir?"

"That is, in fact, precisely what I'm saying. You see, Sergeant, unlike BC McNeil, I actually examined the recordings of the battles at the convention center. The portions that interested me the most were Corporal Popadopoulos explaining the eccentricities of your helmet due to your above-average-sized cranium, your helmet's subsequent switch to IF without your commanding it to do so, and your comment to Private—rather, Sergent Gallagher regarding your sharpshooting abilities."

Now Hastings got up and started pacing. "The reason—the *only* reason—why you were able to liberate Dr. Takeda and emerge unscathed is because your helmet glitched and because the Brotherhood of Nod had a flaw in their defenses."

That last threw Vega. "Sir?"

"The Brotherhood's armor includes an ability to mask from IF. Unfortunately for them, they have yet to work out a way to similarly shield the muzzles of their energy weapons, which generate tremendous heat when they fire."

Vega nodded. That was, in fact, what he'd guessed at the time, though he hadn't thought much about it since, as subsequent events had been more than a little overwhelming.

Hastings tugged on the end of his mustache. "However, that signature could just as easily have been a light fixture, or a random surge in the building's electrical system. You shot at it—probably a low-risk move, since the absolute worst that would happen is some damage to the ceiling, which was hardly a paramount concern at that point. It was from that phenomenal piece of luck that Unit Epsilon derived its victory in the field, for had you not brought down that sniper and his compatriot, they would have picked you all off and taken your survivors prisoner rather than the other way round. Said luck, in turn, derived solely from a freak of nature, to wit, your outsized head."

Retaking his seat, Hastings said, "Oh yes, and then we have your rather impressive takedown of the interrogator." At Vega's confused look, Hastings added, "According to In-Ops, the gentleman you shot was a Nod interrogator whose function was to question Dr. Takeda. He was located there because they wanted him out of the way in case there was an attack."

"I'm surprised they didn't bring him somewhere more secure."

"There was no place secure in San Diego," Hastings said. "Their hold on the city was tenuous at best."

Before he had the chance to even realize what he was saying, Vega blurted out, "They didn't expect to hold the city, they just wanted to strike at us—same as they did the *Philadelphia*?"

That caused Hastings to recoil as if smacked. "Yes, actually. That, at least, is the working theory, but it's rather a good one. GDI forces have been able to expel the vast majority of Nod forces from the Blues over the past day. I suspect it's a personnel issue as much as anything. I doubt the Brotherhood has sufficient troops for such widespread occupation forces. No, they simply wished to, as it were, hit us where we live, to show that we're vulnerable. To that end, I doubt Takeda was ever a target. He was simply unlucky enough to be in the wrong place at the wrong time." Hastings leaned forward. "Just as you were in the right place at the right time when you shot the interrogator with what you yourself described as a talent not a skill. Indeed, your sharpshooter ratings have not improved much since you were a boy—not that there was all that much room for improvement, as they've always been near-perfect. You're a natural, Sergeant. In practical terms, this means that precisely nothing you did in San Diego was due to your skill as a soldier."

Vega shifted in his chair. "Sir, may I speak freely?"

His eyebrows rising, Hastings said, "Very well."

"Sir, I appreciate your candor, truly, but—what do you expect me to do? I don't think I deserve to be a sergeant either. Honestly, it should be Private Bowles with these stripes, not me."

"That was never going to happen," Hastings said quickly. "Someone with that much family on the other side is not someone we can afford to put in a position where he has to give orders that his soldiers are going to doubt."

At first, Vega was going to respond harshly to that, but decided it would be a tactical error. Instead, he just said, "I couldn't exactly turn the promotion down."

"Of course not, don't be ridiculous. That would've been imbecilic." Hastings folded his hands. "Do you recall another part of our conversation the other day at Dix? When I told you to come to me if there were any difficulties due to your parentage?"

"Yes, sir. And I turned you down because I didn't want to disrupt the chain of command."

"I'm afraid that concern has left the building, as it were, Sergeant. You're *part* of the chain of command now, and I fear you may be its weak link. Your natural talent will only go so far. Therefore I want to reiterate my earlier offer. You may find yourself in over your head. If that's the case, I want you to talk to your fellow sergeants, and if that fails, talk to me. Your promotion is as much for political reasons as anything—shining a light on the rescue of Dr. Takeda to show that we can protect our own and that we reward those who do. In times of war, heroes are needed, and the 22nd in general and your unit in particular have become that. But politics and soldiering are a dangerous combination, much like mixing volatile chemicals to form an explosive. I will not see this division brought down, Sergeant."

Vega got to his feet and stood at attention. "If it is, sir, it won't be through my doing."

"I hope to God you're right, Sergeant. Dismissed."

Saluting, Vega waited for Hastings to return the salute, then he turned on his heel and left the office.

Oddly, considering that the major had spent most of the meeting scorching Vega, the newly minted sergeant felt good coming out of it. Hastings was primarily concerned with the efficiency of the division. Frankly, so was Vega. McNeil no doubt wanted to make his division look good to the GDI bosses, but Hastings just wanted a division that did its job. In San Diego, they had, even if it was due to luck.

Sergeant Vega swore that he wouldn't rely on luck, but make sure that the 22nd's skill would win the day against the Brotherhood of Nod.

NINE

Her first night in Atlanta, Annabella's dreams were a disturbing hodgepodge of ti-bos, ti-dies, children playing *bocce* ball while being eaten away by Tiberium, all with a soundtrack of music from the ribs place. She had similar dreams every time she tried to doze, and invariably woke up in a cold sweat.

On her second day, there was a predicted rad shower that was blowing in from R-7, the Red Zone in the central part of the United States. That morning, Mayor Liebnitz showed her a city park where they were growing trees to replace the ones that had been devastated by Tiberium. On a hunch, Annabella left her drone there when they went inside to stay out of the rad shower, which was likely to take up the whole afternoon. The drone had an add-on casing that could be used as weather protection, and she put that on before leaving it by one of the saplings.

After the shower passed, and the scrubbers had gone over the streets to make walking safe again, Annabella retrieved the drone, discarding the casing to be destroyed rather than risk bringing it back home with ti-rot—not that she'd get it past the Charlotte checkpoint in any case. Examining what she'd recorded, she watched the showers destroy the saplings. She decided to make that an add-on to her report that folks could link to if they wanted: the slow death of plant life at the hands of a phenomenon that didn't exist until Tiberium came to the world.

That night, she returned to the hotel, exhausted, and once again struggled with the plastic key. No matter how many times she slid it in and out, the light would not turn green to indicate that the door was unlocked.

"Shite locks, can't even *open* properly," she muttered as she tried for the fifth time.

"May I?"

Annabella turned to see a short man with a thick black beard. He appeared to be of western-Asian descent. "If you can get this door open, I'll kiss your feet."

The man smiled pleasantly. "That will not be necessary. Simply provide your firstborn."

"As soon as I have one," Annabella deadpanned.

Panic suffused Annabella through the haze of fatigue as she realized that she should not be handing over something like this plastic key to just anyone. She pulled back her hand before she could proffer the key, and also activated her spec-cam so she could get the man's bearded face. "Er, actually—"

"You are Annabella Wu, are you not?"

"Afraid not." She provided what she hoped was a sheepish smile. "I get that a *lot*. I think I should change—"

"Please do not lie to me, Ms. Wu. Leaving aside the fact that your inability to use a simple hotel room door belies your status as a person living in a so-called 'blue zone,' there is the simple fact that the hotel's base lists you as the occupant of this room."

Trying not to think too hard about the fact that this person had access to the hotel's private base, she said, "If you knew it was me, why ask the question?"

"Merely attempting to be polite." The man looked back and forth down the hallway. "May we speak in private, Ms. Wu? I have something I wish to discuss with you."

"You just tried to break into my room. Whatever you have to say, say it out here, Mister—?"

The man nodded, apparently conceding the point. "You may call me Mr. Anspaugh. It is not my real name, of course, as that is not something I am likely to reveal to a reporter. And before you ask, I am wearing a device that will interfere with any recording you make. You will retain no record of this conversation."

Annabella wasn't sure she believed that, and she kept recording visual just in case. She also studied his face very carefully, in case he was telling the truth.

"Anspaugh" continued: "My offer is simple. You are one of the better reporters working for W3N. Your piece on the playgrounds of New York was exemplary. I assume you are bringing similar instincts to your piece on the plight of this benighted city."

He seemed to be waiting for a response, but Annabella saw no reason *to* respond. She also wondered where the *hell* security was in this shitehole.

"Unlike your comrades, Ms. Wu, you speak to the human element. Your reports are not about global tragedies and macro trends, but rather about what the news actually means to actual people. We admire that."

She knew the answer to this question, but she wanted it said aloud in case her cam really *was* getting all this: "And who's 'we' precisely?"

"I should think that would be obvious, Ms. Wu. You see, you only provide GDI's truth. But there is a greater truth out there. GDI is losing the war because it clings to a past that no longer has any meaning. Tiberium is the future, Ms. Wu, and the sooner the world embraces it, the better off we shall be."

Annabella looked away for a second to compose herself. She also realized that Anspaugh was *not* using an imager. She'd been wearing one of her own long enough to recognize the fuzziness around the edges that the imager left if you looked closely enough, and she'd spent the last minute or so looking *very* closely at Anspaugh. It was possible that the beard was fake, but the face was definitely his. "I met someone today who 'embraced' Tiberium, Mr. Anspaugh. His stomach exploded a few minutes later. I've seen dying children, whose only crime was to be standing too close to where your precious Tiberium happened to be infesting. I've watched plants die in a rad shower. I can show it to you, if you want."

Anspaugh smiled. "Survival of the fittest, Ms. Wu. Evolution favors those who adapt to changing conditions. Tiberium isn't going anywhere, and we must adapt."

"You're saying Tiberium is part of a natural process?" *And why are you getting into a philosophical debate with a Nod recruiter?* she asked herself.

Chuckling, Anspaugh said, "Natural processes are simply what happens to nature. Tiberium's arrival is no different than the arrival of an asteroid millions of years ago. That changed the face of the planet, and the dinosaurs were unable to adapt, so they died. We must prove ourselves worthier than our saurian forebears. The Neanderthal fought against the Cro-Magnon and lost."

"Bubonic plague changed the face of Europe in the Middle Ages, too," Annabella said quietly. "Are you saying that the people then should have embraced disease? Perhaps worshipped the rats that carried the plague?"

That caused Anspaugh to throw his head back and

laugh. "Well argued, Ms. Wu. Oh, you would be a fine addition to our ranks. But I can see that you have already made up your mind. There is mail in your queue that is labeled TOWNSHIP. Reply to that link if you change your mind."

Anspaugh then bowed and walked toward the lift.

As soon as he was out of sight, Annabella linked to hotel security, provided a description of the man, and said he had tried to break into her room. She then called up what her cam recorded, only to find that it was, indeed, static. She turned to go into her room and found she *still* couldn't get the door open.

Unbowed, she took out her Hand and immediately started doing a recon of Anspaugh's face, and tried to remember all the qualities of his voice that she could.

Security eventually got her in the door—to her embarrassment, she had been putting the key in backward—and took her descriptions and statement, although they found nobody of that description in the hotel. After they left, she checked her mail, and sure enough, one of the shells was labeled TOWNSHIP. It had no text.

She saved it to a folder and started working to see if she could somehow reconstruct her conversation with Mr. Anspaugh.

The next day, after getting even less sleep—between staying up late trying and failing to retrieve what her cam recorded and the bad dreams, which now had Anspaugh looming over each event—she managed to steal a moment alone with Terise.

There was a town hall meeting that Liebnitz was leading, which promised to be stultifying, so she had no qualms about missing it live. Besides, she had bigger fish to fry.

"Shouldn't you be in there recording?" Terise asked when Annabella asked to speak to her in private.

"The drone's got it, on the off chance that something interesting happens—and if so, it'll be the first town meeting in the history of recorded time where something interesting did happen."

That actually got a smile out of Terise. "Good point. I gotta say, Annabella, you look like plastered shite."

"Thank you," Annabella said tartly. "I got a visit last night, and I think you know from whom."

Terise stared at her blankly. "What're you talking about?"

"*Please* don't play stupid with me. You were the only one who knew when I'd be getting back to my room where that Nod recruiter was waiting for me."

"Nod recrui—Annabella, you've gone completely off-net. What Nod recruiter?"

"Somebody from Nod showed up at my hotel room door last night. He knew where I was staying, had access to the hotel's base, and was there right when I got back from a trip only you and I knew about—and anyone else *you* might have told."

"Look, you stupid bint," Terise snapped, "I've never met anyone from Nod in my life. Some people are sympathetic to them, yeah, but that's mostly because they hack off GDI, and lots of folks around here don't like GDI much. But that's just talk. You sure this wasn't a prank?"

In truth, Annabella had no idea, but she wasn't about to say so to Terise. "He was *very* convincing."

"What, exactly, happened?" Terise asked.

Annabella told her all about her conversation with the mysterious Mr. Anspaugh.

Terise looked stunned. "That is seriously insane. They

must *really* want you, to come out in the open like that."
She scratched her chin thoughtfully. "Honestly, you put
that in your report, it'll be worth watching. In other Yellows, they're all over everywhere, but they usually stay
out of—well, the entire area that was *supposed* to be part
of B-2," she added with a wry smile. "As to how they
found out about you, I don't know. They're Nod; they
have resources. Like I said, some folks're sympathetic to
them around here—like, say, a hotel clerk that you
hacked off when you checked in."

Annabella winced. "Patel told you about that, huh?"

"Yup," Terise said with a nod. "We all got a good
chuckle out of it."

"I'm *thrilled* that I got to be entertainment for you."

"Well, it *is* what you do for a living." Terise shook her
head. "Look, lots of people have reason to give your
name to Nod. Getting you to turn would be huge for
them. But it wasn't me. Just because I don't *like* you
doesn't mean I'm going to set you up with the feckers
who blew up the *Philadelphia* and who worship the stuff
I've been watching kill everyone around me. Give me a
little credit, huh?"

Sighing, Annabella said, "You're right. I'm sorry. I
just—that guy really got me all wiggly."

Before Terise could say anything else, the door to the
town hall meeting slid open, and Liebnitz came out, led
by Patel, and being harassed by half a dozen people.

"Smart lady, stayin' out here," Liebnitz said with a
grin as he approached, ignoring the various supplicants.

Patel took on the latter: "Ladies, gentlemen, the meeting's over. You had your chance—the mayor is late for a
very important appointment."

Taking a deep breath, Annabella forced a pleasant

smile on to her face and asked, "What's the appointment, Your Honor?"

"I really wish you'd stop callin' me that. And it's a dinner party."

"Am I invited?"

"It's your last night, ain't it?"

Annabella nodded.

"Then it's best you were invited, 'cause it's your farewell dinner."

"My—" Annabella found herself unable to finish the sentence. "Why do I rate a farewell dinner?"

"You're a guest, Annabella. Southern hospitality ain't what it used to be, but we still know how to treat a guest 'round here. Sal'll take you back to the hotel so you can change. Then he'll take you back to the mansion."

"Th-thank you, Moné."

"You're welcome."

Patel, having shooed away the town meeting vultures, indicated the hallway to the lift that would take them to the parking garage. "Ms. Wu?"

Annabella turned around and took a look at Terise, but she was engrossed in conversation with another of Liebnitz's aides.

With a heavy heart, she let Patel lead her down to the garage.

Annabella had expected the next day's return trip to be a bit more difficult. After all, people didn't travel between Blue and Yellow that often, for very good reason, and to be let back into a Blue after being in a Yellow required special dispensation—emphasized by the fact that the train back was even emptier than the train down. Only one other person was in her car—a bald man in his forties—and there were probably only one or two people in the other car.

But hey, I'm the W3N reporter. I'm special. I get to watch children dying, I get to watch a ti-bo's stomach explode, and I get to be recruited by scary Nod people. Whoopee for celebrity.

As they were pulling out of Charlotte and heading toward the border station, the bald man leaned into the aisle. "Excuse me, ma'am. I'm sorry to bother you, but—aren't you Annabella Wu?"

A fist of ice clenched her heart, as she recalled the last conversation that had started that way. She came within a micron of saying no, as she had to Anspaugh, then realized she was being ridiculous. A hotel that didn't even have proper bioscans was one thing, but this train was made more secure than a sealed drum by GDI. No way this was another Nod person.

Still, there was a catch in her voice as she said, "Yes, I'm she."

Offering his hand, the man said, "My name's Kwame Galiulin. I'm a doctor. GDI had me down in Tallahassee demonstrating some new surgical techniques. What brought you to Yellow country?"

"A story," she said blandly, hoping he'd leave it at that. She really didn't want to get into it, especially since she was peppered with doubts as to what, exactly, her story was supposed to *be. Why did Boyle want W3N to do this anyhow? What good does it do to let everyone know how miserable people are?*

"What about?"

She sighed. People never *did* just leave it at that. "About life in a Yellow."

His eyes widening, Galiulin said, "Really? That's great."

"You think so?" Annabella herself was not feeling particularly sanguine about the story.

"Absolutely. People need to see how other people survive adversity. I mean, look at how these people live. They got no guarantee of a good home, 'cause they gotta pile together away from ti-rot, they got no guarantee of a job, no guarantee of nothin'. But they keep on goin', some of 'em better than a lotta folks I know in Blues."

Galiulin's words triggered a memory. *Blues.* Ironically, the style of music that Terise had introduced her to was called that. Terise hadn't explained the etymology of the word, and it didn't really make much sense to Annabella. True, they were miserable, but they were surviving. Some of them were thriving. *Look at the music they made.*

Before Annabella could reply, the speakers crackled to life. *"Approaching border station."*

Unlike last time, the decon didn't just consist of standing up and getting scanned anonymously. After the train came to a stop at the border station, Annabella saw a large box being placed over each of the train's entrances. Fully-armored soldiers entered that box, which she then realized was an air lock. Four of those soldiers came into her car.

"Ms. Wu, Dr. Galiulin, please, if you'd both stand up." The soldier's voice was filtered through the helmet's speakers. *"You need to remove all of your clothing, please, and also hand over all clothing in your luggage."* As he spoke, another soldier placed a folding privacy screen that was decorated with the GDI logo between her and Galiulin. The final two soldiers were bringing in a pair of what looked like port-a-potties, which confused Annabella; the train *had* bathrooms.

However, she was a bit more focused on the request

for all of her clothes. "What do you mean, all of my clothes?"

Galiulin peered around the privacy screen. "Didn't they tell you on the way down?"

"Not about that, no."

"They shoulda told you that." Galiulin shook his head, then disappeared back behind the privacy screen.

"*My apologies, Ms. Wu, but this is standard procedure. GDI protocol is very clear on this subject. You were supposed to bring a change of clothes when you made the trip down and have it stored here before departing B-2.*"

Annabella couldn't believe this. "Nobody *told* me that! Hell, I got a billion bytes of info on this stupid trip, and nobody *once* mentioned that my clothes'd be confiscated."

"*As I said, Ms. Wu, it's standard procedure. And they won't be confiscated, they'll be destroyed.*"

Throwing up her hands in frustration, Annabella said, "What the hell am I supposed to do, go naked for the rest of the—"

"*We'll be happy to provide a GDI jumpsuit for you to wear for the rest of your trip, but we must insist that you remove all of your clothing, now.*"

For a surreal moment, Annabella thought the soldier was going to order the other three to hold their guns on her if she didn't strip in a timely manner.

"Perfect ending to a perfect ficken trip," she muttered as she pulled her top shirt off over her head, then quickly took the rest of her clothes off. One of the soldiers picked up hers and the doctor's garments, while another took down her luggage. Apparently, the lock she'd paid a hundred creds for was still vulnerable to someone with a GDI military ID, as it unlocked immediately. Her clothing was removed, as were several toiletries. While her instinct was to complain, she didn't bother. *What, if I whine, they'll change their minds and let me keep that toothpaste so I can use it to infect the Bronx with Tiberium? Not ficken likely.*

They also took her glasses and drone. This time, she couldn't beat back the instinct. "Do you have to take those?"

A different soldier said, *"Afraid so, ma'am. It's standard—"*

"Procedure, right, of course." It wasn't as if it mattered: all her footage had been linked to W3N's satellite before she left Atlanta, and she hadn't turned on either of them during the return trip, so she wasn't losing anything by having the equipment confiscated. Penny'd just get her a new set.

Once their various personal items were removed, another soldier held up his (at least, she assumed it was a man—the armor was too thick, and the voice over the speaker too filtered to denote the wearer's sex) arm and looked at the display on a wrist unit of some sort. *"Looks like they're clean, Captain."*

"Good."

Annabella thought that meant they'd be spared any more indignities. This proved a forlorn hope. *Being clean probably just means we'll be allowed back into B-2,* she thought as the soldiers handed her seven small pieces of what looked like rubber—two were flat, four were small and round, and the seventh was wide and flat.

"These are for your eyes, nose, mouth, and ears, to protect against the decon."

"Lovely." Ananbella took them, stuck the small round ones in her nostrils and ears and placed the flat one in her mouth. To her surprise, she could still breathe through both mouth and nose. *Not* just *rubber, I guess.* Finally, she closed her eyes and placed the flat pieces over them.

"Get ready."

Suddenly, her body was pelted from all sides by a thick, steaming-hot liquid. Annabella cried out in pain as the viscous substance flowed over her flesh. After a moment, she was covered from head to toe in whatever it was, and then it hardened. Covered in what felt like a giant rubber suit from head to toe, she wanted to scream, but couldn't, didn't dare open her mouth and it was like she was being smothered and *I'm going to die!*

"All right, you can peel it off now."

Annabella made several incoherent noises, which was the only way she could convey, with the rubber thing in her mouth, that she had no idea how to do that.

"Right, this is your first trip. Hang on."

A feeling that was several orders of magnitude worse than removing a bandage off flesh ripped through Annabella's arm as the soldier peeled the whatever-it-was off her right arm, taking what felt like the first layer of skin off as well. Wiggling her fingers now that they were free, Annabella then immediately grabbed at her neck with her right hand and tore off the covering. When the soldier had done it, it came off in an even strip. But the stuff flaked in Annabella's hands, pulling at her skin.

It took an eternity, but she finally removed it all, the various plugs having come off with it. She could feel little bits of the substance in various parts of her body, and she kept brushing at her legs and torso and arms to get the last of it, until the soldier spoke. *"Stand still, please."*

Then she was pelted again, this time by ice-cold water that was at once a huge relief and devastatingly chilling. Goose bumps rose on her flesh and shivers ran up and down her entire body. Her teeth chattered so fast she feared she'd shred her tongue as the cold water washed away the remainder of whatever that first substance was.

Annabella was hugging herself and shivering and dripping on the train car floor. From the other side of the privacy screen, Galiulin was saying through what sounded like chattering teeth, "Well, that was pretty bracing."

"Not the first word that came to mind," Annabella muttered.

A soldier came in and handed each of them two pills and a glass of water. *"Take these in the port-a-johns."*

Annabella was about to ask what the pills were for, then, upon thinking through why a pill would have to be taken in the bathroom, she decided she didn't need it spelled out.

Folding herself into the portable toilet, she placed the pill on her tongue, then gulped down the water.

Sitting down on the toilet, she instead found herself overcome by nausea and a rumbling in her stomach, which seemed to expand and then contract. The acid taste of bile rose to her mouth, and then she just let go, vomiting heavily into the toilet three or four times, dry-heaving the fourth, her abdominal muscles clenching each time.

Just as that was done, she felt an odd sensation in her belly, and her bowels and bladder then emptied themselves at a great rate.

By the time she was done, she felt physically exhausted, as if she'd run a dozen meters full tilt.

Just when I thought this trip couldn't get any worse, she thought as she stumbled back into the main part of the car.

Galiulin was putting on a pair of denims. Another soldier was holding a jumpsuit out to Annabella. *"Here you go, Ms. Wu."*

Not trusting herself to say something she would later regret, she said nothing, simply snatching the jumpsuit and climbing into it. The fabric rubbed against her raw skin, and she realized that she now knew what wearing a burlap sack would be like.

One of the soldiers had gone into the portable bathroom after she left it. When he came back out, he said, *"We're good."*

"Fotze, you guys just examined my shite, piss, and vomit, didn't you?"

Looking at her like she was crazy—and right now, she wasn't sure she wasn't—Galiulin said, "Whadja expect, Ms. Wu? They gotta be sure you ain't contaminated. Tirot's some nasty stuff."

"So I've noticed." It was easy to believe that Tiberium was bad from people telling you, but there was nothing quite like watching a teenaged boy being eaten alive by the stuff, or a sapling being withered before it had the chance to blossom, to really drive the point home.

"You're both cleared to reenter B-2," the head soldier said. *"Have a nice day."*

Annabella couldn't help it. She burst out laughing.

When she caught her breath, she saw Galiulin's look, which indicated he was now *sure* she was crazy. "If nothing else," she said, "I don't think my day can get any *worse*."

TEN

"*Have I mentioned how* completely *insane this is?*"

"*Several thousand times, Pup.*"

"*Well, it is. Totally, completely, thoroughly, and in every conceivable way cracked up.*"

"*Can't argue with that. Well, I could, actually, 'cause I'm so bored that even arguing with you sounds good.*"

The chatter of Vega's unit over his helmet was interrupted by Gallagher on discreet. "*Vega, can you please keep your dogs from barking? We're supposed to be support, here.*"

"It's not a covert op, Sergeant. We're just buffering 'til they say they need us."

Vega and Unit Epsilon were hunkered down in a small valley in the Madagascar jungle. They were there to support the experimental Mark 3A Juggernauts, which had been attached to the 22nd for this op, which was to take back B-14. Over the past three weeks, the 22nd had become the "fix it squad" for GDIUP. European forces were spread too thin to liberate all the Blues there, so the 22nd had been sent to Portugal to help take back B-5, and then they had been ordered here to B-14.

After Portugal, General Granger had provided McNeil and his people with new toys: Momoa finally had his precious GD3. It had the grenade launcher Momoa had been jacking over, but they also found out that the GD4 was already in prototype form, and it would have a mini-railgun.

The tech guys had also put out new walkers: the Urban Combat Platform Mark 3A Juggernauts. Based on the Mark 3s that were mounted with heavy cannons, these experimental, new UCPs had gun turrets that could turn a full three-sixty, a crew pod that could now hold four, thus giving the walker additional capabilities and backup, and more powerful cannons and an upgraded fire-suppression system. The latter was particularly necessary, since the Mark 3s tended to catch fire at the drop of a hat. Popadopoulos had been going on for about an hour when they were being deployed in the *Huron,* saying that the 3As were being rushed and they wouldn't be any good in the field.

But In-Ops said that Nod had better forces in Madagascar because they were planning to introduce ti-rock into the Indian Ocean, which would engulf at least four Blues in Africa and western Asia, given how fast Tiberium moved on water. That was why air strikes were out of the question. There was too much risk of blowing up ti-rock that would spread and do Nod's job for them.

So they needed to get the new tech out as fast as possible, and that meant putting the new walkers in the field.

Nod had taken over a small town. Battalion 4 was being held in reserve to back up the UCPs in case Nod was able to take them down or in case they failed. Units Gamma and Epsilon were closest, in this little valley, with the other units deployed at various points. Company 6 had engaged some Nod scouts and neutralized them.

But Company 7 in general, and Gamma and Epsilon in particular, were the ace in the hole.

Vega smiled. The phrase reminded him of their most recent poker game. Over the past three weeks, the Company 7 poker games had become legendary, with Vega and Momoa usually putting on a show while everyone else just watched in awe.

The final hand they'd played before the 22nd was sent to Madagascar had been a doozy. Vega had been studying his hole cards intently, his brow furrowing. Not that he had needed to, as he had not one, but two aces in the hole, as well as a deuce. His up cards included another ace and another deuce, along with a three and a four. He'd been betting as if he had a straight—aggressively without overdoing it—in the hopes of lulling Momoa into a false sense of security. Vega was pretty sure Momoa had a flush. It was impossible to be sure. For someone who wore his emotions on his battlesuit in the field, Momoa had an amazing poker face, but with a full house, Vega was willing to risk it.

The two of them and Popadopoulos were the only ones left. Bowles had folded on the first betting round, and Silverstein was gone after the second. Vega wasn't really worried about Geek the Greek, as he'd been steadily losing all night. In fact, he was out of chips, and was now betting upgrades and fast-tracks to equipment, the latter of which were hacking Silverstein off. Momoa, though, had already tricked Vega more than once.

While Momoa had three diamonds showing—a king, a three, and a six—he had no pair up. Although Vega was morally certain Popadopoulos had the worst overall hand, he had a pair of nines showing, so he bet first. "Check."

Momoa tossed five black chips into the already large pile in the center. "Fifty."

Vega tossed in four red chips. "Make it a hundred."

"Fotze," Popadopoulos said, and flipped his cards over. "I'm out."

Momoa didn't even hesitate to put in four red chips of his own. "One fifty."

Not hesitating, either—Vega had the third-best poker hand possible, and it was ace-high on top of that—Vega raised it a third and final time, tossing five blacks and eight reds in. "See it, and up two hundred."

Now Momoa hesitated. Two hundred credits was a lot of money, and that was in addition to the hundreds more that were already in the pot. Whoever won this hand would be the big winner of the game.

Finally, Momoa tossed in eight red chips, then flipped over his hole cards: two more kings and one more six. "Boat."

For the first time, Vega broke into a grin, as he showed that he, too, had a boat: but his aces made his the winning hand.

That broke Momoa's poker face, and his face curled into a rictus of fury. "Crack me sideways!"

"Sorry, you aren't my type," Vega said as he raked in the chips.

Right after that, they'd gotten the call to fall in to the *Huron*.

Now they stood in the valley, waiting for things to start. The battlesuit's cooling system kept the humidity from being too oppressive, but the mosquitoes were playing merry shite with the HUD. A voice sounded in his helmet, that of Lieutenant Lao, the commander of the UCP group. *"We are engaging the enemy."*

Vega set his HUD to show him the approach of the walkers toward the center. The screen inside his helmet lit up with glowing wireframe outlines of the ten UCPs stomping from five different directions toward the tourist center. Next to the wireframes, figures scrolled by showing the walkers' vitals, as well as those of the occupants.

Energy beams were striking the walkers, but the Mark 3A armor apparently was doing what it was supposed to do: the Nod energy beams weren't cutting through it. Vega could hear the high-pitched whine of the energy beams mixing in with the staccato pounding of the walkers' bullets, matching what he saw on the HUD.

Then Vega looked up at Bowles, who had climbed a tree to give himself a view of the battle. "How's it looking, Dish?"

Bowles's voice sounded happy over the intercom. *"There's something incredibly gratifying about watching Nod beams fizzle out like that."*

The UCPs started firing their cannons at the tourist center. "Looks like this might just be cleanup duty," Vega said. "Sorry, Pup. Maybe next time you'll get to play with the grenade launcher."

"Hell with that, Sergeant. I just want my revenge for your boat."

"It was one hand, Pup. Let it go."

"No thank you, sir. I'd rather just win all my money back."

"My money now, Pup." On the HUD the walkers were moving in closer, and Vega tensed up, getting ready to order the troops to move in to help the UCPs secure the place.

Bowles shifted position on the thick branch, trying not to think about how sore his arse was going to be if he stayed up here much longer.

But he wouldn't have traded this view for anything.

One of the walkers started stomping toward a ring of Nod troops. *What the hell?* Bowles didn't understand why that soldier didn't just fire on them. Then he peered more closely and saw that the ring of Noddies were actually spread out a bit. One shot with the gun wouldn't do the trick. *Still, you could just fire in an arc. Why don't they do that instead of wasting time with this shite?*

Two of the Noddies ran away as the walker got close enough, but the other four held their ground—right up until the UCP stepped on them like they were a colony of ants.

Okay, never mind, Bowles thought with a grin. *I'd have paid fifty creds to see that.*

The tide of war had been slowly turning. GDI casualties in general had been appalling, though the 22nd had gotten off comparatively easy, but it was worth it. There had been a scare in North Africa—apparently Nod was developing some kind of chemical weapon there involving liquid Tiberium—but the 3rd, having already taken back Washington, D.C., in B-2 from Nod, took care of that one. All the other Blues were safe, though they were having some trouble in Australia, too. *I'll bet all the money Pup lost at poker that we'll be sent there next.*

While in Portugal, Bowles had been able to meet directly with Anisfeld for the first time since he hired her. They had a nice lunch at this hole-in-the-wall café in Lisbon, but the food was the only good thing to come out of it. Anisfeld was no closer to finding Bowles's family, and she was of the considered opinion that they had changed their IDs after joining Nod and that they didn't *want* Bowles to find them.

"Let me give you some advice, Alessio," Anisfeld had said over dessert and coffee, which was the best espresso Bowles had ever had. "Give it up. All you're doing is giving me all your money, and while I appreciate the work, it's not fair to you. You need to get on with your life."

Bowles had stared at Anisfeld's pretty face for a few moments, then had finished off his espresso before saying: "Without my family, I ain't got a life. Keep looking."

That damn Nod prisoner had sounded so *reasonable* when he went on about how GDI had never really won anything and how they were stuck with ti-rock and all that other gobshite. But Bowles refused to believe him.

The Nod soldiers continued to hold their ground, even though their spicy-arse ray-beams didn't do a thing to the UCPs. *Put that in your mouth and bite it, feckers.*

And then, suddenly, Bowles's helmet went dark. He knocked it on the side a few times, but he got nothing: no HUD, no comms, and he was starting to feel warmer. *Oh, this isn't good,* he thought as he took the helmet off.

As soon as he did, he saw that the Nod soldiers hadn't moved, but the UCPs had all fallen over. *No,* he thought, and he jumped down out of the tree.

As soon as his helmet went dark, Vega ripped it off, since he was blind now. Because he relied on the helmet's various displays, not to mention the communications system, his sight wasn't much improved. It was very odd for Vega not to have somebody talking in his ear, but the mini–HUD unit was just as dead.

Bowles jumped down from the tree. "The walkers just fell over."

"EMP," Popadopoulos said. "Gotta be."

Vega cursed. GDI equipment was supposed to be proofed against an electromagnetic pulse, but it looked like Nod had found a way through their shielding.

Most of Epsilon was cursing and asking questions and making noise, which Vega cut through by yelling, "Quiet! Everyone, *stay here.*"

Then he jogged over toward the very large rock that separated Epsilon from Gamma. Climbing over it, he saw Gallagher and her Gamma troops in a similar state of confusion. Gamma was the only unit close enough for him to talk to. Without their equipment, they couldn't talk to each other, couldn't coordinate, nothing.

"Gallagher, we gotta hit 'em, *now*."

Looking at him like he was six kinds of crazy, Gallagher said, "What?"

"Gamma and Epsilon, up the hill and over to the town while they're not expecting it."

"With what? Our helmets—"

"Don't fire bullets, but our guns do. Sights and readouts may be down, but the actual firing mechanisms of the GD3s and the Nighthawks are mechanical. *They* still work. We don't hit them now, they infect the ocean, and we're done. We gotta do it *now*."

Vega could see the indecision on Gallagher's face for an instant. To her credit, it lasted only an instant, and he knew it was born of her distrust of the nep and his unfair promotion, about which her feelings had not died even though the two of them had been involved in a successful op in Portugal. Vega, obviously, had not gotten them all killed, despite her dire predictions. In fact, during the entire Portugal op, Units Gamma and Epsilon of Company 7 in Battalion 4 had the two lowest casualty rates of any units in the 22nd. Vega knew he was right, and he knew he couldn't be the only one thinking this. While some sergeants and lieutenants might be frozen by the lack of equipment, they wouldn't all be, and with Gamma and Epsilon the closest, they *had* to lead the way.

Still staring at Vega, Gallagher said, "Unit Gamma, let's move out!"

Nodding, Vega climbed back over the rock and ordered his own unit to go up and over. "Sights are down, so just point and shoot."

Momoa snorted. "Sights are for Noddies."

"Let's go, go, go!"

Vega climbed up the branches and rocks of the valley to the pathway that would lead to the town, the weight of his battlesuit and the oppressive humidity almost crushing. The EMP had taken out both the muscular enhancers and the cooling systems. That meant they all had to rely on their own muscles to get them up, and they had to fight the weather instead of ignoring it.

Momoa was the one making the best progress toward the top. Vega said, between grunts as he climbed, "Pup, when you get up there, start running toward the town and firing the GL."

"We're too far away," Momoa said.

"I know that. I just want the smoke from the explosions. The EMP probably took out their equipment, too, but they're prepped for it. Best we can do is make things as invisible to them as possible. Maybe they won't realize they've got two units coming. Maybe they'll think it's more or less than it is."

"You got it, Sarge." Momoa grinned. "Ace in the hole, huh?"

"Two aces, Pup," Vega said as he grabbed a branch and used it to hoist himself upward.

As soon as Momoa clambered over the top of the valley, he started running. Vega and Bowles and a few others made it a second later, and they also started running. Vega noticed that Gallagher was right alongside him.

The grenades exploded in a straight line down the pathway to the town, creating a miasma of smoke and dust. "Stay on the path!" Vega called out, hoping that the soldiers knew to just keep going straight ahead.

Vega then heard the report of gunfire coming from up ahead. At first, he thought it was other members of the 22nd, but the EMP may have fried the Nod weapons, too, so they might have gone back to conventional weapons until their ray-beams recovered.

They came across one of the fallen UCPs. The giant legs were splayed out and up behind it, with the three forward railguns pointed down into the ground.

The smoke from Momoa's grenade barrage started to clear, and Vega could see five troops—Gallagher, Brodeur, Bowles, Momoa, and one of Gallagher's people—taking on Nod troops with their Nighthawks at close range. Given that his specs were probably just as dead as everything else, Brodeur's ability to adapt to being unable to understand what anyone was saying impressed the hell out of Vega.

Vega saw snipers in several second-floor windows of a nearby building, so he fired his GD3 over his troops' heads and at the upper levels.

One Nod soldier got a shot in at Momoa, who fell backward even as he used his own Nighthawk to fire back.

"Pup!" Bowles screamed as Momoa fell. He immediately started wading into them, firing like an off-net.

As he charged forward himself, joined by the remainder of Gamma and Epsilon, Vega heard screams from his left. They were battle cries, not expressions of pain, and he heard the report of GD3s being fired. *I wasn't the only one to think of this.*

Then Vega was barely conscious. He remembered Momoa getting shot, and he remembered running toward the nearest building, and the next thing he specifically recalled was pulling Bowles off the bruised body of a Nod commando twenty minutes later.

What happened between those two events was a blur of sensory overload. He heard gunfire loud enough to make him envious of Brodeur. He saw blood flowing freely. He smelled the odor of rent flesh, exposed guts, and burnt circuitry mixed in with the musky stench of sweat. He tasted the bite of sulfur in the air from all the weapons fire. And he felt the weight of his nonfunctioning battlesuit, even as its surfaces protected him from the worst of the gunfire.

Somewhere in there, the fatigue lessened and the sweat evaporated, indicating that the battlesuits had rebooted and were back online. It wasn't until after he saw Bowles kicking the Nod commando that he thought to put his helmet back on.

But first he needed to stop Bowles from killing the guy. It looked like he was barely conscious, and Vega hoped that meant he wouldn't have the wherewithal to commit suicide. GDI had gotten very few prisoners of any rank within Nod because they all kamikazed.

"You okay, Dish?" Vega asked.

Bowles gave the commando one final kick, then stepped back. "Now I'm fine," he said tightly.

Then Vega replaced his helmet, and he found himself assaulted by GDI chatter, but what caught his attention was Hastings's voice: *"The town is secure. Repeat, the town is secure."*

Vega looked around and spied someone he trusted to do this right. "Brodeur, secure this prisoner for transport back to base."

Smiling, Brodeur just gave Vega a thumbs-up, and then walked over.

Opening a discreet to Hastings, Vega said, "Major Hastings, this is Sergeant Vega. Units Gamma and Epsilon have a prisoner."

"Good to have you back in-system, Sergeant," Hastings said dryly. *"I'm impressed that anyone was left alive after you plowed in. Well done. Your unit will likely get a commend."*

"It was a joint effort, sir, with Sergeant Gallagher."

"*I see. It was a ludicrous, idiotic gesture that only had a marginal chance of success, so I assumed you were solely responsible, Sergeant Gallagher being generally more reasonable than that.*"

Gallagher's voice came over the lines then. "*Major, this is Sergeant Gallagher. We've found the ti-rock stash. My people are guarding it now, but we'll want the cranies in here, stat.*"

"*Of course, Sergeant. Well done. Sergeant Vega tells me you're both responsible for not letting Nod take advantage of their EMP trick.*"

After a hesitation, Gallagher said, "*Sergeant Vega's too modest. It was his idea. I just went along with it.*"

"*Yes, but you were the ranking officer, so you get equal credit. Well done, both of you. Hastings out.*"

A moment later, Gallagher herself walked over. "You didn't have to do that, Sergeant."

"Yeah, I did."

They stared at each other through their helmets for a second.

She was the first one to break eye contact, looking away at the far wall. "C'mon, let's get this place taken care of."

"Sure thi—"

"Sarge!"

That was Bowles, who had wandered off, but was now running right for Vega. "What is it, Dish?" Vega asked.

"It's Pup."

Vega felt the blood drain from his face. He had briefly forgotten that Momoa had been shot. Both Gallagher and Vega ran with Bowles back to the main lobby of the building.

Private Kareem Momoa was propped up against a wall in a pool of blood, only some of which was his own. Vega could see that the battlesuit had attempted to stanch some of the bleeding, but it probably hadn't been able to start until long after Momoa was beyond help.

"I already called a medic," Bowles said.

Kneeling down next to the big man, Vega said, "Hang on, Pup. Help's on the way."

"Looks like I don't get my money back." Momoa coughed up blood after he said that.

Gallagher said, "Don't talk like that, you ficken tibelhead. You'll be fine. You're too stupid to die."

"Don't lie to me, Gallagher. They ain't puttin' me back together from this. Too bad, too. I had plans for you and me."

"Oh yeah?" Gallagher asked. "Unless they involved me kicking you in the balls—"

Momoa laughed, which caused him to cough up more blood. "Nah, I was thinkin' a house in B-6. On a mountain."

"I hate mountains, Pup."

"Yeah," Momoa said, "but you'd grow—grow to like 'em." He coughed up more blood. His eyes were staring straight ahead, not acknowledging any of them. "Hey— hey, Sarge? You there?"

Vega thought, *He can't even see.* "Yeah, Pup, I'm right here."

"Nice—nice job with the—the two aces inna hole."

"Full house always wins."

"Yeah."

Momoa didn't say anything after that. "Pup?"
Nothing.

A medic came running up, and Vega got out of her way, but he knew it was too late. Momoa was dead.

*   *   *

By nightfall, Battle Commander McNeil had made the town's largest building into the 22nd's temporary HQ. He summoned Vega and Gallagher to his office around midnight, right as they were preparing to finally bunk down for the night. The sergeants had both been up for twenty hours, and had spent several hours securing the place, preparing the bodies for transport back to wherever their wills dictated—Momoa's was being returned to his home in Hawaii for burial—but one didn't turn down an invitation from one's BC, regardless of the hour or how exhausted one was.

The office apparently belonged to a travel agency. It was filled with holoposters extolling the virtues of various regions all around the world—all, Vega noticed, Blues—with the walls painted in bright, cheery colors. It was the most unmilitary room Vega could imagine, and McNeil looked slightly ridiculous sitting in the middle of it.

To his credit, the battle commander seemed to realize it. "Join me in a drink, Sergeants?" he asked. "It'll make it easier to sit in this room, trust me."

Smiling, both soldiers agreed, and each took a glass of whatever amber liquid McNeil had poured for himself.

"You did some fine work today, Sergeant Vega. JV'd be proud."

"He is, sir." Vega had actually had a moment to link Dad an hour earlier. It had been a brief conversation, but he assured Dad that he was okay, which was all Dad really cared about.

McNeil threw back some of his drink. "He should be. That was quick thinking. Nod was counting on us being thrown off by flying blind—not to mention the walkers going down." He shook his head. "Ficken cranies. They told me the Mark 3As were ready for the field. Personally, I'm recommending they trash 'em and stick with the Mark 3s for support."

"Yes, sir," Gallagher said.

Vega felt an odd need to defend the Tech Ops crew. "Uh, sir, they also said the GD3s were ready, and they actually were." He sloshed his drink in the glass, not sure if he should actually drink it.

Chuckling, McNeil said, "Good point. Those Noddies are arrogant arses, I'll tell you. And they never stay down. Do you know that I actually killed Kane back in TWII?"

Gallagher blinked. "Excuse me, sir?"

"At least I thought I did," McNeil added with a sigh. "It was in Cairo at the end of the war. Stabbed the psycho right in the heart." Waving his hand back and forth, he said, "It was a classified mission, at least at the time, so GDI put it out that he was in that place in Kenya. Doesn't much matter now, but that's been the story, so we've stuck with it. Still don't know how he managed to come back, but this whole thing has his signature all over it."

Frowning, Vega said, "Well, he's also been showing up in all those pirate casts."

"That could be faked—not easily, but it could be. But no, it's more than that. This is a program he wrote. No doubt about it. There's always some hidden agenda with him. We just need to figure out what it is. Instead, we're busy putting out all these fires he's set . . ."

Shaking his head, McNeil said, "In any case, you're both doing excellent work. You kept your heads in a situation where many soldiers would have panicked—and, in fact, many soldiers *did*. Major Hastings and I managed to put together a strike force to go in after the UCPs went down, but you two were closest. If you hadn't hit Nod before they had a chance to take advantage, we'd be looking at a new Yellow Zone. According to In-Ops, they were only a few minutes away from poisoning the ocean when the walkers attacked, and your hitting them hard meant they couldn't take the time to do that. You gave us enough time to regroup and stop them. Good work."

That surprised Vega—Nod hitting the ocean with tirot was always a fear, but he hadn't known until now that they were that close. "Thank you, sir."

"I've also been talking with our tech people. We need something that can give us mobile C&C in the field. I lost control of my command today thanks to that ficken EMP, but even if we're protected, I need to be able to keep better track of things, so I don't have to rely on people like you and Gallagher getting your heads out of your arses." He took a drink. "Oh, and you'll be happy to know that the first GD4s are coming off the line. Only enough for two companies, but you and Gallagher are gonna be the company commanders who get 'em. Figure it's the least I can do to say thank you."

Again, Vega was surprised. "Th—thank you, sir."

Gallagher frowned suspiciously. "Sir, we're not company commanders."

"Yes, you are—Lieutenants." McNeil leaned back in his chair and let out a long breath. "I wish I could say that this is good news—and it is, in a sense—but you two are being promoted as much because we need lieutenants as anything else. We lost a lot of good people out there when the EMP hit, and the Keepers are spread too thin to be able to get replacements from elsewhere. We lost Lieutenants Gnaizda, Giughan, and Lemish, so Goodier's taking over Company 2, Gallagher, you're getting Company 6, and Vega, Company 7's yours."

"Yes, sir," Gallagher said.

Vega said nothing, and McNeil obviously noticed Vega's sudden discomfort, and prompted him. "What is it, Lieutenant?"

"Nothing, sir, I just—" He decided to take some of the drink. It smelled like lighter fluid, and a quick sip indicated that it would have to improve tremendously to taste that good. His throat burned, and his brain felt like it had been rattled around inside his skull.

Grinning, McNeil said, "That shite packs a wallop, doesn't it?"

Vega tried to say, "Yes, sir," but it only came out as a croak. He cleared his throat, then said, "I was just thinking about Pup, sir. Er, Private Momoa. He was always looking forward to the next BAG. He was really juiced for the GD4s."

"Momoa was one of the ones we lost, as I recall."

Surprised that McNeil would remember the name of one of the many privates who died in the engagement, Vega said, "Yes, sir, he was. He was a good soldier, sir. We'll miss him."

Raising his glass, McNeil said, "To Private Momoa— and all the others who fell."

For that, Vega was willing to choke down the drink once more.

ELEVEN

"The thing that strikes you the most about living in a Yellow Zone, though, isn't really what you expect."

Penny Sookdeo sat at her desk, watching the large-scale holo of Annabella Wu in the center of her office. The reporter had a perfect voice for this sort of thing: soft, pleasant, not too throaty, not too high-pitched. It was ideal for conveying information, and for setting the listener at ease. Combined with her face, which was attractive without being threateningly beautiful, it was easy to see why she was one of Penny's better on-cam personas.

Still, the one criticism Penny had had of her was a lack of *gravitas*. It was a minor complaint—most W3N news didn't require any kind of *gravitas*, after all—but it was still holding her back a bit.

The holo changed to a variety of scenes that matched Annabella's words:

"Yes, there is terrible overcrowding"—Penny saw an office that was jammed full of people trying to work— *"and massive restrictions on what you can wear, or where you can go, or what you can eat."* Two people climbing into jumpsuits. *"GDI troops are everywhere."* Troops walking down an Atlanta street. *"Weather is more dangerous than the worst tornados and hurricanes*

and earthquakes of the PTE, as ion storms damage property"—a view of a screen showing an ion storm, followed by a pockmarked street—*"and rad showers kill vegetation easily."* A sped-up view of a sapling being slowly choked and killed by infested rain. *"Illness is commonplace, and Tiberium poisoning can happen under the most mundane circumstances."* An image of someone with sores from Tiberium poisoning. Then it cut back to Annabella. *"While I was not allowed to bring my cam into the hospital, I did witness a person who ingested Tiberium die when his stomach ruptured and I saw a thirteen-year-old boy whose body was being eaten away by Tiberium."* Now a view of a house that was surrounded by armored guards, with Tiberium infestation visible on some of the ground around it. *"This house was overrun by Tiberium, and its dozen inhabitants infected due to a faulty shutter. But none of this is news to anyone who is paying attention. While the immediacy of it can be overwhelming, it is not what one comes away with when one is in Atlanta."*

Now the images jumped around from a bunch of children playing *bocce* to a group of musicians on a stage to a crowd of people enjoying dinner. *"These people's lives are devastating in ways that can seem unimaginable to those of us fortunate enough to live in a Blue Zone, but they also continue to* live those lives. *Children finishing their* bocce *game when they know an ion storm is imminent. Musicians sharing their art. People enjoying each other's company."* Now the mayor's office. *"Mayor Moné Liebnitz is as tireless a public advocate as you're likely to find. It would be easy for him to give up, to accept defeat and simply go through the motions. But he continues to fight for his constituency. GDI soldiers are fighting their third war against Nod right now, but to*

Moné Liebnitz, that's a secondary concern, because he's still fighting the same war humanity has been fighting since 1995. And he's fighting it with dignity, he's fighting it with honor, and he's fighting it with spirit. And as long as people like him and his staff continue to fight, there's a very good chance we'll win."

Then an image came up of a computer rendering of a male face. *"Of course, the war may be fought closer to home than Mayor Liebnitz is expecting. Yellow Zones are generally a hive of Nod activity—most of their strongholds are in Yellows, after all—but Y-6 in general and the southeastern coast in particular have generally stayed free of Nod's influence. I say generally because this man approached me at my hotel and tried to recruit me to Nod's cause."* Back to Annabella herself. *"Naturally, I turned him down. He argued that Tiberium was part of the natural evolution of society, but what I saw in Atlanta just tells me that it's no different from any other disease we try to eradicate before it kills us. That's what Tiberium is, that's what Nod is, and that's what the good people of Atlanta are fighting against every day."*

Menus to the right of Annabella's recording gave her viewers the opportunity to see other aspects of the story, including interviews, full coverage of the concert, views of the city from a variety of perspectives, the rad shower, the ion storm, and more, but Penny didn't bother with those. She had seen what she needed to see.

"What did you think?" asked a soft, pleasant, not too throaty, not too high-pitched voice from the other side of the office.

"I like the fact that you kept the Nod guy's face on so long. Too bad you're cutting that part."

Annabella blinked. "What?"

Penny smiled. She'd been waiting for something like

this. "You're cutting out everything about the Nod recruiter. Instead, we're giving it to GDI."

"What!?" Annabella rose to her feet.

Having expected this reaction, Penny said, "Calm down, Annabella. This is good for you, too."

"We're *censoring* it?"

"No, we're letting the professionals know that Nod's getting active in Y-6 again and they need to deal with it."

Throwing up her hands, Annabella said, "So, what, we just turn this over to GDI? That's *completely* wrong, Penny! Our job is to report the news, and this is *definitely* news."

"Yes, it is. It's also something GDI would really like to know and do something about."

"That's their problem," Annabella said harshly.

"No, it's ours. Sit down."

"Penny—"

Leaning forward in her chair, Penny said, louder: "Sit down and shut *up*."

Annabella, for the first time, seemed to notice that Penny wasn't in a mood to be trifled with. To be fair, Penny hadn't really put on her game face, as it were, until now. She had expected Annabella to react negatively, after all.

After Annabella fell into rather than sat in the guest chair, Penny folded her arms on the desk. "A free press also means we're free *not* to run something, especially if it serves the greater good."

"And how are we serving the greater good by—"

Letting out a breath through her teeth, Penny said, "If you'll stay shut up, I'll tell you."

"Sorry." Annabella didn't sound remotely apologetic, but Penny let it pass.

Penny leaned back. "Let's say we run the story as is.

Here's what happens: GDI finds out at the same time as everyone else that Nod's stepping up recruiting in Y-6. Not too surprising, they've been stepping up recruitment all over since they blew up the *Philadelphia,* but Y-6 is mostly on GDI's network. Still, if GDI finds out at the same time as everyone clicking on W3N, they get hacked off at us for not sharing it with them. Plus, of course, *Nod* sees it and they lock down further and they're harder for GDI to trace. *Plus,* GDI is wary of us and may start cutting off access or just generally making our lives miserable.

"All of this," Penny added quickly before Annabella could interrupt again, "in order to preserve something that *isn't actually part of your piece.* Watch it again, Annabella. You're talking about heroic people there, and then you branch off into something completely different that's really about *you,* not the story."

In a tight voice, her arms folded defiantly across her chest, Annabella asked, "So what happens if we don't run it?"

"I have a friend in Giddy-Up's In-Ops. She can take this and use it to try to trace Nod quietly, with a minimum of fuss."

A light started blinking on Penny's holo, indicating that she had an incoming link. Reaching up to touch the light, she saw who it was from and chuckled. "Speak of the devil, this is that friend now."

"Hold on," Annabella said before Penny could activate the link. "I haven't agreed to let you do this to my story, yet."

Penny was getting tired of this. "You don't *get* to agree to anything. You did this story as a W3N employee using W3N clearance and W3N equipment. It isn't your story. It's our story." She touched the hold light, which would let Telfair—or, more likely, one of Telfair's adjutants—know that she couldn't take the link yet. "I realize this has never come up before, but that's the way it is. And what's more, you *know* that. You're just hacked 'cause this is something that happened to you."

Annabella shook her head. "It isn't *just* that, I—" She let out a long breath, and slumped in the chair. "Okay, it *is* that. This guy tried to come into my *room*, Penny! And he was bigger than me, and I was exhausted, and if he *had* tried anything physical, which, Goddess bless, he didn't, but if he had . . ." She trailed off and shuddered before finally saying: "I don't know what I would've done, to be honest, but it probably would've involved a lot of screaming and trying to run away very fast. And then there was the whole ficken decon procedure after that and—" Letting out a burst of laughter, she shook her head. "I'm sorry."

Giving the reporter a look she hoped was encouraging—Penny wasn't sure it worked; she was better at intimidation than encouragement—she activated the link. A display with the GDIUP logo and the words HOLD PLEASE appeared over the desk.

Then, moments later, the pleasant Asian features of Sandra Telfair appeared. *"Penny, how've you been?"*

"Insane as usual. Too much news, not enough net space."

"I wish I could say I sympathize. Look, Penny, it's always good to hear from you, but you might have heard that there's a war on, and I—"

"Sandra," Penny interrupted, pointing at Annabella, "this is one of our reporters, Annabella Wu."

"I recognize her. Pleased to meet you, Ms. Wu, but I'm afraid—"

"She just came from doing a story in Y-6. While she

was there, someone from Nod walked up to her in her hotel and tried to recruit her."

Telfair started to speak, then stopped. *"They're recruiting openly in Y-6?"*

Annabella squirmed in her seat. "Well, they tried to recruit *me* directly, but to do it, they had to have access to the hotel's base, which probably means someone gave it to them."

Nodding, Telfair said, *"Yeah, probably. You have a recording of this?"*

"He was jamming it, but I have a physical description. And he wasn't using an imager."

"How do you know that?" Telfair asked, more than a little snidely.

Undaunted, Annabella said, "Because I use one every day, and I know how fuzzy they can be at the edges. Trust me, this was his face."

"Fine. Let's see it."

Penny grinned. "Not so fast. W3N will be happy to turn over this information and keep it out of Annabella's report."

Telfair raised an eyebrow, and prompted: *"If?"*

"You let one of my people tag along with one of your divisions."

"We've been over this, Penny. Granger doesn't want a reporter rewriting the code."

"Oh, don't feed me that shite, Sandra. Reporters have followed the military around during wars for ages. You guys have been trying to block this, but think about what it'd do for morale. The soldiers get to be profiled on the net, and the civilians get to see the everyday life of the people fighting the battles, learn who they really are. It'll be good for everyone." She smiled. "And if you don't, then you don't get the Nod recruiters."

"We can find them without you."

"Not if we let Annabella's report go through *in toto*."

Telfair stared at Penny for several seconds. Penny just leaned back in her chair. Telfair had absolutely no choice, and she knew it, she was just stalling while trying to figure out if there was any way to gain the upper hand.

Penny added: "C'mon, Sandra, you know I wouldn't have even linked you if I didn't already know what the answer was going to be."

"I'll have to ping Granger with this. If he doesn't thumb off, it's no deal." She shook her head. *"Assuming he does, did you have a particular division in mind?"*

Chuckling, Penny said, "Funny you should ask. I was thinking one of your two golden groups would be nice: the guys who took Washington and North Africa, or the guys who took San Diego and Madagascar."

"Make it the 22nd. They took San Diego. They're shipping out to Australia, and I think their BC'll be more amenable than the BC of the 3rd. Besides, the 22nd's getting some of our new field weapons, and if they work, it'll be good to get it out there that they do work. Show Nod we can play the propaganda game, too. And, in return, you give us everything on Nod and keep it off the net, right?"

"Absolutely."

"Spicy," Telfair said dryly. *"I'll be talking to Granger in an hour, and I'll bring it up then."* She smiled. *"I should be able to put enough armor on before that to protect me from his going thermonuclear."*

"Remind him what a great person I am," Penny said, deadpan.

"Didn't he try to get you fired once?"

"One of millions. Take care, Sandra, and let me know as soon as Granger thumbs off on it."

Telfair's face disappeared from over the desk, which revealed Annabella staring incredulously at Penny. "You're trading my data for a story?"

"Happens all the time, Annabella. Reporters trade spicy intel that would be harmful to be let out in public for stories they wouldn't get otherwise all the time. Now you should go home, and get some sleep. Maybe take a few days."

"No." Annabella said the word harshly, like she was revolted at the very notion. "I can't go home."

Penny stared at her. "What?"

"I can't go home! I can't go back to my nice little flat with its wonderfully efficient House that I get to live in by myself and keep living here. I need to—" She had shaken her head. "I need to get out of Blue. Let me be the one you send to go with the 22nd." Holding up a hand to stave off Penny's objection, Annabella added, "I know I've got another nine months before I hit my three years, but I'm ready for this. Please?"

About to refuse on general principles, Penny thought about it a moment. Everything she said to Telfair was true, but it was also true that Annabella did the type of reporting this piece needed. It was a natural extension of the playground story and what she did in Atlanta. "All right, tell you what. You do what I told Sandra we'd do, and tell me about the *people* instead of the usual gloss, and it's worth breaking the rules a little."

Annabella let out a sigh of relief. "*Thank* you." Then she smiled. "So why'd Granger try to have you fired?"

"I made the massive tactical error of running something he said when he thought there weren't any cams around."

Smirking, Annabella asked, "So how come it didn't work? Granger's not someone you crack around with."

Penny smirked right back. "He made the massive tactical error of thinking that I don't have friends on the Council of Directors. In any case, as soon as Granger goes ripshite, I'll carve out the Nod parts and put your piece up. I confidently predict it'll have our second-highest clickrate of the year." She didn't have to say what was likely to keep the top spot. Nobody, it seemed, had grown tired of watching the *Philadelphia* explode. More people were watching the *Philadelphia* blow up than Penny would have believed possible. But then, in this fear-filled climate, people were hungry for information—any information—even if it was something they already knew.

Annabella silently stared down at the floor.

For the first time, Penny noticed the bags under Annabella's eyes. "Think you can handle one night in your flat?"

"Maybe." Annabella's tone didn't inspire confidence.

"Well, try it. You're no good to me exhausted. Get a good night's sleep—and maybe a good day's sleep after that—and then we'll send you off to war."

"Okay." She got up. "Thank you, Penny."

Penny nodded. "Honestly, Annabella, you're the best person for the job. So don't crack it up."

TWELVE

Lieutenant Ricardo Vega sat alone in barracks, cleaning his GD4. He shared this space with the other lieutenants in Battalion 4, but none of them were present. He'd had the rank for a week now, while they secured B-14. Ever since the promotion, Vega had taken to wearing his battlesuit sleeveless, the same way Momoa had, out of respect for the Angry Puppy's memory.

He was watching a W3N report on the war effort. Acting Director Boyle was giving a press conference, standing at a metal podium that had the GDI logo emblazoned on the front.

Vega was amused by the fact that none of the reporters asking questions could be seen. All the cams were on Boyle, whose thin mustache looked laden with sweat.

"Director Boyle, do you feel that GDI's victories in North Africa and the confiscation of Nod WMDs is a turning point in the war?"

Boyle smiled. *"The only real turning points in a war are its start and its finish. Until then, we will relish every victory and try to learn from every defeat."*

"I see Boyle got a better speechwriter," said a voice from behind Vega. Turning, he saw that Gallagher had entered.

"I guess," was all Vega said in response.

"Why do you watch that shite, anyhow, Puke?"

"*Will* you stop calling me that?" Vega asked, as he always did when she called him that. He wondered if she'd stop if he stopped complaining about it, then decided he'd never know, because he had no intention of ceasing his complaints about it.

Another reporter spoke up. "*What about the Nod activity near Sarajevo in Y-1?*"

"*I'm sorry, but I do not have reliable intel on the new Nod temple in Sarajevo at this time.*"

Gallagher lay down on her bunk. "What an arse that guy is. Do we have to watch this?"

"Sorry, *Harley's Day* is a rerun."

"Beats the shite outta this tibehead."

The same reporter followed up: "*That's what you said about the Casabad lab. But clearly somebody in the military had the intel.*"

"Wow," Gallagher said, "a reporter with brains. What're the odds?"

"*Evidently,*" Boyle said, "*but one simple communications error is nothing to start a controversy over. The situation has been rectified, I assure you.*"

Vega finished cleaning his GD4 and started putting it back together. "He's just hacked off because Granger didn't tell him about sending the 3rd into North Africa."

"Yeah, well, Granger's the brains of the outfit." Gallagher closed her eyes. "I need a nap. Can we please turn this shite off, Puke?"

Reaching up, Vega touched the holo that made the feed louder.

"Crack you dead, Puke." Gallagher rolled over and put her pillow over her head.

"*Does that mean you're now making all the strategic military decisions?*"

That got Gallagher to take the pillow off. "Oh, *hell* no."

Vega smiled. "This oughta be good."

"Now that's what I call jumping to conclusions."

"We should be so lucky," Gallagher muttered.

"Look, will I be deciding how many tanks to deploy?" Boyle asked. *"What kind of missiles to fire? What color camouflage to wear? Of course not."*

"For starters," Vega said, "the only camo we have is black."

"But I will be involved in all the important decisions from this point forward."

"I really wished I believed in God right now," Gallagher said.

Vega finished putting his GD4 together and stowed it under his bunk. "Why?"

"So I could pray to somebody that Boyle's talking out of his arse."

"He's a politician: He's *always* talking out of his arse."

He was still talking. *"Believe me, Nod will reap what it has sown. And Kane has sown the seeds of his own destruction."*

Gallagher was shaking her head. "I'm gonna throw up."

"Good, then I can call *you* Puke."

The barracks door slid open to reveal Captain Opahle. "How're my favorite lieutenants?"

"Spicy, Cap," Gallagher said. Opahle used to refer to them as her favorite sergeants. "We—"

The holo went staticky all of a sudden. "What the?—" Vega stood up.

After a second, the static faded, coalescing into the Nod insignia.

"Shite," Gallagher muttered, "another ficken pirate cast."

Sure enough, Kane's smug face appeared in place of the Nod insignia. *"Mr. Boyle is correct about one thing.*

Nod will reap what it has sown: the seeds of GDI's destruction. Righteousness has only one allegiance and that is to the oppressed—our Sacred Brotherhood—inheritors of this glorious Tiberium world. Look to the skies, my children, for a new dawn is rising in the east. Ascension awaits the faithful."

The static returned.

"He needs to be killed," Vega said, shaking his head.

"I *told* you to turn that ficken thing off."

Opahle cut Vega's response to Gallagher off. "If you two children are done?" They both clammed up. "McNeil and Hastings want to see us."

"About time," Gallagher said, practically jumping off her cot. "We been sitting on our arses way too long."

Vega laughed. "Fotze, Gallagher, we've only been out of the field for a week."

"A week too long, you ask me." Gallagher followed Opahle out the door, with Vega stepping out behind her. "The more we're out there, the faster this shite'll be over."

Vega, Gallagher, and all the other lieutenants in the 22nd, as well as the four captains, sat in a briefing room, with McNeil and Hastings standing at the front. A holo was showing a map of Australia. Standing up front with the battle commander and the major was a woman who was dressed in fatigues but wore no rank insignia. She looked maddeningly familiar to Vega, but he couldn't place her.

As they sat down, Gallagher said, "Fotze, I was hoping we'd be going to Sarajevo."

"Maybe they'll just send you," Vega said with a grin.

"People," McNeil said, and his voice caused everyone to quiet down, "we have three things to cover here. First of all, we have new toys once again. We have enough GD4s to go around. Not just Companies 6 and 7 will be issued them."

"About damn time."

"The pets get all the good shite!"

Gallagher smiled. "We actually know how to fire 'em, d'Agostino—at something other than our feet."

Before d'Agostino could respond to the slander, McNeil said, "Settle down. When we took San Diego back from Nod, we were able to capture a couple of their rayguns, as well as one Dr. Takeda. Well, Takeda's earning his creds. He managed to figure out how to make it work." McNeil picked up an item off the desk that Vega hadn't noticed. The stock and trigger were the same as on a GD3, but they were under a big, boxy piece of metal. A plastic tube served as the muzzle. From the way McNeil hefted it, the weapon carried a certain weight. "Ladies and gentlemen, I present the EW1."

Captain Henry raised his hand.

Hastings said, "Captain, if you have questions, they can wait until the briefing has ended."

McNeil shook his head. "I know what you're gonna say, Henry. These are ti-powered weapons."

Vega and Gallagher had already known that, but apparently several others hadn't, as a groan went through the room.

"Look, I know how you all feel about that, but we're *losing* this war, and the main reason why is because they can shoot beams of energy and we're still firing bullets. We're a lot better at firing bullets, and they're talking about having the GD5s be able to switch from grenade launching to railgun with the push of a button."

The groans turned to ragged cheers.

"But"—that quieted everyone down—"we need to keep up with Nod if we're to have any chance of winning. That means we need the EW1s. Right now, we've only got enough for one company. Any volunteers?"

Nobody said anything. Sighing, Vega raised his hand.

Gallagher muttered, "You're outta your ficken mind, Puke."

He whispered back, "Don't call me that." Louder, he said, "My guys'll be rated on these things by the weekend, sir."

McNeil said, "You'd better be, Lieutenant Vega, because that leads me nicely to the second part. GDI *finally* freed up an occupation unit to relieve us here"—more cheers from around the room— "so we've got a new assignment. Major?"

Hastings enlarged the holo of Australia. Yellow dots were all around Sydney, with blue dots in the city itself. "After the attack on the *Philadelphia,* Nod invaded Sydney, along with all the other Blues. Unlike the other Blue incursions, GDI forces have only been able to *hold* them off, not *drive* them off. In-Ops believes that Kane's second in command is in charge of the mission for them down there." Hastings touched a glowing bar to the right of the map, and it changed to an image of a blond-haired woman with penetrating eyes. "This is General Kilian Qatar. If our intel is correct and she is Kane's right hand, then this may just be a holding action in preparation for something greater. It's also possible that she's to distract us from whatever it is Kane is doing in Sarajevo."

McNeil quickly said, "But we don't know what's going on there. Anyhow, it's not our problem. Australia is. Assuming existing GDI forces haven't been able to drive Qatar back"—he grinned—"then the 22nd gets to do what it always does."

Captain Henry said, "Pull other people's arses outta the fire?"

Hastings almost smiled. "Got it in one, Captain."

"We'll be moving out in the *Huron* on Sunday morning," McNeil said. Then he walked over to the redhead. "Which brings us to this charming woman. This is Annabella Wu from W3N."

Vega snapped his fingers and whispered to Gallagher, "*That's* where I know her."

"Yeah," Gallagher said, "she's one of W3N's talking heads. And you know what McNeil's about to say."

"She's been assigned by W3N to do a story about the 22nd. Apparently, we've become legends in more than our own minds. People are talking about us, and they want to know who we are."

D'Agostino said, "They're gonna be disappointed."

For the first time, Wu spoke up. "Let me be the judge of that, Lieutenant."

"Ms. Wu is here as our guest," Hastings said, "therefore I expect her to be treated—"

"Like one of our own?" Henry asked.

"No, Captain Henry," Hastings said, "I want you to treat her *well*. Having said that, you are under no obligation to speak to her if you do not wish to be on the record, as it were. However, if you do refuse, please do so politely."

Wu added, "Or not. I don't expect any of you to treat me with anything but disdain."

McNeil said, "I, however, do expect that. And if I hear any complaints from Ms. Wu, the person she's complaining about may not live to regret it. Am I understood?"

"Yes, sir," several people, including Vega, said immediately, followed more slowly by the rest of the officers.

"Good. You're all dismissed except for Vega and Opahle."

Everyone got up. Gallagher leaned over to Vega.

"We're so screwed it's not even funny. Reporters follow-ing us *and* Nod ray-guns? Fotze, we might as well surren-der now."

Except for Opahle, Hastings, and McNeil, everyone cleared the room—even Wu, who presumably went to find someone to interview. McNeil smiled and said, "Looks like I win the bet, Major."

"Yes, sir," Hastings said blandly.

McNeil then explained, "I wagered Hastings that you'd be the first to volunteer."

Looking at the major, Vega asked, "If I may, sir, who'd you bet would volunteer?"

"To be honest, Lieutenant, I didn't think anyone in the 22nd was that stupid."

Sardonically, Vega said, "Thank you, sir."

Opahle elbowed Vega. "Lieutenant."

Hastings held up a hand. "No, no, Captain, that's all right. In retrospect, I should have known better. Lieu-tenant Vega has done quite the job of defying expecta-tions. And I do mean that as a sincere compliment, by the way."

"Thank you, sir," Vega said again. Then he turned to McNeil. "Sir, may I speak freely?"

McNeil nodded.

"Sir, I didn't want to say anything in front of the oth-ers, but—what kind of risk are we facing? If the EW1s are powered by ti-rock—"

"None whatsoever," said a voice from behind him. Vega turned to see Dr. Joseph Takeda entering the room, looking much better than he had the last time Vega had seen him. His dark hair was neatly combed, most of the cuts and bruises had healed, and his thin mustache was neatly trimmed. "Private Vega, it's good to see you again.

Ah, I see it's lieutenant, now. Congratulations. It's well deserved, I'm sure."

"Thank you, Doctor." Vega refrained from pointing out that it was his dumb luck rescue of Takeda himself that had a lot to do with the promotion in question.

"In any event, the guns are completely safe. The only way you can get Tiberium poisoning from it is if it explodes." He smiled grimly. "If that happens, the so-called ti-rot is the least of your troubles. The energy discharge of this weapon overloading and exploding is such that everything in a one-meter radius will be vaporized."

Opahle started twirling her braid. "Uh, Commander, Major—that raises the question of what can cause them to explode."

McNeil looked at Takeda. "Doctor?"

"Only another explosion," Takeda said. "If there's a method of overloading it, we haven't found it, and we looked. These guns are *safe,* Captain."

"See?" McNeil said. "Nothing to worry about." He looked at Vega. "Assuming your people know what they're doing."

"They do, sir," Vega said without hesitation.

Opahle nodded. "All right. We should issue them to Company 7 right away and start their training."

"Absolutely," McNeil said. "Good luck, Lieutenant."

Vega nodded, wondering what he had let himself in for. McNeil and Takeda were trying a little *too* hard to sell the safety of the weapons. From Takeda, he'd expect that, but he'd been hoping for a bit more skepticism from the BC. Vega could also tell that Hastings was a lot less sanguine about the whole thing.

Once they left the room, Vega said, "Captain, with

your permission, I'd like to keep the GD4s issued to Company 7 when we go to Australia."

"Why don't you wait until you've seen the EW1s in action?"

"Learning how to use them isn't what I'm concerned with, ma'am. Qualifying on the firing range is one thing, but in real combat, especially if we're going against Kane's SIC, we need to have familiar weapons as backup in case something goes wiggly—and something *always* goes wiggly in the field."

Opahle seemed to consider the point. "All right. I'll authorize it."

"Thank you, ma'am."

"Any way we can use these things to zap the skeeters?" Bowles asked.

"It ain't a precision weapon, Dish," Zipes said. "But I'm there with you, sib, I tell you."

"No shite, but I still—"

"Close it!" Sergeant Brodeur said. He'd been elevated to command of Unit Epsilon after Vega's promotion, which Vega had been grateful for. It was bad enough Bowles was being cracked by GDIUP because of his family, but Brodeur was a good soldier whom tech had allowed to be just as productive as anyone despite his hearing loss. And even when the tech had failed, he signed on with everyone else and did as well as anybody in taking B-14 back, and better than most. Zipes had been moved over to Epsilon to replace him, and a greenie named Ida Spahiu had replaced Momoa. Spahiu had arrived from Basic the day after they secured the island.

"Ready target!" Brodeur then said. Popadopoulos nodded, and touched a control on a box he was carrying. The rest of Unit Epsilon was down on one knee—several of them brushing away the ubiquitous mosquitoes—their EW1s at the ready.

Takeda had instructed the soldiers on the differences between the EW1 and the various GD-model weapons. These differences were minimal and mostly related to recoil and weight. Company 7 had spent several days practicing with them. Now the unit was going into the jungle outside the town to train against "live" targets, to wit, holos that Geek the Greek had programmed to imitate Nod ground troops. Right now, it was Epsilon's turn, and Vega was supervising it himself.

"And, go!" Brodeur said. Several streams of green energy flowed forward at the holos. A few people fell backward, not expecting the recoil despite using the weapons for several days, and at least two people didn't fire at all.

Brodeur walked over to the two in question: Golden and Spahiu. "Hold!" he yelled. The Nod holos winked out. Brodeur looked expectantly at the two privates.

Spahiu looked up in frustration. "Jammed, sir."

"It's an energy weapon, Private, there's nothing to jam. Let me see," Brodeur said, holding out his hands. Spahiu handed up the weapon.

"Well?" Vega prompted, after Brodeur had looked it over.

The newly minted sergeant then aimed it forward, but nothing happened. "I'd say the firing mech's busted, sir."

In a long-suffering tone, Popadopoulos said, "Lemme take a look."

He jogged over and took the weapon from Brodeur, which left the sergeant to stare down at Golden, who was staring straight ahead. "Private? You jammed, too?"

"No, sir."

"So what's the problem?"

"I ain't usin' no Nod weapon, sir."

Brodeur put his hands on his hips. "This is a GDI weapon, Private. It's been issued to you, and you will become proficient in its use."

"Crack that," Golden said. "This thing's gonna give me ti-rot, and I ain't firin' it."

"It's not gonna do any such thing, Private."

Spahiu then said, "How do we know that, sir?"

"Because people a lot smarter than any of you told us so."

Zipes said, "What, that Takeda crany? He ain't no thing. He just all they got left after they blew Mobius's arse up. The crack he know, anyhow?"

Vega heard someone walking up behind him. His heart sank when he saw it was Annabella Wu. *Fotze, that's all we need.* Two MPs were behind her. They were serving as her escort.

Vega had already given Wu one interview, which was one more than he was entirely comfortable with, but he also felt that if the other soldiers were talking, he should as well. And the interview had actually gone well. But he really didn't want her here now, and he stepped up to her, hoping to keep her from seeing the ugly scene that was about to play out on the testing ground. "Can I help you, Ms. Wu?"

"My drone's been here since the test started, Lieutenant," Wu said with a sweet smile, "so trying to keep me from finding out that Private Golden's insubordinate is pretty much a forlorn hope."

Vega sighed. He hadn't realized her damn remote cam was here. Somebody should have told him.

Wu looked over at the tableau. "And he's not the only one."

Bowles was standing now, as were many of Unit Epsilon.

"Hey, c'mon, we gotta keep up with Nod. With these weapons, we can take 'em down."

"Doin' fine without 'em," Zipes said. "But then, you're a ti-die, ain'tcha, sib? Whole family's gone Kane on us. Stands to reason you'd go too."

"What, the con's lecturin' me? Crack off, Zipes. I'm here 'cause I hate ficken Nod, not 'cause I'm too wiggly to stay in prison."

"That's *enough*!" Vega said. "Ten-*hut*!"

Those who were still kneeling got to their feet and the entire unit now stood at attention.

"What kind of ficken soldiers *are* you people, anyhow? This is just the latest BAG. So it uses ti-rock. So the hell what? Yeah, it's what Nod would do. Know what? It's what we'd do, too. Ti-rock ain't goin' anywhere, so we might as well use it."

"You don't *use* Tiberium," said a voice from behind him.

I don't need this, Vega thought. "No one invited you to speak, Ms. Wu."

"Too bad, 'cause I'm speaking anyhow. I've seen what that stuff can do, Lieutenant. I watched a man who'd ingested Tiberium die in front of me because his stomach literally exploded. I've seen children with ti-rot, and it's a sight you never, *ever* want to see close up. You don't *use* Tiberium, Lieutenant. You try to keep it from killing you. This shite's *vile,* and I don't blame any of your soldiers for not wanting to get anywhere near it."

Vega gritted his teeth. "You know what I like less, Ms. Wu? Good soldiers dying. I've watched Nod use these weapons to slice off people's limbs. The best soldier in this unit is dead because of these weapons, and I want to give some of that back. Like Sergeant Brodeur said, people smarter than us say that these weapons are safe, and we've been ordered to believe them. Any of you don't like that, I'm sure I can find someone to escort you to the brig." Turning to Brodeur. "Sergeant, finish the test. Anyone who refuses to fire will be under arrest for insubordination."

"Yes, *sir*."

Golden was giving Vega a murderous look, but Vega chose to ignore it.

Popadopoulos handed the EW1 back to Spahiu. "Should work now, Private."

"Thanks," Spahiu said, although she held the weapon the way one handled a poisonous snake.

"Ready target," Brodeur said. Popadopoulos nodded.

The Nod holos reappeared. Unit Epsilon all got down on one knee once again.

"And, go!"

More streams of green energy struck the targets. To Vega's relief, nobody fell over.

To his annoyance, one weapon went unfired. Vega gritted his teeth a second time. He liked Golden despite his tiresome hypochondria—which, he suspected, factored into his vehemence against using the EW1s—and he had been wounded in the line at San Diego. And he didn't entirely blame Golden for his reluctance to use a ti-rock-based weapon. Vega shared the apprehension. But he also understood the chain of command, and while Vega didn't have to volunteer, he also thought it was best that his unit be the ones to do it. For Momoa, if nothing else.

But he had already said what would happen if anyone disobeyed. Dad always said the road to a breakdown of discipline was to not follow through on threats.

"Private Golden," Vega said, "you are under arrest for insubordination." Turning to one of Wu's MPs, Vega said, "Corporal, will you please escort Private Golden to the brig?"

The MP saluted. "Yes, sir!"

A deathly quiet came over the clearing as the MP did as he was told. First, the corporal confiscated Golden's EW1, his GD4, and his Nighthawk. Then he led Golden toward base camp at a quick jog.

"Carry on, Sergeant," Vega said to Brodeur.

As Brodeur started the test up again, Vega walked over to Wu. "Ms. Wu, if you ever speak out of turn when I'm talking to my soldiers again, I will have *you* put in the brig. I don't care what kind of access you're supposed to have, the minute you disrupt unit discipline, you become a problem."

Wu started to say something, then stopped. "You're right. I'm sorry."

That surprised Vega. "You're apologizing?"

"I'm not supposed to insert myself into the story. I'm reporting on you guys, not on me. So I broke my own rules in addition to yours." She let out a breath. "It won't happen again, Lieutenant. And, if you don't mind my saying so, it took a lot of *chutzpah* for someone with your relative lack of experience to arrest one of your soldiers like that."

"I have the rank, Ms. Wu. That comes with responsibilities that have very little to do with how long I've been in uniform."

Smiling, Wu said, "Good quote, Lieutenant. I'm going to keep watching the test, if you don't mind."

Indicating the testing area with a hand, Vega said, "You have free access, Ms. Wu."

For his part, Vega walked back toward base camp. He was going to need to explain Golden's arrest, not to mention filling out the paperwork on it. *I just hope this locks off anymore insubordination . . .*

THIRTEEN

Penny Sookdeo took a seat in her office and checked her mail. She'd just finished a tiresome meeting on the subject of ways to improve their subscriber base and clickrates—which pretty much boiled down to "do your jobs better," advice Penny didn't really need—and knew that her mail was going to be full of nonsense she was in no mood to deal with.

Then she saw one of the shells was from the military account GDIUP had set up for Annabella: it was her first report from the field, all nice and edited and waiting for Penny's final review.

One of the best moments in the meeting for Penny had been when one of the officious twits presiding over it—Penny considered it a point of pride that she didn't know any of their names—said, "You know what our viewers would really like to see? Some reporting from the field. I don't mean the usual press conferences with Granger and that funny-looking guy with the hair in his ears, I mean real ground-level stuff. Get one of the brighter faces to do it—Blair or Frank or what's-her-name, the one who did that thing on Atlanta."

"Annabella Wu?" Penny had said, smiling.

"Yeah, her."

"Funny you should mention that," Penny had then

said. "Annabella's just joined the 22nd. She's with them right now, reporting from the field."

The officious twit's face from that point forward had resembled a pickled prune, which had given Penny great pleasure.

Before opening Annabella's report, Penny called up the current W3N feed. William Frank was talking about the Nod temple in Sarajevo and how reports from GDIUP indicated that they'd be raiding the temple very soon, in what officials said could very well be the decisive victory in this war, babble, babble, babble. One of William's greatest skills as a reporter was parroting GDI's gobshite with a straight face.

She consigned William to a flatscreen on her wall, just in case something interesting happened. That wasn't especially likely, but ever since the *Philadelphia*'s destruction, Penny had learned the value of keeping one eye on the breaking news, since she could even be surprised in her own house.

Annabella then appeared in the center of her office. She still had the same qualities that made her a good reporter all along, but Penny noticed that her mouth was set a bit more firmly than it used to be, and there was something behind her eyes—as if she was thinking about what she was saying.

"This is Annabella Wu, reporting from the front lines for W3N." She smiled, though Penny noted it wasn't the vapid smile she used to have. *"Actually, we're not on the front lines yet. As I speak, I'm on a troop transport, the* Huron. *This gigantic plane—and* plane *isn't really an adequate word for it, nor is* transport—*is what takes the 22nd Infantry Division of the Keepers to where they need to go."*

The image had pulled back, placing Annabella in a

corner of the field, while behind her, a plane that looked like a giant condor came in for a landing. As she spoke, several tanks came out of a hatch that opened in the bottom, and only then did the scale of the *Huron* truly become meaningful.

Penny shook her head. *She's right. The thing's huge.*

Annabella went on: "*In the opening weeks of TWIII, the 22nd has received a reputation as Giddy-Up's problem solvers. After the devastating attack on the* Philadelphia, *the Brotherhood of Nod then invaded several Blue Zones. Most were repelled with ease, but the city of San Diego wasn't so fortunate—until the 22nd arrived.*"

Behind her were some satellite images of the 22nd, led by Battle Commander Michael McNeil, retaking the San Diego Naval Yards, as well as some ground-level shots of tanks overrunning the base that GDI had been kind enough to release.

"*In both Portugal and Madagascar, the 22nd continued their good work. I asked the soldiers of the 22nd what they thought was the reason for their success, and got some—interesting answers.*"

A large-nosed man with a mustache and a caption that read MAJOR ALBERTO HASTINGS, SECOND IN COMMAND, 22ND INFANTRY DIVISION appeared. Images of the retaking of San Diego continued to play in the background. Hastings spoke with a British accent: "*We fight by the book—even if that book needs constant revision. But we are professional soldiers, and winning wars is our job. If we don't succeed, then we deserve to be fired—or, in our case, fired upon. The attrition rate for our profession is rather high, it's true, but it needs to be.*"

Hastings was then replaced by a bald man with dark skin and darker freckles under his eyes, the caption identifying him as CAPTAIN RYON HENRY, BATTALION 1 COM-

MANDER. *"We're a team. It's teamwork that keeps us together, and it's teamwork that will keep those ficken Noddies down. These are good people fighting a good fight."*

Now a woman with blond hair and a small braid down the left side of her head appeared: CAPTAIN MONIQUE OPAHLE, BATTALION 4 COMMANDER. *"Discipline. Training. We're soldiers. This is what we do."*

Another woman, LIEUTENANT TERA GALLAGHER, COMPANY 6 COMMANDER, came on screen. She had short curly dark hair and a determined expression. *"We've got right on our side. Anybody who thinks ti-rock is natural is out of their minds. It's a disease that we need to carve out of our bodies before the infection kills us all. And the Noddies are just another symptom of that disease, and that needs to be treated, too. I mean, c'mon, ti-rock's the wave of the future? When you get cancer, that's not the wave of the future. That's you with a death sentence. We gotta treat ti-rock and the Noddies like that."*

"We're right, they're wrong." This was a blond-haired man with intense blue eyes that scared Penny even on the holo. His caption read PRIVATE ALESSIO BOWLES, COMPANY 7. *"It don't get no simpler than that. The Brotherhood of Nod is evil. Period, end of ficken sentence."*

Penny started making notes for Annabella. The first was to talk to Sergeant Bowles some more. *There's a story there.*

Back to Annabella. *"The tenor of most of the responses was along those lines, with one exception."*

"We've been lucky." This was a good-looking young man with dark skin and hair and a genial face. No caption accompanied his three-word statement, and that was all he said before the image cut back to Annabella. Now she was standing in front of a group of soldiers firing what looked like ray-beams from an old sci-fi movie

in the background. *Interesting,* Penny thought, *I thought only Nod had those. If GDI's been developing them, why haven't they said anything?*

Realizing that this was something that would probably have to be edited out when GDI's oversight office got their hands on it—one of the conditions of Annabella's story was that GDI had full approval over all content, which was completely nonnegotiable as far as GDIUP was concerned—Penny made another note.

Annabella was speaking: *"While most of his fellow soldiers were spouting the expected platitudes about teamwork and noble causes, Lieutenant Ricardo Vega, one of the 22nd's company commanders, took a more realistic view."*

Back to Vega, who now had a caption: LIEUTENANT RICARDO VEGA, COMPANY 7 COMMANDER. *"I'm sure most of the guys are saying the usual, and they're not wrong, really. I mean, we do have teamwork, we are fighting the good fight and all that, but—"* The lieutenant took a deep breath. *"I studied history in college, and I've been fighting this war, and, well, we've been lucky. There are no winners in a war. There's just folks who lose a little bit less than the other guy. Wars are lost by smart people doing stupid things. Napoleon invading Russia, the Japanese bombing Pearl Harbor, that kind of thing. Right now, both sides are just losing a little bit at a time, until someone does something stupid."* Vega then broke into a grin. *"I just hope it's them and not us."*

Annabella was now walking across a field showing several soldiers firing those ray-beams. *"Lieutenant Vega's story is an interesting one. He comes from a family of soldiers—his father was wounded in the line of duty during the Second Tiberium War—and he hadn't been with the 22nd for more than an hour when the call came to repel* the Nod invaders of San Diego. Since then, he's moved quickly up the ranks to become one of the most decorated soldiers in a heavily decorated division. But when asked about his accomplishments, Lieutenant Vega is surprisingly modest."

Vega now looking down, his cheeks flushed. "The medals are spicy, yeah, but I don't think about them too much. Mostly I think about the guys who didn't make it. I mean, great, I get a piece of metal or a ribbon I can hang on my dress blues, but that ain't gonna bring Momoa or Kelerchian or Lipinski or McAvoy or any of the others back."

Back to Annabella with the ray-beams. "This, I believe, is why the 22nd has been so successful: These soldiers are realists. They know how tenuous their victories truly are, and how precious. They also know that victory can be taken away from them at any time—if not by the Brotherhood of Nod, then by the very substance over which they are fighting."

Now another soldier, whose caption read PRIVATE IDA SPAHIU, COMPANY 7. "Ti-rock scares the shite outta me. I really hate that Nod attacked right when we were on the verge of figuring out ways to get rid of it. We need to win this war so we can get back to what's important."

Another soldier, an Asian woman with pale skin, a flat face, and a wide mouth appeared, her caption reading SERGEANT EIKO NAKAGAI, COMPANY 7. "I used to be a shield in Tokyo before I joined Giddy-Up. I've faced riots, I've faced killers, and I've faced Nod troops. None of that scares me. Tiberium, however, scares me a great deal. My parents both got ti-rot when I was a child." The sergeant smiled grimly. "You don't worry about the piddly shite after that. Kane talks about how Tiberium will save us, but I watched my mother and father get eaten *alive and die slowly. If that's saving, I don't wish to know from it."*

Annabella again. *"One member of the 22nd has a particular animus for the Brotherhood of Nod, though."*

Now it was Bowles. *"My entire family all joined Nod. I couldn't believe it. They said that Tiberium's taking over, and by fighting it, we're fighting nature. Like that's part of any nature God created. Crack that noise, sib, 'cause I ain't peepin'."* Bowles looked like he had to get himself under control. *"They kept trying to convince me to go with 'em, but I wouldn't have any part of it. That's why I signed up. If I can't prove to them that what they're doing is evil, then I can do what I can to stop it. I'm just grateful I'm with the 22nd."*

Penny deleted her first note.

Now Annabella was standing next to another soldier in the ray-beam field. Penny recognized several of the soldiers who were working with the guns, including Vega.

"One of the reasons why the 22nd is an elite division is because they have been the testing ground for new technologies in the field. I'm here with Sergeant Joshua Brodeur. Twenty years ago—indeed, three years ago— Sergeant Brodeur would not have been able to enlist."

Penny paused the playback, because something caught her eye on the flatscreen report. The caption under William Frank read GDI TROOPS CAPTURE NOD TEMPLE.

Putting William on the main holo, she watched as her employee spoke.

"Reports are coming in that GDIUP soldiers have taken the Nod temple in Sarajevo. However, while Kane is believed to have been present in the temple, he has not been captured. GDI Acting Director Redmond Boyle is about to speak to the press, and we're about to switch to that live."

Penny got up and ran to the main control room.

In the center of the room, a holo was running. The new press secretary for GDI, whose name Penny suddenly found she couldn't remember, was standing at a podium. Penny walked over to her director, Anh DiFillippo. "Hi, boss," Anh said, "fun day, huh? Ready 2," she added to her comm.

The press secretary said, *"Ladies and gentlemen, Director Redmond Boyle."*

As the press secretary stepped aside to let Boyle onto the podium, Penny muttered, "Not 'acting' anymore, I see."

Anh chuckled. "Maybe they realized he hasn't *been* acting like a Director."

"Thank you, ladies and gentlemen of the press, but I'm afraid I only have time for a statement and a brief holo. There will be no questions. Several weeks ago, the Brotherhood of Nod, in a cowardly and unprovoked attack, destroyed the GDSS Philadelphia. *Today, the GDIUP has at last begun to exact a proper punishment for this crime. As of 0600 GMT this morning, GDIUP forces have secured the aboveground portions of the Nod temple in Sarajevo. As of five minutes ago, I ordered one of our orbital ion cannons to be redeployed for a surface strike on that selfsame temple. Kane, the leader of Nod and the man who ordered the deaths of the men and women who died on the* Philadelphia, *is sealed in a basement below that temple, and in thirty seconds, he will pay the ultimate price for that crime."*

Anh's already-pale face went even whiter. Penny asked, "What is it?"

Blinking, Anh turned to look at Penny, and she saw fear in the Director's eyes. "We got a link from Cassandra about half an hour ago, saying a source was telling her that Nod had liquid Tiberium in Sarajevo. If they hit it with the ion cannon—"

Several reporters were trying to get Boyle's attention on the holo, and Anh shook off her shock and said, "Cue 2," which changed the view to the other reporters. They were all talking over each other, but Penny's lip-reading skills were sufficiently good that she knew that at least two of them had heard the same thing Cassandra had.

"*I'm sorry,*" Boyle said, "*but I don't have time for questions.*" He then looked to the side and nodded. A holo appeared in front of the podium a moment later.

Anh's assistant director said, "We're getting a direct link to that holo."

"Put it up," Anh said.

Now the holo in the center of the control room—which was going out to anyone who was linked to W3N live right now—was showing the same view the reporters were seeing, which was from a cam in orbit. According to Anh's status board, which Penny peered quickly at, the cam was on a GDI weather satellite. It was probably the one closest to the ion cannon in question, which was one of six GDI had placed in orbit years ago as a last-ditch weapon.

Looks like Boyle's finally dug his last ditch, Penny thought. "Anh, put up a link on this story to anything we've done in the past on the ion cannons."

"Got it." Anh nodded to the AD, who carried out the instruction.

The cannon was rotating on its axis. It didn't look like much from this distance. Against the backdrop of the planet it was orbiting, it was just a small metal tube. Intellectually, Penny knew that the cannon was a kilometer long, and had enough power to keep the lights on in the entire Western Hemisphere for six months.

Then the cannon stopped rotating, and Penny realized she was holding her breath. *Fotze, some grizzled old newshound you are.*

What at first seemed a trick of the light at one end of the cannon turned out to be the growing glow of the cannon firing up.

If you looked at it very closely, you could actually see the beam of charged particles as it sizzled through the atmosphere, but at a casual glance, it was as if a white beam instantly appeared, linking the tip of the cannon to the ground on Sarajevo.

Penny had seen explosions from orbit before. The really, really big ones, the ones that were the most devastating, as in Hiroshima- and Nagasaki-level big, looked like small bubbles popping from orbit. It was difficult to imagine them as destructive from that remove, and that was one of the reasons why Penny had never liked showing explosions from orbit. It diluted the impact, which defeated the purpose of showing an explosion in the first place. It was also why GDIUP, when it first demoed the original Mark I ion cannons back in the day, used orbital images to show those explosions. They wanted people to look at it and say, "It worked!" rather than seeing several kilometers' worth of devastation and thinking, "This is horrible!"

The explosion that resulted from the ion cannon's strike on Sarajevo was considerably larger than a small bubble, and Penny had no trouble imagining it as destructive from any remove.

Penny had seen all the demos of the Mark IVs when they were first deployed a few years after TWII ended. On their best day, they didn't have that level of destructive force.

Which means Cassandra's source was right, and we just blew up liquid T. Fotze.

"He's gone," the AD said. "Boyle bolted."

Anh snapped her fingers, and said, "Cue 1," and the holo reverted to the podium, which was now empty. The press secretary stumbled forward and said, *"Uh, Director Boyle has some pressing GDI business to attend to. Thank you, all."*

The reporters all blurted out a thousand questions, most relating to the death toll from the unexpectedly large explosion. The press secretary, however, disappeared as fast as Boyle had.

"Cue William," Anh said, and the holo went back to William Frank.

Penny looked over to the desk where William was sitting. To his credit, the reporter—who had also been live when the *Philadelphia* went down—was composed and professional when his cam went live. "Ladies and gentlemen, for the first time since they were deployed seven years ago to replace the Mark IIIs used during the Second Tiberium War, GDI has engaged one of its Mark IV ion cannons. Designed as a peacekeeping initiative, the six cannons send streams of charged particles from orbit to a terrestrial target—"

As William described the cannon by way of filling until someone provided some hard info for him, the AD said, "We're getting some reports in from the field."

"Link 'em to William," Anh said. "Goddess bless, what did we do?"

Penny had no answer. She just put a hand on Anh's shoulder and said, "Just keep the news coming."

She went back to her office, unsure if she'd even be able to look at Annabella's report on the 22nd now.

FOURTEEN

As the world exploded around Ricardo Vega, he said to nobody in particular, "Remind me next time I volunteer for something to keep my ficken mouth shut."

Naturally, Gallagher's voice sounded in his helmet. *"I did tell you that, Puke."*

"Crack off, Gallagher," Vega said as he held down the trigger on his EW1, watching as the green beam sliced through several Nod. Next to him, Bowles had put the railgun attachment on his GD4 and was using it to plow through several more.

GDI had the high ground in this spot in Y-4, in the midst of the Australian Outback, which was good, since half of them had had to abandon their primary weapon.

The good news was that, when the EW1s worked, they worked beautifully.

Unfortunately, the problems that Spahiu was having with her weapon were endemic to the model. According to a lengthy lecture from Popadopoulos on the subject, the shielding of the power source was so thick and the connection to the rest of the gun's systems so fine that the littlest thing sent it out of whack. In the controlled conditions of practice, everything was mostly spicy, with only occasional crackups like what happened with Spahiu.

But in the chaos of the battlefield the EW1s were pretty regularly rattled, and as soon as that happened, they stopped working.

Gallagher and Vega had been sent to this road in order to check out some intel from In-Ops saying that a Nod strike force was in the area. They were supported by three G-150 Mammoth tanks and a Mark 3 Juggernaut UCP, both from local Giddy-Up forces.

As Vega cut through the dozen Nod troops that seemed to just pour out of nowhere on either side of the road, Bowles ran forward, screaming and firing the railgun some more. "Dish, hold the line!" Vega screamed, but it didn't seem to do any good, as Bowles was determined to shoot as many Nod soldiers as possible.

"Fotze." Vega ran forward after Bowles, not willing to let him kamikaze. "Private, get your arse *back* on the line!" he said as he zapped the two Nod who were converging on Bowles.

Bowles took a breath, and then ran back with Vega to the line. "Yes, sir. Sorry, sir."

Ahead of them, the Mammoths and the Juggernaut were plowing through the Nod troops, who were not able to penetrate the armor even with their version of the EW1.

This is no way to run a war, Vega thought. The assault force they were facing was much bigger than In-Ops had indicated, and Vega was starting to think they'd been set up to come after this force in order for Nod to take out the 22nd.

Vega wasn't happy, and if he survived this nightmare, he fully intended to talk to Major Hastings about it.

His EW1 finally gave out right after he sliced through a perfectly good rock.

Throwing it angrily to the dirty ground, he pulled his

GD3 off his chest—he didn't trust the GD4s yet—and fired three grenades at the four Nod soldiers who were advancing on his position.

To make matters worse, the road they were on was taking them dangerously close to the border of R-8, Australia's Red Zone. For the moment, the weather was holding, as the prevailing winds were toward the Red, but the last thing Vega needed was an unexpected rad shower.

Vega watched as one of the UCPs took on a Nod tank. The latter looked like the Sydney Opera House after taking some particularly good psych meds, and its weapons turrets glowed green with ti-rock. The walker, though, did what it did best, shells pounding the sleek curves of the tank until it exploded in a green-tinged plume of fire.

"Stay back from that!" Vega yelled into his helmet. The last thing he needed was the entire company getting ti-rot from an exploding tank.

Then a whine started sounding in the back of his head. At first, he thought the helmet was going wiggly on him—*Dammit, Geek, you said you* fixed *the problem with my big head*—until the whine grew louder and louder, and was very obviously coming from outside.

Within seconds, it grew so loud, Vega couldn't hear anything else, not the chatter in his helmet, not the reports of the weapons, nothing. In part that was because it was also getting darker, even though it was early morning and the sun had only just risen a little while ago.

The weapons had stopped firing, because people were looking up. Vega did likewise.

A giant shape was plummeting to the earth, screaming through the air at speeds Vega wouldn't have believed possible. Vega couldn't make out the shape, as it was consumed by the flames of atmospheric entry.

He checked with EVA, which told him that the unidentified object was on a trajectory to land in R-8 in about two seconds.

Two seconds later, a massive quake threw Vega to the sandy ground. Even as he fell, knowing the battlesuit would cushion the impact, he screamed, "Gallagher, what the hell *was* that?"

"Cracked if I know, Puke."

Then there was more whining in the air, but this wasn't as loud as the first one.

Looking up and toward the Red where the UO landed, Vega saw what looked like nothing more than a buzzing cloud flying right toward them. All the GDI soldiers were horrified—they knew their new enemy was not from this earth, but they were in shock at what they saw when the swarm came into view—insectlike creatures with sharp razors. There were hundreds of them, all dark, all with tapered sides like insect wings, all with faceted plating, headed straight for the battlefield. According to EVA, they'd be within striking distance in one minute.

To his surprise, the next thing Vega heard in his helmet was the voice of BC McNeil himself. *"People, I just got word that after we blasted the shite out of Sarajevo, six UOs headed toward Earth. Our esteemed Director fired on them, at which point the six UOs became thirty-nine UOs, which have all landed on Earth. Do not engage these—whatever the hell they are—but if they engage you, defend yourself as necessary, using whatever force is necessary."*

Chatter was flying fast and furious after that, with the entire division asking McNeil questions he probably couldn't answer. Vega instead linked Gallagher on discreet. "Gallagher, what in ficken hell is going—"

"Dunno, Puke, but I've been serving under McNeil longer than you, and I've never heard him sound like that. Some nasty-arse shite's goin' down. But hey, the tidies ain't doin' shite, either. Maybe take advantage?"

"Works for me." He was about to switch to a general link to order his people to engage Nod while they had their thumbs in their ears, when he looked up again. "Uh, Gallagher, we may have bigger problems."

The UOs started firing beams that looked depressingly similar to those that came from the EW1s.

And they were firing on both Nod *and* GDI troops.

Vega did switch to the general link. "All units, we got new bad guys. Fire on these things, everything you got! Go, go, go!"

Annabella Wu stood behind Battle Commander Michael McNeil in the *Huron*. "Ficken hell, I'm losing control again," McNeil muttered. Then louder, he said, "Memo, link to Granger's people and ask him again when that damned C&C prototype's gonna be ready."

Silverstein sighed and said, "Sir, the answer won't have changed from what it was yesterday. They're still testing it."

"We can ficken well test it in the field. We *need* this." He sighed. "Will someone *please* get the ficken Orcas moving? Our people're getting *toasted* out there."

Annabella's cam was active, of course, and her drone was following the 22nd. In fact, she was probably getting a better view of what they were doing than McNeil was, though she wasn't about to share that. She actually wanted to know more about this C&C prototype he was talking about, but that was for another time.

Right now, she was much more concerned with the third front that had just been added to the war.

She had played Bill Frank's report over and over again, unable to entirely believe it. The report had had a holo attached, which showed the images provided by GDI Sat-3. Annabella found herself punching it up again, rather than watch as the aliens decimated the soldiers she was just starting to get to know and like.

The satellite's images were of the vast emptiness of space, broken only by the blue strip of the upper atmosphere of Earth on the bottom, a small dot in the center, and six more dots on the outskirts. Those latter dots were the unidentified objects that the Jet Propulsion Lab had detected moving toward Earth very soon after the liquid-T explosion in Sarajevo.

Several streams of light issued forth, one from the dot in the center, others from unseen points off the satellite's field of vision. The text display identified all of those as the beams from ion cannons—just like the ones that had devastated most of Europe only the day before.

The cannons struck their targets, and one would have expected to see them destroyed in much the same way the Nod temple was.

Instead, in a process that on this display looked frighteningly like cellular mitosis, the six dots that represented the alien ships (and Annabella felt ridiculous even using that phrase, but what else *could* she call them, especially given what she was seeing on the battlefield?) instead split off into several dozen dots, all of which careened toward Earth at a great rate.

She then switched to Bill's report. *"According to what we've been able to learn, there are thirty-nine UFOs, and their trajectories are taking them to Red Zones. We repeat—and we're still waiting for confirmation from GDI on this—the six objects that were headed earth-*

*ward have now split into thirty-nine objects that are
minutes away from making planetfall in Red Zones
across the planet. At this time we cannot verify this completely, but all our sources are saying the same thing:
each of these objects will land in a Red Zone within the
next few minutes."*

"Ficken Nod," McNeil muttered. "I know this is part
of their plan. It *has* to be."

"If it is," Hastings said dryly, "it's rather a bad plan.
Those aliens are destroying Nod troops right alongside
ours. Besides, Kane's dead, I doubt that—"

"Kane's been dead before," McNeil snapped. "He
said to look to the skies, and we should've listened to
him. Our friend Acting Director Boyle played right into
his hands. It was right after they blew up Sarajevo that
the UFOs moved toward Earth, and firing on them just
made things worse. Make no mistake, Major, we're not
fighting a new war, we're fighting a two-front war."

"Then someone should tell the Nod troops out there,"
Hastings said, "because they're dying, too."

Annabella muttered, "A smart person doing something stupid."

McNeil whirled on her. "I beg your pardon, Ms. Wu?"

"Something Lieutenant Vega said, Commander. He
said that wars are lost by smart people doing something
stupid, and I'm wondering if firing those ion cannons on
the aliens wasn't it."

Hastings shook his head. "I doubt that Director Boyle
would ever be mistaken for a smart person."

Silverstein then said, "Sir, I just got pinged by HQ.
They're recalling the EW1s. Apparently, Takeda's design
had some flaws, and in the rush to get them out to the
field, they missed it the first time. The containment units
start—leaking, sir."

"What impeccable timing," Hastings muttered.

"I'm *so* glad we wasted time, effort, and lives saving his crany arse in San Diego," McNeil said. "Well, nothing to be done now, and Company 7's the only one they were issued to. I just hope they don't start—leaking, was it?"

"Yes, sir," Silverstein said.

"Out there. Or if they do, Vega deals with it."

Annabella shook her head. Golden had been the only member of Unit Epsilon to refuse to use Tiberium weapons, but eleven other members of Company 7 had also refused. Vega had put them in the brig, too. She wondered what would happen now, and what effect Vega's actions would have on the company's morale.

Of course, this assumes they survive . . .

The alien device functioned in much the same way as the UCPs, but it looked more like a giant scorpion, its ti-rock-enhanced beams firing both from the nose and from the stinger in the tail.

As Vega watched, their own UCPs were engaging, but railgun shells seemed useless against the aliens.

One of the beams from the alien walker lanced through the air and hit Zipes. The beam not only sliced through his flesh, but also his EW1, which then exploded in a green-tinged plume of flame.

"Zipes!" Bowles yelled, and started running toward him.

Vega cried out, "Dish, get *away!*"

But Bowles backed off on his own as soon as he saw the green crystal that was already spreading across Zipes's battlesuit and the parts of his body that had been exposed by the alien beam.

Zipes started screaming in agony. As Vega watched, the ti-rot spread faster than he'd ever seen, creeping across his body and his battlesuit like fungus over a tree.

Bowles then walked up to him and shot him six times.

Before he could fire off a seventh round, Vega grabbed his arm and yanked it back. "Are you cracked in the head, Dish? Why'd you?—"

"He was already dead, Lieutenant!" Bowles said. "You saw. The ti-rot was gonna get him, and I'd rather he died at a friend's hand."

More alien beams sliced through the air, making it impossible for Vega to continue the conversation. They both dove out of the way, albeit in different directions. Even as he did, Guthrie's voice sounded in his helmet. *"Lieutenant, my EW1 is—"*

Vega saw a large rock, and started running toward it for cover. "Is what, Sergeant?"

"Leaking, sir. I've already tossed it, but it's leaking ti-rock, and—"

Fotze. "Be careful, and if these tibeheads get too close, throw it at 'em."

"Yes, sir."

Then he tried to open a channel to McNeil, but got no response. *Ficken aliens must be jamming.*

He dove behind the rock, to find Spahiu right there with him. Her EW1 was on the ground next to her. She was staring straight ahead.

"Private, pick up your weapon," Vega said as he took aim at the alien tanks that were right behind the insect-like assault walkers. They looked like manmade tanks but much faster. "Private!"

Spahiu spoke in a very small voice. "Not real."

Turning, Vega saw that Spahiu was rocking back and

forth very slowly. Grabbing her shoulder, Vega said, "Private Spahiu! Ten-*hut*!"

She didn't move.

"Dammit, Ida, get your head out of your arse! You've got a job to do!" Vega wondered how many other soldiers on both sides were similarly paralyzed. These aliens—*and don't I feel totally off-net even* thinking *that?*—were like nothing he'd ever seen before. He wasn't at all surprised that Spahiu was wiggly.

But he couldn't afford for her to stay that way.

"Private Spahiu, the enemy is firing on us! You're a Giddy-Up, and you have a job. What's your job, Private?"

Spahiu said nothing, but she had stopped rocking back and forth.

"What is your *job*, Private?"

"To—to shoot the enemy before they shoot us, sir."

Vega smiled under his helmet. "You got trained by Sergeant Caselberg, too, huh?"

"Yes, sir."

"Now pick up your weapon, soldier, and let's get to work."

"Yes, *sir*," Spahiu said as she grabbed the EW1, took aim for a second, and then fired on an alien walker.

Her beam sliced right through the nose, causing it to fall to the ground. A second later, the walker fell over, making a loud beeping noise.

The UCP then moved in and fired its cannon, not at the outer shell, but the innards that Spahiu's shot had exposed.

A second later, the alien walker exploded.

So the only weapons that work are the ones that leak ti-rock and will give you ti-rot if they're damaged. Typical.

He opened a wide channel. "All units, the EW1s are the only weapons working against the aliens." He hadn't been able to pay close enough attention to see what kind of effect the Nods were having, but since some of the aliens were damaged, and since conventional weapons had been useless, it stood to reason that their energy weapons were as effective as the EW1s. "Anybody whose EW1 is functioning, use it *now,* repeat, use it *now!* If it isn't working, ping Geek the Greek and get him to fix it!"

Gallagher then came on. *"Puke, I'll have my guys buddy up with yours. Bullets work on the insides, so Company 7 can set 'em up. Company 6'll knock 'em down."*

"Didn't know you bowled, Gallagher. Too bad we don't have missiles."

"We fight with what we got, not with what we don't got."

"Yeah, yeah." Vega opened wide again. "Company 7, you all copy that?" Various affirmative noises came through. "Let's do it." He turned to Spahiu. "Private, you're with me. You up for it?"

Spahiu hesitated. "Not really, sir, but I'll do it anyhow."

"Good soldier. All right, let's go, go, go!"

As they ran out from behind the rock, Spahiu started firing wildly ahead of her, not really trying to hit anything in particular, just trying to hit *something.*

"Easy," Vega said to her. "Use the HUD, find a target."

"Yessir."

"Find anything that looks like a cracked-up insect."

That got a chuckle out of her. "Yes, sir."

As they ran forward, Vega heard a more familiar whine. He linked with EVA, and was pleased to see that the Orcas were finally joining the party.

Gallagher's voice sounded over his helmet. *"About ficken time McNeil gave us some air support."*

"Yeah, but it looks like the bad guys have their own," Vega said, as he noticed a second swarm heading toward them. These "bugs" were smaller than the ones in the first wave of alien tech, but much more numerous.

"Gallagher, Vega, this is Johanssen. We'll take care of the flying bug squad."

"Johanssen, what cracked off-net put you in charge of the Orcas?"

"Natural selection, lay. Watch me work." Vega could hear Johanssen's grin.

The Orcas flew overhead and engaged the "flying bug squad."

Keeping one eye on that battle on his HUD, Vega focused his attention on the two alien walkers that were heading toward them. Spahiu just held down the trigger on her EW1 until it carved through the walker, which was too busy carving a hole of its own in one of the Mammoths.

Vega tried to ignore the screams of the soldiers operating the Mammoth.

The other two Mammoths, having realized that their shells were having no effect on the aliens themselves, started firing at the ground under them, hoping that destroying the ground would work. Vega then ordered his people to focus on anything that was left wiggly by that.

We're ficken sitting ducks out here, Vega thought. The entire area was mostly open air, with few places for cover. It was why it was the ideal spot for Nod to ambush them, and it made it impossible to use any kind of tactics beyond "keep shooting until you can't anymore."

But the aliens had made it from R-8 to the battle in only two seconds, so it wouldn't be long before they made it to any of the heavily populated areas of Y-4 or, worse, B-9.

"Sergeant!"

Vega whirled to see that Spahiu was looking down at her EW1. Following that gaze, Vega saw that green ooze was creeping out one of the corners of the box that contained the ti-rock power source.

A buzzing sound got both their attention. Some of the "bug squad" that Johanssen and his Orcas had engaged had broken through and were heading toward them. They were no bigger than a person. Vega concentrated and fired on them.

So did Spahiu. Only she did any good, as the EW1 beams sliced right through them.

"Dump the weapon, Private, before—"

"No, sir."

Vega whirled on her. "Private Spahiu, I order you to dump the weapon before it kills you."

"I drop this weapon, the aliens kill me, sir. I prefer to go down fighting." She kept firing. Her voice sounded almost disconnected, a dull monotone, as if they were around the poker table.

Her EW1 blew open a few more alien devices that looked like smaller versions of their walkers—more like dragonflies than scorpions. Vega immediately fired on the holes she made, and the machines were destroyed.

Vega had no idea how long they kept at it, but every time he stole a glance at Spahiu's EW1, he saw that the green ooze was spreading further from the corners of the weapon. Bits of it were getting on her battlesuit. *We need to end this and get her to a medic.*

However, that would take more time than she had.

Before Vega even realized it had happened, he found himself surrounded by the hideous insectlike things. He was also almost out of ammo, which was the only reason why he knew he had to have been out here for at least an hour.

Spahiu kept firing and firing and firing, even as the tirot spread up the arm of her battlesuit. Vega fired in her wake, trying to hit what was exposed by the EW1's beams.

Then one of the alien beams sizzled through the air near Vega's head. He fired back on instinct, and said, "Spahiu, nail that thing!"

Nothing happened.

Turning around, he didn't see Spahiu—then realized she was on the ground at his feet.

All but her head, which had started to roll across the sandy ground.

I'm sorry, Dad, Vega thought as the aliens closed in on him.

Then half a dozen of them exploded in a fiery conflagration that blew Vega backward. He landed on the ground, his suit protecting him from the impact. There were still dozens of them around, but this had at least made a hole in their numbers.

He ran.

A person in a Nod uniform said, "Move your arse, heathen, or it'll get blown off."

Vega only hesitated for a second. *Any port in a storm,* he thought, and ran toward the Noddies, firing blindly behind him with the GD3.

* * *

It was over another hour later. It was impossible to say who was winning, but suddenly the aliens retreated back toward R-8.

Vega found himself standing next to a Nod soldier. It wasn't the one who'd rescued him, as he—or she, it was impossible to tell sex in a battlesuit—had been killed five minutes later.

The soldier said something in a language Vega didn't speak.

"If you're saying this is some crazy shite, sib, I'm right there with you."

"My English not good," the soldier said. "But agree is very cracked up."

Vega turned to look at the soldier. "Why'd you fight with us?"

"Was ordered to. Besides, is *our* world. Humans. Not them. Why you fight with us?"

Grinning, Vega said, "Didn't have much choice." He hesitated. "I'm going to find my people. And next time . . ."

"Next time, I kill you, heathen."

"Just as long as we understand each other," Vega muttered as he turned and—making sure the Nod soldiers didn't follow him—ran back eastward, toward where EVA told him Gallagher was. He figured that was as close to a field base as they had until the *Huron* finally came and got them.

On the way, he realized he had to step lightly. The ground was awash in green crystal and liquid alike. The once-pristine ground was pocked with impact craters. Vega wondered how much of it was from actual weapons fire, and how much was from the liquid T that was now spilling all over the Outback, whether from failed EW1s or the innards of the alien infantry.

He was also grateful for his battlesuit, because it kept the odors out. Most of it wouldn't bother him, but Vega knew what dead bodies smelled like, and there were plenty of them to go around, Keeper and Nod alike. Some had been torn apart by energy weapons. Some were riddled with shrapnel from explosions. Some were covered in the green death of ti-rot, which could have come from any one of a dozen sources.

According to EVA, there were only forty-one survivors of the three hundred GDIUP troops assigned to this detail. None of the Orcas made it back, though they had also taken out a good chunk of those little bugs that had almost taken him and Spahiu out.

A sudden wave of nausea overcoming him, he used EVA to track Spahiu. He ran over to her decapitated body, saw the ti-rot that had already claimed the entire left-hand side of her corpse. Of her head, there was no visible sign, though EVA tracked it to a spot about half a click away.

Leave it to body pickup, he thought, and kept on toward Gallagher.

Then EVA informed him that the *Huron* had landed. When he arrived, he saw McNeil, Hastings, and Opahle waiting for him.

"You did good work," Opahle said after returning Vega's salute.

"Thank you, ma'am, but we owe a lot to Nod."

"I *beg* your pardon?" McNeil said.

Gallagher was running up to them. "Lieutenant Vega's correct, sir. The Noddies were fighting alongside us. Without them, we'd all be worm food right now."

One of the nearby soldiers cried out, "Sir! Nod on approach!"

Vega turned to see a single Nod ground vehicle, which looked like an old Volkswagen Bug with body armor and truck wheels, heading toward them. However, it wasn't running the Brotherhood of Nod flag. Instead, it bore a white flag: the universal signal for a truce.

"Let 'em through!" McNeil said, though Vega detected a not-so-subtle undertone of reluctance.

The vehicle pulled up to the *Huron*. About a dozen GD3s and two or three EW1s were trained on it as it came to a halt.

When the doors opened, three Nod soldiers with rifles of their own popped out, along with a woman wearing a major's ti-too, and no headgear.

She looked right at McNeil. "You are Battle Commander Michael McNeil?"

"Yes. And you have fifteen seconds to give me a good reason not to blow you back to whatever hell spawned you people."

The major cocked her head and smiled. "Very eloquently put, Commander. My name is Major Kumato, and I have a proposal."

"Make it a fast one. You now have eight seconds."

"My people are willing to die for their cause, Commander McNeil, so I will ignore your tiresome posturing. These alien creatures, wherever they came from, are no friends of ours."

His arms folded defiantly, McNeil said, "I dunno. Looks to me like they share your love of ti-rock."

"It is true that the invaders seem to have tamed Tiberium in ways we can only dream of. But they also have viciously attacked us, and they do not seem to care about our ideological differences. And if they do not, then we cannot afford to, either."

"What are you proposing?" McNeil asked, though Vega had figured it out, so he couldn't imagine that McNeil hadn't.

"A truce—one that lasts long enough for us to eradicate these aliens. Failing that—at the very least, cooperation in destroying the towers these things are constructing."

"Towers?"

Kumato gestured, and a holo sprung up next to her. It provided a map of the world. Most of the landmasses were denoted within a neutral brown color, except for the regions GDI had designated as Red Zones. This being a Nod map, those regions were indicated with a Tiberium-green. The eight Reds (or, in this case, Vega thought darkly, Greens) had black dots in them: four in the central United States in R-7; six in R-6 in the northern region of South America; five in R-2 in central Africa; two in R-5 in the South Pacific; four in central Australia in R-8; five in R-4 in southern China; six in R-3 in western Asia; and a rather distressing seven in R-1, which covered southern Europe and northern Africa, and was also in the region where Tiberium was first discovered.

"Each of those dots represents a tower being constructed by these aliens. Both your troops and ours have attempted flyovers, only to be shot down. However, I believe that our combined forces can destroy the towers. I don't know what they're for, but since they went to the trouble of attacking us in the hopes of keeping us from noticing . . ."

"I can't authorize any kind of truce, General," McNeil said, "and neither can you."

"With Kane's death," Kumato said, "General Qatar is in charge now. She has authorized my approaching you."

"You expect me to believe he's really dead *this* time? For that matter, you expect me to believe Qatar's okay with this?"

"I understand why you of all people are skeptical, Commander, but we don't have time for this. I speak for the Brotherhood now. My troops will attack the towers with or without your help. With your help, humanity stands a better chance of survival."

McNeil still stood with his arms folded. "Give me a minute." He then gathered Hastings, Opahle, Gallagher, and Vega close to him and out of earshot of the Nod troops. "Thoughts?"

Vega hadn't expected this opportunity to speak up, but he also knew that any objections were best raised in private. He said, "Sir, the only reason any of us are still alive is because the EW1s were the only effective weapons against the aliens *and* because the Nod soldiers helped us. I spoke briefly with one of them, and he said that they didn't want to be invaded any more than we did."

"Lieutenant," Hastings said, "the EW1s are being recalled. They don't work."

"They *do* work. Yes, they leak and they kill you if anything on it breaks"—unbidden, the images of Spahiu's decapitated body and of Bowles killing Zipes before the ti-rot could take him slammed into Vega's consciousness, but he thrust them out and continued speaking—"but they're also all we got. Maybe this can be a step toward actually achieving peace of some kind."

"You want to make *nice* with these tibeheads, Puke?" Gallagher said.

Quietly, Opahle said, "That *is* what the P in GDIUP stands for, Lieutenant."

McNeil looked at Hastings. "What do you think, Major?"

Hastings tugged at the ends of his mustache. "I think we've seen enough death for one day. But I also think we'll see more if we don't remove those towers from the field of play."

He turned to Opahle. "Captain?"

Opahle started twirling her braid. "She's going out on a limb, sir—and that limb is an olive branch. We should take it."

To Gallagher, he said, "Lieutenant?"

Gallagher said, "Sir, we only have her word for it that those towers even exist."

"No, actually, we don't," McNeil said. "Before we lost contact with In-Ops, they told us about those towers. The map they linked to us is a perfect match for what Kumato just showed us. What's more, the towers are surrounded by force fields of some kind."

Vega shook his head. Force fields were the stuff of science fiction he had read and watched as a kid. *Yes, so are ray-beams. Accept it.*

McNeil went on: "If we take out those force fields, we can nail the towers with the ion cannons. But somebody needs to go in there and take out the generators."

"Sir," Vega said, "we stand a better chance of making it to those generators if we use the EW1s—and if we fight alongside Nod."

Gallagher added, "Even if Lieutenant Vega's right, sir, we shouldn't trust Kumato as far as I can throw the *Huron.*"

"Oh, trusting her doesn't even enter into this, Lieutenant, believe me." McNeil unfolded his arms. "All right."

He turned and walked back toward Kumato. "The aliens have kept us out of touch with my superiors, so I can't authorize anything beyond here and now—but here and now, I say, for the sake of humanity, let's take these aliens down."

FIFTEEN

Company 7, along with a regiment of Nod soldiers, took the lead on the attack on the towers. There wasn't time to retrofit any of the UCPs or air support with the EW1s, so instead Vega and his people rode the two remaining Mammoth tanks into the Red Zone. With silent apologies to Momoa, Vega had changed into the full battlesuit, with every body part covered. That was the only way to enter a Red.

As it was, this would be a suicide mission for most of them. One rent in a battlesuit, one hole in a tank, one hull breach in an Orca, one exposure of the inside of a UCP, and that was it—the ti-rot would happen sooner rather than later. As it was, whatever equipment they brought into the Red would have to be destroyed once the op was over to avoid contamination.

Assuming, of course, they lived through it.

The Nod vehicles and aircraft that accompanied them were sleeker in design, going for curves and points where GDI tended toward a boxy, angular style. It certainly made it easy to tell who was who which, if nothing else, cut down on "friendly fire" incidents, since there was no mistaking a flat, squared-off Giddy-Up tank for the triangular Nod ones.

Vega sat quietly in the Mammoth alongside Balidemaj, Bowles, Ndoci, Simon, and, to his surprise, Gallagher. Brodeur, Guthrie, Ellis, Kahrl, Minaya, and Nakagai were in the other one. There were only a dozen EW1s left, and only eleven people from Company 7 who were rated on the things and weren't either in the brig or dead. Gallagher, it turned out, had trained herself on the EW1s back in Madagascar, a fact confirmed by Guthrie. She said it was because she wanted to be ready in case she found herself with only an EW1 standing between her and death.

"Thanks for coming, Gallagher," he had said to her as they boarded the Mammoth.

"What, you think I'm gonna let you get all the glory, Puke?" she had replied with a cheeky smile.

"Don't call me that," he had said automatically.

Vega had written a letter to his father, and asked Memo to link it when and if the jamming was ever broken. Bowles had done likewise to that PI he'd hired, telling her to keep up the search even if he died, but now if she found Bowles's family, to tell them how he died.

The surprise was that Bowles was coming at all. When McNeil had described the mission to the entirety of what was left of the 22nd, it was put in terms of a call for volunteers, not an order, since he knew that plenty of Keepers would be uncomfortable working with the enemy. Vega would have put Bowles at the top of that list.

Bowles had said, "Didn't you notice? Those feckers are using ti-rock. Hell, I heard someone telling Opahle that their armor was made of a 'Tiberium composite,' whatever the hell *that* is. Don't you know what that means, Lieutenant?" Before Vega could answer, Bowles had said: "They brought that shite here! *They're* the ones responsible for *all* this hell we been livin' since '95. And if it means blowing them away, off our world, I'll fight along Kane his own cracked self."

"Okay." Once Bowles had explained it, Vega understood. "So what'd you write to the PI?"

"I named her as the beneficiary of my pension," Bowles had said. "So she'll be able to keep workin' on it."

Vega supposed that was as close as Bowles could get to leaving his pension to his family. "Look, Dish, about Zipes—"

Defensively, Bowles had said, "You gonna toss me in the brig?"

Shaking his head, Vega had replied, "No. I wanted to apologize, actually. You did what you thought was right, and it's not as if Zipes was gonna make it out of there alive." The image of Spahiu's head slowly rolling on the Outback earth came back into his mind.

"Thanks, Lieutenant," Bowles had said quietly.

Now they were approaching R-8. No one spoke in the Mammoth, not that Vega could blame them.

The tank's driver, a surprisingly cheerful lieutenant named Neil Albert, said, "Comin' up on it, kids. We've now entered R-8."

"Shouldn't there be a fanfare or something?" Bowles asked.

"Yeah," Ndoci said, "like the lights all going dark or something."

Balidemaj chuckled. "We should all look fish-eyed now."

Albert said, "We'll reach the first tower in ten."

That was quick. Vega looked at Gallagher with a questioning glance.

"Whatcha lookin' at me for, Puke? It's your company. I'm just appended."

"You're the senior lieutenant, Lieutenant," he said with a small smile. "I'd say it's your op."

"Fine. Everybody, move it! We've got aliens to boil!"

Annabella had been given a few extra drones for this assignment, and she had sent one of them in with the 22nd, knowing that it would be destroyed before it would be allowed to leave R-8, but she set it to link to GDI's satellite as it went.

Living in a Blue all her life hadn't prepared her for the ugliness of life in a Yellow. Spending three days in a Yellow, though, she had thought that she understood the true effect of Tiberium on the lives of the people of Earth.

She had seen pictures of Reds, of course, and film. Everyone had. They were the first things they showed you in school, making sure kids knew exactly what kind of world they were living in.

But that didn't prepare Annabella for what she saw in the images the drone was sending her now, standing in the small corner of the flight deck of the *Huron* that Hastings had assigned to her.

She had seen Atlanta after a rad shower and after an ion storm, and she had seen what Tiberium could do to people at Laubenthal Memorial Hospital, but that didn't prepare her for the way the land in R-8 had been corrupted.

It was like the arm of the teenager with the green death, only a thousand times worse. Entire acres of land that was once covered in grass and trees were the sickening green hue of Tiberium. What few trees were left were decaying and rotting and crystallized. The sky was a dark purple color as ion storms swirled and rad showers pelted the dying ground. A miasma hung over the entire area.

Nothing grew here.

Nothing *lived* here.

Except the aliens, who seemed to be thriving in it.

The 22nd started to engage the enemy, protected by their battlesuits, which had been sealed tighter than a drum against the Tiberium that was in the very air. They were now all standing on the edges of the two G-150 Mammoth tanks and firing their EW1s at the aliens, who were firing right back. Alongside them, the Nod troops were doing likewise, and behind them, two more tanks, and half a dozen Orcas were providing backup.

Annabella wasn't sure how she felt about GDIUP troops fighting alongside the same people who blew up the *Philadelphia*. She was, however, completely sure of two other things: that she liked the idea of the planet being overrun by aliens with a proclivity for Tiberium even less, and that she was sick of watching people shoot each other. She now understood why Penny didn't let anyone cover combat until they'd been working for three years, simply because they would lose any greenies who went straight into this nightmare.

"Greenies"? Great, now I'm talking like a Giddy-Up.

To distract herself from the carnage, she linked to W3N's current feed. Bill Frank was talking to some crany or other—a west-Asian woman with her hair done up in a bun.

"Here to shed some light on these enemy structures is Dr. Emel Ibrahiim, Research Manager of GDI's Future-Tech Lab."

Annabella sighed. Of course, they were talking about the fight against the aliens. What else *would* they be talking about? For centuries, humanity had dreamed of first contact with aliens, everything from peaceful coexistence to misunderstanding leading to conflict to an out-

and-out invasion. Like most people, Annabella had lived in fear of the latter being the case, and now an entire species' worst fear was actually happening.

"First of all, Dr. Ibrahiim, congratulations on your escape from Munich."

Ibrahiim smiled. *"Thank you, William. It was most harrowing."*

A link came up on the flatscreen Annabella was watching, from which one could watch the report on the rescue of Munich.

"I can only imagine . . . Now what can you tell us about these strange Red Zone towers?"

Leaning forward in her chair, Ibrahiim said, *"As with everything involving invaders, Tiberium is key. They utilize the green crystal in ways we cannot imagine. We know, for instance, Tiberium fuels their craft and weapons, and we know these towers are made from Tiberium composite material. What we do not know is purpose of towers. We have only theories."*

Very useful, idiot. Annabella thought, then retracted the thought as uncharitable. She knew all this already, but she'd also been following BC McNeil around for a week.

"Fascinating," Bill said. Annabella smiled, because he sounded genuinely fascinated, even though Annabella knew for a fact he had no interest whatsoever in science. *"And just what are those theories?."*

"Could be Tiberium refineries, missile silos, even planetary destruction system. Need to get closer—not so easy."

Annabella turned to look at the drone's feed. She could see Vega and Gallagher, right at the forefront of one of the Mammoths, leading the way. The aliens were giving as good as they got, and Annabella couldn't help but notice that there were three fewer members of Company 7 hanging onto the sides of the tanks. *No, Dr. Ibrahiim, not easy at all,* she thought. And the 22nd weren't there to study the towers, but to destroy them.

A month ago, Annabella would've been repulsed by the very idea of destroying the first aliens who made contact with Earth. She was still repulsed by the idea of doing it with Tiberium-powered weapons, but she understood the need for it.

Bill said, "*No, not so easy at all. Thank you, Dr. Ibrahiim,*" then turned to face the cam. "*Whatever these towers are I think it's safe to say they were not built for the benefit of mankind.*"

At that, Annabella rolled her eyes. As closing statements on a report went, that ranked down around the bottom ten of Bill's career.

The next report was from Cassandra Blair talking about another Giddy-Up regiment that had had success against a tower in R-1 in Rome. Annabella turned it off. *This isn't an improvement.*

Of course, she could go through and pick and choose a story to watch, but she suddenly found herself as disgusted by the very concept of the news as she was by the notion of watching more combat.

Yet she found herself suddenly riveted as a G-150 plowed through the alien forces. It was like watching bug spray in action, and Annabella quickly grabbed her Hand and made a note of that simile.

Only four people were left on the tanks by the time they made it through the final line of defenses the towers had. Once that happened, the Orcas came screaming in and leveled the generators for the force fields. Unfortunately, in order to get close enough to do that, the Orcas had to fly right in range of the alien ground forces, and their Tiberium-enhanced ray-beams, which they fired with a precision that made Annabella wonder if they were fully automated. Three of the Orcas and one of the Mammoths were completely vaporized by the alien weaponry, but the towers were now vulnerable.

"Fall back!" That was Vega. *"Generators down, fall back, back, back!"*

One of the other soldiers in the flight deck said, "Ion cannons in position, Major."

Hastings, who was standing behind that soldier, turned to McNeil, who sat in the center seat. "The 22nd will be out of R-8 in three minutes, sir."

"Then count it down from three minutes, Major."

Annabella turned back to the drone's feed. She didn't instruct it to stay with the Mammoth. It recorded the two tanks that remained, as well as the lone UCP and few Orcas that survived the assault. Almost as few Nod troops retreated as well, though Annabella noticed they went in a different direction.

The three minutes took forever. Several of the alien constructs went after the retreating troops. Others tried to repair the generators. *Fotze,* Annabella thought. She turned around. "Commander, they're trying to repair the generators."

"What?" McNeil got up and walked over to see what her drone was showing. "Hell. Fire the ion cannon now!"

Annabella prayed to the deities, which she hadn't been on the best of terms with since she saw a man's stomach explode in an Atlanta hospital, that the survivors of the 22nd would make it out without being caught in the ion cannon's backwash.

She watched, transfixed, waiting for the cannon's blast.

It came astonishingly quickly. One minute the tower sat there, a giant monolith of green metal—probably more of that "Tiberium composite" Ibrahiim was talking about—reaching for the sky, and the next moment it exploded into a billion pieces as white fire flowed through it and destroyed it.

Then the screen went dark, the backwash having destroyed the drone. *But it would've been wiped out anyhow, and Penny'll love that image.*

The technician said, "A-SAT's reporting all four towers in Australia are down."

Nobody cheered. Too few people were coming back alive from R-8 for that.

SIXTEEN

The *Huron* came equipped with a medical bay that included a quarantine unit for anyone who might have ti-rot. Everyone who was wounded in R-8, as well as the bodies of those who were killed, were all moved into that unit after the towers were destroyed. Of course, the former would be the latter before long. Everyone who was wounded in a Red got the ti-rot in a matter of minutes, because any wound meant a battlesuit breach.

Vega stood at the glasteel window that separated the QU from the rest of the medical bay and watched as Private Alessio Bowles slowly died.

The 22nd's medic, Lieutenant Scheeler, had told Vega he could stay for only a minute, that her patients needed their rest. Vega had thought that the stupidest thing he'd ever heard—they'd be resting permanently pretty soon—but said nothing.

"How you doin', Dish?" Vega asked, knowing as he said it that the question was absurd. Bowles's entire left biceps was a hunk of boiled meat, green slime that could've been infection or ti-rock oozing out of the wound. Bowles was paler than a paper towel, and his eyes were red-rimmed.

"Feelin' great," Bowles said with a ragged smile. "Doc's got me onna *good* drugs."

Vega provided a ragged smile of his own. "That explains your love-hate relationship with consonants right now."

"Crack me entirely, Lieutenant."

"It shoulda been you," Vega said suddenly.

"Huh?"

"After San Diego, you shoulda been made sergeant."

"Been over this," Bowles said. "I'm lucky t'be a Giddy-Up. Rank don't mean shite. 'Sides, I prolly woulda been in R-8 anyhow."

Annabella Wu walked in, interrupting whatever reply Vega would have made to that. "What're *you* doing here?" Vega asked harshly.

"The private asked me to be here," Wu said in a quiet voice.

"S'okay, Vega," Bowles said. "I asked t'do one last innerview."

Looking at Vega, Wu said, "Unless you have some objection, Lieutenant?"

Vega had several, but they were all selfish, so he didn't voice them. "Go ahead, Ms. Wu."

Wu looked at Bowles. Vega recalled that she had a cam in her glasses. "Just start talking, Private Bowles."

Looking right at Wu, Bowles said, "This's a message for my parents, case anyone ever finds 'em." He tried to lift his left arm. "Got wounded in a Red. Like they tol' us in grade school, Red means dead. Got the ti-rot, and that means I ain't gonna live much more. Mom, Dad, Brian, Rika—*this* is whatcha worship. *This* is why our family ain't a family no more, 'cause you guys decided t'worship somethin' that's killed me. Nice goin'."

"Lieutenant Vega, report to the wardroom."

Vega looked up. "I gotta go. You okay, Dish?"

Bowles nodded. "Just gotta do this, y'know. An' hey, Vega?"

"Yeah?"

"If y'get th'chance, find Steph an' thank'er for me. I left a link for her, but I wan' her t'get somethin' in person, y'know?"

Nodding, Vega said, "No problem, Dish."

"Thank you."

It took a supreme effort for Vega to leave the medical bay, feeling quite sure he wouldn't see Bowles alive again.

He arrived in the wardroom, where McNeil, Hastings, Opahle, and Gallagher were all waiting.

"Take a seat, Lieutenant," Hastings said. Vega did so next to Gallagher, and wondered why he'd been summoned just then.

"Okay, people," McNeil said, "the *Huron*'s en route to R-1."

Vega blinked. He hadn't even realized that the *Huron* had taken off.

"Almost all of the towers are down, but there's one still up. The first force that tried to take it down was repelled—by Nod troops."

Gallagher snarled. "I *knew* we couldn't trust that bint."

"We've lost all contact with Kumato," Hastings added. "And EVA's scans picked up a platoon of Nod troops coming into Australia and raiding Qatar's HQ. I suspect that Kane's death has put some dissension in the ranks," the major added dryly.

"Either that, or Kane's actually alive, and is hacked off that his people teamed up with us," McNeil said. "In any case, that alliance is worm food. Which leaves us with

Italy. The 3rd and the 22nd will be leading the charge against the last tower. The 3rd'll be focusing on Nod, while we take on the aliens with our new toys."

"Sir, we're down to only eight of the things," Vega said. "The other four hit critical leakage in R-8. And only three of us still active are rated on them."

"What do you mean 'still active,' Lieutenant?" McNeil asked in a dangerous tone.

Opahle stepped in. "Four people are in the brig. They trained on the weapons, but then refused to use them in the field. And there are a few more in the brig who refused to even be trained."

McNeil closed his eyes. "Shite! Lieutenant, I'm not about to tell you how to run your unit, but what the *hell* are you doing putting that many good soldiers in the brig?"

Vega felt his cheeks get hot. "Sir, they disobeyed orders. I didn't have much choice."

"I support his choice, Commander," Opahle said. "Especially since it was *your* orders they were disobeying."

"So do I, for what that's worth," Gallagher put in. She shot Vega a look.

Vega was blindsided. *Gallagher's supporting me? My feet are icy; it got cold in hell . . .*

McNeil stared at Vega for several seconds, to the point where Vega feared that beams like those from the EW1 would shoot from his eyes and fry him alive.

Finally, he said, "Fine. We're also testing out a new toy. I'm sick of having to run C&C from two clicks away, especially when aliens keep ficken up our comms. We think we've plowed through that, at least, but the cranies have been workin' on something that'll allow us to have a mobile C&C so I can run things from the field. The stuff'll be waiting for us at the staging area in Monte Carlo, as well as the new Dragonflies."

"Dragonflies?" Opahle asked.

Grinning, McNeil called up a holo, which showed something that looked like the offspring of a UCP and an Orca, only it was smaller than either one, based on the image of the person standing next to it to provide scale.

"One-person transport, can move me from place to place as needed. Plus I'll have a full holo view of the entire battlefield. It's based on the tech that gave that deaf sergeant of yours, what's his name—"

"Brodeur, sir," Vega said.

"Right, him—it's based on the stuff that lets him be one of us." Looking at Opahle, Vega, and Gallagher each in turn, McNeil added, "Nothing against the work you've all done, but it does me no good to stand around on the *Huron* with my thumb up my arse. The rank is *battle* commander, and that means I command the battles. It's past time I started doing it, and finally the tech's caught up to the point where I can."

"However," Hastings added, "the equipment hasn't been tested yet."

"Which," McNeil said with a smile, "is *why* I'm glad I have nothing against the work you three have done. Bat 4 is all that's coming with us into R-1. Bats 1, 2, and 3 are needed to provide relief for our forces elsewhere in Europe, so Major Hastings will be leading them there. We're barely holding the line in a lot of places, and Nod troops are getting nasty again now that the towers are down. It's like I said, this is a two-front war, now."

For some reason Hastings shifted uncomfortably in his seat at that.

"You three," McNeil continued, "will be the front line of attack, breaking through the aliens with the EW1s so the Orcas can come in and blast the shite out of them. We got a whole fleet of A50s waiting at Monte Carlo, too."

Hastings added, "The A60s went back to the drawing board. They kept leaking fuel."

"Just what you want in a combat plane," Opahle muttered.

"They have, however, rolled out the G10 Bull APCs," Hastings said, "which have portholes through which you can fire the EW1s from the safety of *inside* the tank."

Thinking of Bowles's dying in the QU from a wound received while standing outside a Mammoth, Vega was grateful for that.

"We'll hit Monte Carlo in three hours. Catch a nap if you can, people, it's gonna be a long day."

As the energy beams from the alien invaders sizzled past his head, Vega realized that he hadn't gotten a good night's sleep since he joined Giddy-Up. He wasn't sure why he was thinking of this now, but the thought wouldn't leave his head, even as he used his EW1 to blast several holes in one of what In-Ops was now referring to as an "annihilator": a giant tripod device that fired from three flexible, coiled turrets that looked like a mix between a three-armed octopus and the hydra from Greek myth.

However, this one didn't grow back another head if you cut it off, as Vega demonstrated when, with several shots near the base of the annihilator with his EW1, he managed to expose enough of the thing's innards for the APC to take it down.

Technically it wasn't his EW1. The weapon he'd been issued was leaking ti-rock all over everything after the first ten minutes, so he tossed it at a Nod soldier who was part of a platoon trying to keep the 22nd from engaging the aliens. That platoon had broken through the 3rd's lines, and had succeeded in killing Golden and Nakagai. Vega was now using Golden's gun.

The time Vega was supposed to have spent napping was instead spent in the *Huron* brig trying to convince someone, anyone, to recant their position and join the battle in R-1. Golden finally had been convinced, as had Mercier and Janssen.

And now he's dead. Like Spahiu, like Dish, like Pup, like—

He cut the thought off. There wasn't time. He remembered what Dad always said: "The first rule of war is that good people die. Accept it, get over it, move on."

McNeil's voice sounded in his helmet: *"Keep moving forward, people. We're almost there!"*

Brodeur contacted Vega on discreet. *"Didn't he say that half an hour ago?"*

"He didn't say it now," Vega said as he took cover behind the ruined superstructure of an old building, the metal pocked green with ti-rock. "It's just a text loop on your readout."

"Hilarious, Lieutenant," Brodeur said.

Then McNeil's voice came back. *"Vega, you've got two floaters on your six. They're behind that ridge. Keefer, Palmer, you two are closest. Take out the ridge so Vega has a shot."*

The aliens were relentless. Every time Vega thought they had taken care of all of them, a thousand more sprung up. *Maybe they are hydras,* he thought as the two Orcas flown by Lieutenants Keefer and Palmer did a strafing run over the ridge behind Vega. He waited until the smoke cleared, using EVA to locate the floaters— In-Ops's unofficial name for the shaggy, levitating things that were only slightly bigger than a human—and then Vega jumped up firing the EW1 at where his HUD told him they were.

"Nice shooting, Lieutenant. Gallagher, firm up over there. You're about to be overrun."

There was only one reason why Vega was still alive and why the 22nd and the 3rd even had a chance of coming out of this with anything like a victory, and that was the prototype. McNeil was able to run the entire battle from right there on the field, and reposition assets as necessary.

Two tanks came rolling up behind Vega, shooting down the remnants of the floaters now that Vega had exposed their insides. On discreet, Vega said to Gallagher, "We done good. Looks like our set-'em-up-and-knock-'em-down idea's working. Especially since we need to limit usage of the EW1s."

"First of all, Puke, it was my *strategy, not yours."* He heard multiple reports from Gallagher's EW1. *"Second of all, all limiting usage does is make these ficken things last longer, and I'd just as soon they were gone forever."*

Vega started running forward, hoping that the power node they needed to take out was somewhere close. EVA couldn't get a bead on it, so they had to keep plowing through aliens—and taking on casualties by the dozen—until they found it.

"First of all, don't call me that, and second of all, these weapons are the only reason we stand any kind of chance."

"No, McNeil's gizmo is why we stand a chance. Every other unit in Giddy-Up did fine without them."

"And had twice the casualty rate." Vega ran past a

burned-out, ti-rotted shell of what was probably once a beach resort.

When he ran past that onto the crystalline remains of the beach, he saw the power nodes.

Looking up, he saw the tower in the distance, which was where the 3rd was focusing their attack. It was huge, unfaceted, dark, glowing, and—there was no other word for it—evil. The tower seemed to come with its own built-in sense of foreboding, and Vega felt frightened just looking at it. He also saw several more devices that obviously belonged to the aliens, based on the design, at the very top of the structure. Were the aliens trying to make it bigger?

Then he realized they were putting a roof on it. *Fotze, it's almost done!*

"Commander, I found the nodes."

"Everybody, converge on Vega, now!" McNeil said. *"Everyone, go, go, go!"*

Several glowing globes—far more than there'd been in R-8—were embedded in the ti-rotted sand. Vega started firing on them with Golden's EW1.

Another stream came from behind him, and his HUD told him Brodeur had joined up and was firing as well.

Two of the aliens came out of nowhere and started firing on them.

Vega dove for cover. Brodeur didn't. The beam cut right through his head, splitting it open like a grapefruit.

"Brodeur!"

Another EW1 blast came from the west, and Vega saw Gallagher taking out the aliens who'd killed Brodeur. That snapped Vega back to reality. *Accept it, get over it, move on.*

Now Keefer said, *"Sir, we've got the nodes painted."*

"Fall back, everyone. Fall back!"

Glancing down at Brodeur's mangled body, which would surely be vaporized by the Orcas' air strikes, Vega only hesitated for a second before running quickly away. The APC—which had been on its way to provide support—was turning around also, and Gallagher and Vega both managed to hop on to its side as soon as it was done rotating, and then it beat a hasty retreat. *These feckers are a lot faster than the Mammoths.*

McNeil then said, *"Keefer, Palmer, they're out of range. Do your thing."*

Vega turned and watched as the two Orcas flew overhead, dropping their payloads onto the remnants of what used to be a beautiful beach in Italy.

As soon as the missiles struck the earth, Vega looked up at the tower. The slight green glow it had had dimmed to an inert black. Even more impressively, the aliens started to fall from the top of the tower.

"All right," McNeil said, *"let's take the tower now. Swann, Greenberger, Bousquet, you're up. Bomb the shite outta that thing."*

As McNeil spoke, the tower started to glow again, this time with a much harsher, brighter green.

Three more Orcas flew through the purple sky, dropping their payloads just as Keefer and Palmer had—but the missiles stopped short of the tower and exploded in midair, as if they had struck something.

"Fotze," McNeil said. *"Another ficken force field."*

Vega almost laughed involuntarily, but locked it down quickly.

Then the tower glowed even brighter, and a green wave of energy seemed to slough off it, like a snake shedding its skin, only the energy wave spread outward like ripples in a pond, heading right for Vega.

He jumped off the APC, as if that would help, only to feel like he'd crashed into a brick wall.

Vega collapsed to the ground in spine-shattering agony, the world went black . . .

EPILOGUE

The next thing Vega saw was a field of white that penetrated the gloom. After a second, he realized that it was the ceiling of the medical bay on the *Huron. How the hell'd I get here?*

"You're up," a voice said. The speaker sounded like she was in a cave very far away. Scheeler's round, pale, freckled face appeared, looking down on him. "How do you feel, Lieutenant?"

Groggily, Vega said, "Feels like there's this gnome drillin' through my skull with 'bout five different kindsa power tool."

She smiled. "Sounds about right."

"Wha' hit me?"

Looking down to make notes on her Hand, Scheeler said, "Cracked if *I* know. It's not like they tell *me* anything."

"How'd I get here?"

"That I *do* know." She set down the Hand. "McNeil saw that all you guys that were close to the big bad monolith were all unresponsive, so he diverted some others to get you, including some of the 3rd. Good thing, too, 'cause they hit it with more air strikes."

"So th'tower's down?"

Scheeler shook her head. "Nope. But the aliens are all

gone. As soon as the power nodes went down, all the alien tech all over the planet imploded. Not even any remains left."

With a supreme effort, Vega made himself smile. "Thought they didn't tell you nothin', Doc."

"They didn't. It's all stuff I overheard. Or I'm lying. Get some rest, Lieutenant. You've earned it."

Scheeler touched something, and Vega felt even more groggy, then fell asleep again.

He woke up to see Gallagher's face. " 'Bout time you woke up, Puke."

"Don't call me that," he said automatically. The headache had calmed to a dull roar. "How long I been down?"

"About a day. We're back in B-2. Apparently there's gonna be a parade."

Vega frowned. Then he remembered what Scheeler had told him. "War's over?"

"Yes," said Gallagher.

"What about Nod?"

"The few we've heard anything from have surrendered, believe it or not. Heard that a platoon went to Qatar's HQ in Australia after we left. Place was completely cleaned out of everything—except Qatar's corpse."

Wincing, Vega said, "That's not good."

"With Kane dead, there's probably factions beating up on factions." She grinned. "Great for us, though, since most of what was left of their best forces were in R-1, and we took 'em out. Well," she added with obvious reluctance, "us and the 3rd."

"Do we *have* to give them credit?" Vega asked with a grin.

"I sure as shite don't plan to. Anyhow, with Kane dead

and Qatar dead, I don't think Nod'll be a problem for a while." She shook her head. " 'Course, the BC's convinced that Kane *ain't* dead. It's some wiggly-arse shite, I'm tellin' ya."

Slowly, Vega turned his head toward the QU. "Dish?"

Gallagher lowered her head. "He died while we were fighting. And we weren't able to get any of the bodies out of R-1."

Vega hadn't expected them to. A tibc-infested corpse wasn't something you took back even to a Yellow, much less a Blue. Brodeur and the rest weren't going to have their remains moved. Besides, the air strikes Scheeler had mentioned had probably vaporized anything they left behind.

"That last tower's still up?"

"Yup. It's pretty wiggly. The thing's gone completely inert. I figure if the war really *is* over, the cranies can take a look at it." She snorted. "Beats the shite outta makin' more EWs."

"We were their swan song, huh?"

"*Oh* yeah. S'like I told that reporter lay, ti-rock's just the shite you fight. You use it, you get burned. Sometimes literally."

Again, Vega winced. "You didn't actually *say* 'the shite you fight,' did you?"

Gallagher chuckled. "Nah, didn't think of it 'til just now. Maybe I should find her."

"Fotze," Vega muttered.

Then he noticed something. The bar on her arm had changed.

"You got promoted?"

At that, she broke out laughing. "About *time* you noticed, sib! Fotze, I thought I was gonna have to shove the new patch in your face. And I ain't the only one, *Captain*.

McNeil'll do the honors when Scheeler kicks you outta here, but you got bumped up. Shite, all of us who made it out did."

Vega couldn't entirely believe it. He'd joined Giddy-Up just a few months ago, in a time of peace, thinking he'd serve his time, maybe become an officer someday. The day he finished Basic and joined his unit, the *Philadelphia* was destroyed, the world was plunged into a war, and now Vega was a captain less than a year out of Basic.

"Listen, Vega," Gallagher started.

That got his attention. She'd always referred to him by rank or as "Puke."

She hesitated, then said, "I owe you an apology. I thought you were just some cracked nep that didn't deserve to even *be* in the 22nd, much less get promoted so fast. Especially after San Diego, when Dish *did* deserve it. But after all we been through—" She put a hand on his shoulder. "You're a good soldier. I'm proud to have served with you."

Reaching up and putting his hand on Gallagher's wrist, Vega said, "So'm I, Gallagher."

Rolling her eyes, Gallagher said, "Oh, fotze, Puke, just call me Tera, will you?" She smiled. "That's what my friends call me."

"Actually, my friends all call me Vega."

"Not Ricardo?" She chuckled. "Or Ricky?"

"*Hell,* no," he said emphatically. "Honestly, I'm okay with Puke. I've kinda gotten used to it. And besides, it reminds me of Golden, y'know?"

They sat in silence for a few minutes. Vega remembered the practical joke he'd played on Golden back on the *Huron* on the way to San Diego, what seemed like a lifetime ago—Golden's lifetime, in fact.

Finally, Gallagher removed her arm from his shoulder, and he let go of her wrist. "I better go before Scheeler descends on me. I'll be there when you get those captain's bars."

"Good," Vega said with a smile.

"Get some rest, Puke."

"Yes, ma'am."

Penny Sookdeo turned her attention from the latest in a series of reports on the end of the war, confirmations that the aliens had stopped being a threat almost as fast as they had become one, and reports of Nod stragglers surrendering to GDI forces, to check the latest link from Annabella.

As soon as Penny activated the link, she winced. On the holo, she looked like someone about ten years older than Annabella Wu actually was.

"*I'm standing in the wardroom of the* Huron. *Just an hour ago was a ceremony to provide promotions to all those members of the 22nd who survived the Third Tiberium War*"—the image switched to a woman being given a promotion, the caption reading MAJOR MONIQUE OPAHLE, FORMERLY CAPTAIN—"*which would appear to be over, with the repelling of the aliens and the apparent collapse of the Brotherhood of Nod.*" Now the person being promoted was Ryon Henry, according to the caption. "*Of course, as long as there is Tiberium, the war never really ends. With the considerable damage done to so much of the planet, with so many attacks on Blue Zones, who knows if the zone map will remain as it is now?*" The images cycled through several more promotions. "*And there is the knowledge that we are not alone in the universe. Was the attack from space an isolated incident, or the prelude to a full-scale invasion?*"

Back to Annabella. *"These questions don't have easy answers, but if we are to have any hope of surviving, it will be because of people like those of the 22nd Infantry Division of the Global Defense Initiative United Peacekeepers. One of their soldiers said something to me that bears repeating."*

The image changed to that of Ricardo Vega, a piece Penny remembered from Annabella's first link. *"There are no winners in a war, there's just folks who lose a little bit less than the other guy."*

Back to Annabella: *"One of the reasons why we're all still alive to talk about this is because the 22nd lost a lot less than the other guy. It's true that they have earned the respect of their fellow soldiers and of GDI's Council of Directors for their excellent work in integrating new technologies into the battlefield, whether the mobile command-and-control successfully tested by BC Michael McNeil in Italy, the Tiberium-based weapons used by Lieutenant—now Captain—Ricardo Vega and his troops in Australia, or the equipment that allowed the deaf Sergeant Joshua Brodeur—who died in Italy—to function as a soldier. But that is not what separates these soldiers, nor what makes them special. It is this: They know the stakes, they know the risks, and they go anyway. They stand against the forces of darkness and they say that nobody's gonna hurt you tonight, not on my watch. We live in a terrible world, one laden with disease and death and disaster, and it's easy to give in and say that there's no hope.*

"But I have seen the face of hope, and it belongs to these men and women who have chosen to serve the world by defending it against those who would destroy it, or let it succumb to the horrors of Tiberium. And I have been proud to observe them, and honored to know

them. I hope, through my efforts, you have gotten to know them as well, for they deserve to be known—and they deserve to be respected. This is Annabella Wu, reporting for W3N."

Annabella's image winked out. Penny hadn't even realized that it had just been a simple shot of the reporter after the clip of Vega. McNeil, Vega, and Brodeur had been shown briefly when their names were mentioned, but that was it. And Penny had been completely riveted by it.

"Certainly not gonna admit *that* to anyone," she muttered. Instead, she put the link up on W3N immediately with no changes or additions. The world, after all, needed to see it.

Kane watched several dozen news feeds at once: W3N; Nod's religious news service; and several other independents from around the world.

They all showed the same thing.

The Third Tiberium War was over. And the alien invasion that had served as that war's climax had been repelled.

At least, that was what people believed.

Suddenly, Kane bent over, pain slicing through his chest. Unsurprisingly, Brother Eamonn was at his side in an instant. Turning around, he screamed at one of the other acolytes: "Summon a doctor, immediately!"

"No!" Kane said in a ragged voice, even as his hand clutched his chest tightly. "I am fine. It is the usual pain."

Not for the first time, Kane cursed Michael McNeil and his persistence. Kane had had his escape route well planned from the Cairo stronghold, but the thrice-damned soldier had found him and impaled him. It had taken him years to recover from the wound.

It was one of many certain deaths Kane had survived over the years. The latest was the easiest, by virtue of his being very far underground. GDI hadn't known about all the subbasements here in Sarajevo, and they certainly hadn't known about the liquid Tiberium. Between the cannon strike and all the fighting, Europe would be one big Red Zone before long.

Kane shook his head, cursing himself for the weakness of using GDI's repugnant terminology. The attempts to classify the world by colored regions was absurd, and self-defeating.

Luckily for Kane, his faith was strong. And the plan had always been a long-term one in any case.

The pain finally subsided, and Kane straightened. "I am fine. We must prepare, Brother Eamonn. Phase Three has at last commenced."

Eamonn nodded, and went back to his task.

Kane continued watching the reports, most of which came back to the same image: the alien monolith in southern Italy, not far from where humans had first discovered a strange green crystal in 1995 and called it "Tiberium" because it was discovered on the shores of the Tiber.

The other thirty-eight towers had simply been diversions. The last tower was all that mattered. All of it had been very carefully planned: provoking a war with GDI to force them to use their ion cannons on Kane's liquid T, thus gaining the aliens' attention ahead of the original timetable.

Not everything had gone to plan, though. He hadn't expected Qatar's betrayal, but she'd paid the ultimate price for that.

Briefly, Kane prayed for the souls of his followers who had died in the war—except Qatar and those who followed her. In the short term, he knew that sacrifices would be made, and all those who followed Kane knew that death was a distinct possibility—though he supposed they all expected to die fighting GDI, not the heretofore unheard-of aliens. Their souls, however, were in good hands, for they had died in the service of Nod and of Tiberium. Ultimately, that was all that mattered—to them, and to Kane.

The plan remains. Kane smiled. For years, he'd been building to this moment. *Now, to quote a long-dead poet, surely some revelation is at hand. For inside that tower lies the true secrets of Tiberium, and with them control of* everything.

He shut the feeds off. There was still a great deal of work to be done.

NOT THE END . . .

ACKNOWLEDGMENTS

Primary thanks must go to my editor, Tim Mak, and my publisher, Scott Shannon, who were the ones who brought me into this project in the first place. Tim in particular has been an excellent sport under some trying circumstances, and I hope I didn't drive him *too* crazy.

Secondary thanks have to go to all the wonderful people at Electronic Arts, who are *way* too numerous to mention by name. I will single out David Silverman, who served as liaison between me and Tim and the other folks there, but I have to also give props to the game developers I talked to both during my visit to EA's offices and over e-mail and by phone since then, all of whom were tremendously helpful and supportive and inspirational. If this novel is at all successful in tying into the Tiberium Universe of *Comand & Conquer,* it's due to these guys' infectious enthusiasm and hard work.

Tertiary thanks to: my agent, Lucienne Diver, for her tireless work in making my life better; Marcus and Aoki, the cats, for being cute and affectionate; the Forebearance, especially The Mom; *Kyoshi* Paul and all the folks at the dojo for everything, in particular the hiking trip to New Paltz; the Paul Simon *Graceland: The African Concert* DVD (which also featured Hugh Masekela, Miriam

Makeba, and Ladysmith Black Mambazo), which proved to be an inspirational soundtrack to write to; and especially my girlfriend for kicking my butt when I needed it. (Falling in love with a fellow writer can be *very* handy . . .)